Lynna's Promise

Curse of the Conjure Woman
Book Three

Kitty Margo

First Edition November 27, 2013
Second Edition May 30, 2024
ISBN: 9780985928087

ISBN: 9780985928087

Dedicated with Love

to

my amazing grandchildren.

Jaiden

Jordan

Cadence

Clara

&

Rae,

my heartbeats.

Chapter 1

Trinidad
1855

A flood of vivid memories and conflicting emotions overwhelmed Lynna as she stepped inside Joshua's cabin on the *Windjammer*. Her hand lovingly caressed the finely carved cherry bedpost, unleashing a wealth of passionate memories that caused her body to tingle.

She meandered around the room, touching a compass, a sextant, and a logbook as she thought back to how thrilled she had been to be leaving France to experience her first sea voyage, having no idea of the heartache that awaited her in the new land.

The majority of her suffering had been a welcoming gift from Suzanne Fletcher, a nightmare unto herself. Lynna had been greeted by pirates, shipwreck, voodoo, and sickness so severe that she prayed for death to release her from the agony. Yet, far worse than all the trials and tribulations she had encountered along the way, was being forced to abandon her precious son.

She gazed out the window to watch the gently rolling swells of the Caribbean in darkness. She heard the sails being raised, and snapping as they filled with wind. She felt the ship lurch and heard timbers groan when the mighty ship was set in motion. Joshua would be at the helm, steering the *Windjammer* out to sea, and far away from Trinidad.

She was surprised to realize she had mixed feelings about leaving the lush island paradise she had grown to think of as home. Why did the thought that she might never return to the island cause a sharp ache in her breast? Of course, it was the fact that she would dearly miss Lisbeth.

And Sean.

What of Sean?

"I believe we's gwine make it outta heah alive," Rob announced, from the doorway. A delicious aroma filled the air as he strolled across the room to place a tray on the table. "Ain't no pi'ates aftah us dat I kin see."

"That is certainly welcome news." Lynna beamed a brilliant smile for the gentle giant. "I wouldn't care to witness bloodshed on my behalf."

Rob reached into his pocket and withdrew two oranges as his lips curved into a sheepish grin. He tossed her one. "I brung 'bout a bushel of oranges, and lemons, and plums from de island. I don't reckon dat pi'ate gwine miss dis lil bit of fruit."

"There are hundreds of fruit trees at Devereux Acres." Although Lynna's mind was far from the orchard, she attempted to ease his mind. "I doubt a bushel will be missed."

Rob wore a puzzled frown. For the life of him, he could not understand why Lynna didn't want bloodshed. Sean Devereux had kidnapped her from her home, and stole her away from her son.

Shouldn't she want to see him strung up from the nearest yardarm? "Buttercup, you ain't gots ta answer me if'n you don't wants to rat now, but I's gots ta know sumphin'."

"What is it, Rob?" Lynna had no desire to have the discussion that she knew was coming.

Rob shuffled his huge feet, scrubbing his massive hand over his bald head. "I needs ta know whut dat pi'ate done ta you. If'n he made you do anythin' agin yo' will, I wants you ta tell me." Rob's mind wandered to thoughts best left to rest in the darkest recesses of his mind. His hand squeezed the orange until juice ran through his fingers and dripped on the floor. "Cause if'n he did, I aims ta kill him fo' it."

Lynna held onto a table as the ship shuddered and headed toward open water. When the vessel was parallel to the island, she glanced toward the house on the hill. The sight caused her heart to flutter when she saw a candle flickering in Sean's window.

Was he watching her go?

Had he found her note saying only that her husband was alive and they were returning home to their son?

When she felt composed enough to answer Rob's question, she turned to him with a bright smile. "I give you my word, Rob. Sean did not force me to do anything against my will. In fact, he was a perfect gentleman during my entire stay on the island."

"Humph," Rob snorted, not believing a word of it. He knew Sean Devereux, and the man was no gentleman, perfect or otherwise. He couldn't figure out why Lynna felt the need to protect the filthy scum, but it was obvious that she did. "I ain't neber know' him to act like no gen'leman befo'."

"Sean and his grandmother were always kind to me," Lynna reminded him, standing to drop the orange on Joshua's desk. She smoothed her skirt with nervous fingers as she faced the goliath with her hands on her hips. "You mustn't concern yourself with some ridiculous notion of defending my virtue, Rob."

"I cain he'p it, Buttercup." Still, he had plenty of time to find out the truth since making the difficult decision to leave his treasured island and return to civilization. He only prayed that he wouldn't live to regret it.

Relief washed over Lynna when Joshua edged around Rob's massive bulk and through the door, effectively ending the conversation that she never wanted to have.

"I reckon you two be wantin' to be alone," Rob sounded irritated by the interruption. He wouldn't rest until Lynna told him the truth of what had happened at Devereux Acres. He wouldn't judge her regardless of what she said, for she was an innocent victim, but he *would* seek revenge on her behalf.

"Whatever gave you that idea?" Joshua chuckled.

Rob cast a stern glance his way, warning Joshua that he was not in a jovial mood at the moment. "I be on deck if'n you needs me, Buttercup." Rob knew how badly Sean Devereux wanted Lynna, and he would wager the man hadn't left her untouched during the months she resided under his roof.

"Thank you, Rob." Lynna breathed a deep sigh of relief and hurried to his side, standing on her tiptoes to reach around his neck for a hug and a loving kiss on his rough cheek. "It's so wonderful to have you back in my life. You will never know how much I missed seeing your smiling face each day."

Rob returned her hug and stood her away from him, determined to continue their conversation the next time they had a few minutes alone. "G'night, Buttercup"

As the door clicked shut behind Rob, Joshua took his exquisite wife in his arms. "Alone at last. I can't count the nights I have dreamed of this moment."

As Joshua unbuttoned his shirt Lynna couldn't resist rubbing her hands across the firm muscles of his sun-bronzed chest. She jerked her hand back when her fingers came in contact with rough, ridged skin. She slipped the shirt over his shoulder and gasped in horror as his chest was revealed. "Joshua, what… happened?"

He took her hand and placed it on the ugly scar. "A souvenir from Suzanne, my love."

"A… souvenir?" Lynna cringed as scalding tears filled her eyes to stream unchecked down her cheeks.

"Yes, my love. Trust that only my inability to move a muscle could have kept me from you and our son." He swiped at the tears shimmering on Lynna's sooty lashes. "It took months to recover from the wound to my chest."

"The wound is so close to your… heart," she whispered.

"I am a very lucky man. Come sit with me while I explain why I was unable to come home to you." He led her to the window seat and drew her on his lap. "I was shot, Lynna. Thinking me dead, Suzanne had her henchmen dump my body in a ravine on the North and South Carolina border."

Lynna's was left speechless by the pain that lingered in his eyes.

"God was smiling on me that day, because a young mute girl named Clara found me and she and her grandmother nursed me back to health. If Clara hadn't stumbled upon me when she did, I wouldn't be with you today. I lost a great deal of blood and was unconscious for weeks."

Lynna could only imagine the pain he had suffered after taking a bullet to his chest. "If only I had known where you were I would have come for you immediately."

"Of course you would have, but there was no way you could have known. Suzanne made sure of it. It's a miracle that I lived long enough for Clara to find me."

"Suzanne visited me almost daily after you disappeared, Joshua. She comforted me while I cried on her shoulder, always telling me how sorry she was for my loss. She assured me that she was steadfastly praying for your safe return." Lynna gazed up at him, her eyes glistening with fear. "Suzanne drove me to the docks to meet Sean the night we left Charleston."

Joshua wiped a tear from her soft cheek and his hand lingered to caress her silken skin. "They were both in on the kidnapping plot."

"How do you know this?"

"I was able to... persuade Suzanne to confess everything."

A frightening thought struck Lynna. "First you, then me. What if Suzanne takes it in her mind to... harm our son while we are both away?"

"I personally dropped Suzanne off at the county jail, so don't worry about her being released any time soon. When your father found out that Suzanne was behind both our disappearances, well, livid is putting it mildly. He vowed to see Suzanne punished for her crimes and was already corresponding with several of the best lawyers in the country when I left Sea Grove to find you."

"All Suzanne wanted in this life was you, Joshua. I can't for the life of me understand why she would try to kill you."

"My guess is that it was simply a case of *if I can't have him nobody can.* But that is enough talk of Suzanne. I have you all to myself for at least the next eight weeks and I don't intend to waste a minute of it."

"At least?" Lynna turned to him with a confused look.

Where did he think she was going?

"I would wager that once we return home we will have the addition of a bouncing little toddler in our bed. One who will remain in your arms until you have sufficiently smothered the child with enough love to allow him to return to his own bed."

Lynna smiling dreamily. "You know me well don't you, darling?"

Joshua kissed the tip of her nose. "I know you will be a wonderful mother to our son. I know your homecoming will make your father the happiest man alive." He placed another soft kiss on her cheekbone. "I know you are the answer to many, many heartfelt prayers. I know you love spring mornings and loathe thunderstorms." His mouth slid across her cheek to nibble on her earlobe. "I know you speak several languages fluently."

"How do you know?"

"Your father was bragging," he teased. "I know that when you are with child you eat everything that isn't nailed down."

"You are incorrigible, Joshua Jordan." She laughed, enjoying his lively banter.

"I know you are without doubt the most beautiful woman I have ever seen." Just before his lips met hers, he whispered, "I know that I love you more than life itself."

His moist mouth slid across her lips, his tongue flicking out to do a sultry dance with hers that caused her insides to quicken. His fingers slid up the back of her head, piling her hair on top as his long fingers massaged her scalp and sent delicious shivers racing along her spine. He backed her against his desk and pressed his full length against hers. "I know that if I don't make love to my gorgeous wife I will explode."

Without another word he raised her dress, making short work of removing her shoes and the bothersome undergarments that accompanied them. As his mouth once again sought hers, he lifted her to sit on the edge of the desk.

A desk that was exactly the right height.

Afterward, they held each other close, neither moving as they waited for their breathing to return to normal.

"Where were we?" He reached behind her to unfasten the stays on her dress and lift the cumbersome garment over her head. "While it is not my intention to sound greedy, you are mine until we dock in Charleston and I intend to enjoy every second until I am forced to share you."

Lynna leaned her head against his broad shoulder as his hands moved to caress her bare skin. "I still can't believe you're alive. I remember so vividly when Sean told me you were dead." She shook her head to dispel an avalanche of painful memories that threatened to overwhelm her. "Those days, and my sickness, were a living hell worse than anything I could have imagined."

Joshua nuzzled her silky hair, remembering his own particular form of torment. "I have become well acquainted with hell on earth as well, my love. When I found out that Sean Devereux had taken you…"

"He didn't harm me in any way, Joshua." As usual, she was quick to jump to Sean's defense. "Please, don't forget that if not for Sean, I would be dead."

Joshua's hands stilled. "How can I forget when you remind me at every turn?"

"I don't mean to keep bringing him up." She tried to pull away, yet he held her pressed against his broad chest. "It's important to me that you realize the truth."

"While I realize that I should be grateful to the man for saving your life, it is difficult at best,

Lynna. Can't you understand?"

"Of course, I do."

"I'm not sure that you do. What if I suddenly had a change of heart and decided to welcome Suzanne back into my life with open arms? How would you feel?"

Lynna stiffened at his words, the mere thought causing a chill to shiver along her skin. "I see your point."

And she did.

Nonetheless, she would be forever grateful to Sean Devereux. "Let's change the subject and speak of this another time. For now, I only need to hear about my son."

With Beau being one of his favorite subjects as well, Joshua was only too happy to oblige. At the same time, he knew he would be even happier if he never had to hear Sean Devereux's name fall from his wife's luscious lips again. "Beau is perfect, and being the spitting image of his father he is devastatingly handsome."

"Of course, that goes without saying," Lynna teased, as Joshua lifted her and carried her to the bed. "Was Beau taking steps when you left?"

"He hadn't gained the courage to turn loose and stand on his own two feet, but he was pulling up and crawling from room to room with a gaggle of females always at his heels." Joshua joined her on the bed, pressing the length of his lean torso against hers. Every nerve ending in his body came to life as her soft supple curves slid across his hard lean torso. "You feel like my own little slice of heaven." His lips found hers in a kiss that sucked the very air from her lungs.

Lynna had another question about her son on the tip of her tongue, that was temporarily relocated to the back of her mind. It was difficult to form a rational thought at all when her husband filled her so completely, making her forget all else.

"I'm sorry, my love. It has been too long and your body feels too good. Next time, I will see to all your needs. You have my word."

Fortunately, he always kept his word.

Lynna was exhausted and too excited to sleep. She fingered the silky hair at Joshua's nape as she ran her toe up his leg. "Tell me more about Beau?"

He turned on his side to face her and smooth the damp hair from her forehead, tracing her sensuous lips with his finger. "Between Clara and Malinda his feet rarely touch the floor. Mother insists that he will never learn to walk if they don't put him down."

Lynna's eyes brimmed with unshed tears upon the realization that she had already missed several important milestones in her son's first year of life. Sitting. Crawling. Most likely his first steps. She hastily brushed away a tear. "Do you think Beau will remember me at all?"

"You must remember, darling, that he was only a few days old when you left. Besides, even if he doesn't it will only take a few days for him to fall head over heels in love with his mother all over again." He tilted her chin as he gazed into her watery eyes. "We will be a family at last, Lynna."

"That will be a dream come true.*"* *My family, together.* "I can't wait to meet Clara and

Lucille and thank them for saving your life."

Joshua chuckled as Lynna moved to rest her head against his heart. "Let me warn you ahead of time that Clara considers Beau to be her charge and is very possessive of the child. She and Milly are forever at odds because of it." His hand moved down her back to rest on her hip. "Beau needs a sister so they would each have a youngster to spoil rotten."

He felt her body tense beneath his hands as he raised up on his elbow to look into her eyes. "What did I say to upset you, Lynna? Is it too soon for talk of another child?"

"What? No, of course... not," she stammered. "I was... just thinking of Beau."

"Don't worry about Beau, my sweet." Joshua settled beside her. "If we have good winds at our backs we should be in Charleston in a few months. Sometimes, I worry that you might be bored with plantation life after your many adventures of late."

"I long to be bored." Lynna's hand slid up his neck and along his finely chiseled jaw. "I pray that I never have to leave my son or Sea Grove again. I can be happy wherever I am as long as I have Beau by my side." Goosebumps raced over her skin when she remembered saying those exact words to Sean. "And you, my darling. As long as I have you by my side."

Lynna released a blissful sigh as his moist mouth slid down her neck. She needed this man as she needed the blood that flowed through her veins, the air that she breathed, her daily bread. "I love you, Joshua Daniel Jordan."

He paused, raising his head to look with deep longing into her azure eyes. "As I love you, Lynna MaKensie Rhodes Jordan. It is my most fervent wish that I never have to spend another day in this life without you."

As they clung to each other with limbs entwined, afraid the other might disappear in the night, Joshua knew he wouldn't find peace until he had some answers. "There are a few things I need to get off of my chest, Lynna. Until now, I haven't been able to find the words."

"Tell me," she mumbled, sleepily.

"I need you to know that... whatever... happened in Trinidad, you can tell me. You were kidnapped by a despicable pirate and cannot be held responsible for anything that transpired while you were held captive. I will continue to love you no matter what transpired between the two of you. You thought I was dead, so even though it will kill me to know that he... I just need the truth."

"Sean never forced me to do anything against my will, Joshua." She tilted her head back to gaze at her handsome husband as her hand trailed up his chest and behind his head to pull his mouth down to hers, silencing any questions for the time being. "I'm exhausted. Shall we try to get a few hours sleep before we greet a glorious new day?"

A vise that had gripped his heart like an iron fist slowly loosened. Still, Joshua would not rest until Sean Devereux was no longer a threat. He knew beyond a shadow of a doubt that Sean would come after Lynna.

Any man would.

He vowed the pirate wouldn't live long

enough to ever lay hands on his wife again.

Chapter 2

Mississippi
April 1856

Suzanne Fletcher Jordan lifted the heavy hoe with bruised and calloused hands, peering into the huge orange glow of a blazing summer sun. It had to be well over ninety degrees in the late May heat and the thick humidity made it feel like she was struggling to breathe underwater.

Even though she gave it her best effort, she could only raise the hoe a few inches above the ground. This small exertion caused muscles in her body that had *never* been used to scream with agonizing pain. Nonetheless, she continued the monotonous motion over and over, having no desire to feel the bite of the guard's whip again.

Once had been more than enough.

She hastily swiped at a single tear as it scorched a trail down her sunburned cheek, and sniffled as she drew a calming breath before anyone could notice her moment of weakness. They would only laugh at her foolishness for crying around a gang of seasoned inmates. She hated to cry, unless it was to get her way. It was indeed a rare occurrence when it happened for any other reason, until recently.

Some days the thought of spending the next five years in this hellhole completely overwhelmed her and she briefly gave vent to the pain. But crying was a sign of weakness in a place like this that she could ill afford. Weakness would get you killed in the Mississippi Women's Prison Farm.

She touched a sore finger to her tender face, her once pale, unblemished face that had been the envy of many. Having been forced to work in the open field under the unrelenting sun for months now, the punishing rays had baked her skin until it was as scaly and tough as shoe leather.

She hadn't looked in a mirror recently, as there were none in the prison, but she could feel wrinkles beginning to form on her forehead and spread like spider webs in the creases beside her eyes.

She swiped a hand across her furrowed brow as a pained sigh slipped from her lips when she recalled the nightly applications of buttermilk her mother had insisted she rub on her face. It worked to keep the freckles at bay and promote the smooth, porcelain skin so cherished by Southern women. What a wasted effort that had been.

Sweat streamed between her breasts in rivulets, causing the already coarse, itchy, ill fitting, mud caked and tattered homespun gown to chafe against her raw skin. This caused a pained memory of the many watered silk and satin ball gowns of every style and color imaginable that hung in her wardrobe at Magnolia House.

She recalled the soft lacy chemises and satiny nightgowns that were folded neatly in her chifforobe. She had so many comfortable muslin day dresses that she could go a fortnight without being seen in the same dress twice, and each dress had an adorable little hat and matching parasol to protect her from the ravages of the sun.

What I wouldn't give for a parasol now.

It was far too late to worry about her skin. The damage had been done and could not be undone. Her days of being the belle of the ball had most likely ended the moment she stepped foot inside the penitentiary. Society as a whole seemed to not only frown upon, but also be extremely unforgiving toward incarcerated women. At any rate, all her parasols were in her bedroom at home.

Home.

Would she ever see the magnificent plantation house again? Did she want to? Did she want to see her traitorous parents and hear more lies fall from their deceitful lips?

We cannot abide the thought of you in prison Suzanne, honey, and we will use every available resource to keep it from happening.

While it's true that you have made some mistakes, you don't deserve to rot in prison for them.

We just want you someplace... safe.

However, we do think you need... help.

There is a lovely asylum in New York where you could get... treatment for your problems.

Help you to think about the consequences of your actions.

Move on from... Joshua and Lynna and leave them in the past where they belong.

Meet someone new and start a whole new chapter in your life.

Even though her parents had spent a fortune on her defense, defending her with every breath, forgetting what it was like to sleep through the night without being awakened by nightmares of their daughter in a hellish prison, and stood by her every second of the trial, in Suzanne's mind it wasn't nearly enough.

Since being convicted and sentenced to prison she had twisted the facts in her mind until she was convinced that her parents were to blame for her landing in the penitentiary.

They simply had not done enough to prevent it.

Her warped reasoning assured her that her parents, a matched set of deceptively evil charlatans, had sat in the courtroom and watched as she was sentenced to five years of hard labor, without lifting a finger to stop it.

Her mother, with her swollen and red rimmed eyes, shedding what Suzanne was convinced were fake crocodile tears. Her father, with his sorrowful face and dismal shake of his head when she begged him to get her out of this horrible mess and take her home.

Suzanne was smart enough to realize that when it came to the justice system money talked and bullshit walked. Still, the courtroom battle had been a clash of the titans. The lawyers hired by Silas Fletcher of Magnolia House against the lawyers representing Jeremiah Jordon of Sea Grove. They were neck and neck during the trial. Heated words. Accusations. False witnesses. Outright lies from her lawyer.

Jeremiah and Silas had been true friends. Two of the most profitable plantation owners in the South, they had enjoyed their time together immensely. Until the trial, when they became sworn enemies. They had sat on the edge of their seat and wheeled chair during the heated confrontation, eying each other with contempt when Jeremiah refused Silas's offer to admit Suzanne to a mental health facility. Jeremiah had vehemently *insisted* that Suzanne do hard time. In truth, Jeremiah wanted Suzanne behind bars to protect his family.

The trial was a circus show and the spectators loved it, crowding the courtroom to overflowing each day. The riveted audience never knew how any given day would turn out. The defense would have a banner day, then the prosecution would rally forth with a winning salvo. This went on for weeks, until the lawyers' back and forth ramblings made observers in the crowded courtroom dizzy to watch.

Finally, after two weeks of arguments, Suzanne began to notice a tiny glimmer of hope in her father's weary eyes.

The glimmer faded with lightning speed when Nathan Rhodes and his entire team of esteemed lawyers strolled into the courtroom one rainy afternoon, joining the prosecution. With more wealth than that of Magnolia House and Sea Grove combined, Nathan had run the show from that day forward.

After Nathan was sworn in he stated that Suzanne had attempted to murder both his daughter and her husband and had almost succeeded with both counts. When he loudly demanded that justice be served, for all intents and purposes the trial was over.

Suzanne would always remember the grin

and conspiratorial wink Nathan and Jeremiah exchanged before leaving the courtroom, while her mother's heartbreaking sobs were the only sounds to be heard.

By the end of that day, Suzanne had been in a carriage headed deeper South with two burly, tobacco chewing, smelly guards. Even she had tired of sex by the time she arrived, sore and abused, at her home for the next five years.

Upon her arrival at the women's penitentiary, against her tears, flat out begging, and vehement objections, she had been sent to work in the cotton field the following morning.

A cotton field.

Hell on earth, and a torture unlike anything she could have imagined.

After the first week of working in the field from sunup to sundown, her hands were a mass of blisters that had broken open and left raw, stinging sores. It didn't take many days of wielding the hoe before the blisters became rough calluses that marred the appearance of her once beautiful hands.

She leaned the hoe against her chest and held her ruined hands in front of her, and cringed. What nails hadn't been chewed down to the quick were jagged and broken.

She glanced down at her bare, filthy feet, raw and bleeding from being dragged through mud and sharp rocks. They were crusty with dirt and had at least a week's worth of mud jammed under her toenails. At first she had been thoroughly appalled by the sight of her feet at the end of the workday, diligently scraping mud out from under her fingernails and toenails each night after returning from the field.

She had long since given up on such frivolity.

It was pointless.

Her arms and legs were a mass of scrapes, scratches and bruises. Suzanne still carried the scars from the many scuffles during her first week of being incarcerated, when she had haughtily informed the guards of just exactly who they were dealing with. That had been her biggest mistake. Now they sought her out to ridicule and make the rich girl the object of their jokes and jeers.

One hand automatically went to the rat's nest of her hair, feeling unimaginable sorrow when she was unable to force her fingers through the knots of her once glorious mane. A sob caught in her throat as she jerked her hand away and swiped it across her forehead to prevent sweat from dripping into her stinging eyes.

She would never survive five years of this hell. She wasn't like the other degenerates who had been thrown into this cesspool. She had been born to wealth and opportunity. Yet, the guards didn't seem the least bit impressed by her privileged upbringing.

After only ten minutes in the blistering heat of a cotton field she had sweated until water could be wrung out of her dress. Still, Suzanne and the other inmates were only allowed the luxury of a dip in the river once a week to wash their stinking bodies and hair. Each and every prisoner smelled worse than polecats.

It was a travesty. An outrage. Suzanne Fletcher Jordon hoeing cotton.

And having body odor.
All thanks to Joshua Jordan.
No.

Her life would be perfect if Lynna had never entered it.

Suzanne jerked the hoe with a vengeance, chopping grass and weeds as her eyes flashed with righteous indignation. She imagined Lynna's smirking face in the dirt each time she brought the hoe down and smiled maliciously as she dug the blade between the eyes of her nemesis.

Imagining her revenge was Suzanne's only source of entertainment in this waking nightmare, to the point that it had become the driving force in her wretched existence. She smoothed the hair from her face and leaned back to straighten her stiff muscles and remove the kinks in her spine.

"Get back to work, Fletcher," Mona, the fat, red-faced guard, wheezed, waving her detestable whip in the air with a flourish. "You ain't got time for all that exercising." She chuckled, winking at another guard sitting atop a horse a few rows down. "Besides, Maxine will give you all the work out you need."

Maxine was Suzanne's cellmate, and probably the meanest female she had ever had the displeasure of meeting. The poor thing wasn't much to look at, and had about as much class as a warthog. Somewhere in her thirties, she had dull brown hair with a considerable amount of premature gray around her hairline. Her two front teeth had been chipped in prison riots and her skin was irreparably damaged from years of hoeing under a sizzling sun. Still, she ruled the prison population.

With self-preservation being her main objective during her stint in this miserable detention center, Suzanne had immediately made friends with Maxine. Close friends.

Intimate friends.

Suzanne swallowed bile that rose in her throat just thinking of the vile, disgusting acts she had been forced to perform on Maxine. Since there wasn't a man on the entire premises, what other choice did she have? Maxine had ways of getting things accomplished that none of the other inmates could and, better still, she had the ear of the warden.

After the things Suzanne had done to Maxine she damn well better be able to accomplish a miracle for her. Without missing a beat in her hoeing, Suzanne glanced down the rows toward the miscreant with naked hostility, her face flaming as she remembered the events of the previous night.

Maxine felt eyes on her and looked up to wink lasciviously, causing shivers of revulsion to rush down Suzanne's spine. She flinched, seething with anger when the odious reprobate licked her lips and rubbed her hand over her crotch in anticipation of future endeavors.

Suzanne was convinced that work in the fields, heinous as it was, might be preferable to a night in Maxine's hammock.

It was almost dusk when the guards called quitting time. Heat lightning danced across the sky and bats swooped low around their heads as the seventy eight prisoners breathed a collective sigh, watching as the last dying rays of sunlight fell below the horizon.

Suzanne was so exhausted she could barely lift her feet. Her arms ached and her legs, feet, and every other part of her body throbbed with each beat of her heart. She lifted her skirt to her knees in hopes of feeling a cooling breeze on her legs and made the mistake of glancing at Maxine who was near salivating at the sight.

Thank God it wasn't bath day.

Suzanne may have been forced to do unspeakably horrible things, but she had made one point perfectly clear from the get go. *Whatever* she touched, with any part of her anatomy, would be squeaky clean.

Hearing the supper bell, Suzanne and her fellow inmates headed toward the dining hall. Meals consisted of a small bowl of porridge, a biscuit, and a small cup of warm milk for breakfast and lunch, and she was starving. She prayed there would be meat added to the vegetable soup for supper. Maxine had advised her to enjoy the fresh vegetables while she could, for when the garden was done it would be porridge, bread, and milk three times a day.

She hadn't had a piece of meat since arriving in Mississippi, so just thinking of the smokehouse back home filled to overflowing with pork, beef, and venison caused her mouth to water. That made her think of her parents, the traitors, sitting down to a veritable feast and not even giving her so much as a passing thought.

"Two more days til we git baths." Maxine sidled up beside her as they entered the dining house, practically drooling. "You ready for Maxine to make you holler girl?"

"Um… sure," Suzanne lied, glancing around at the many sets of eyes focused on them. She was no more liked by the inmates than she was the guards. "I can hardly contain my enthusiasm."

"Me neither, sugar lump." Maxine's eyes moved down Suzanne's shapeless dress. "I done been here two years and this has been the longest week yet. Since I can't stop thinking about you, I done come up with a plan to convince the warden to let me and you take a bath three times a week."

A horrified gasp flew from Suzanne's lips before she could stop it. *Three times a week?* Having to lie still while a disgusting pig mauled her and expected way too much in return? She could not bear it. She would rather be dead.

She relaxed as a hastily laid plan began to form in her mind. If Maxine, pitifully ugly thing that she was, could convince the warden to make her life easier, Suzanne had to wonder what someone as stunningly beautiful as herself could accomplish. Well, after a bath, substantial grooming, and clean clothes.

Why, if the warden was of a certain persuasion, she could have the woman eating out of her hand in no time. First, she had to meet her, and she would need Maxine's assistance for that.

She turned to the short, stubby little woman and beamed. "Why, Maxine, I think that is a simply marvelous idea. However, I have just have one tiny request and I sincerely hope you can honor it for little ole me."

"Just name it, sweet cheeks." Maxine lifted a lock of Suzanne's hair to twirl around her filthy finger, inhaling deeply of the scent of sweat and dirt.

"I would like to meet the warden myself," Suzanne purred. "The majority of the women here, with the exception of you of course, are rather ill bred and I would love to carry on a discourse with someone more like... myself. I simply pine for an educated discussion."

"I understand exactly, darlin'. Why, I hate to see a fine filly like you having to wallow in the mire with this bunch of illiterate swine." Maxine swallowed her drool, making her Adam's apple bob. "Put your trust in me, sugah. I will obtain you an audience with the warden within the week."

"I just knew I could count on you, honey," Suzanne simpered.

The warden couldn't possibly be any more disgusting than you are.

"Why, I do declare, I don't know what I would do in this simply dreadful place without my big, strong Maxine."

Chapter 3

Suzanne finger combed the mass of tangles as best she could, convinced that the knots in her hair would have to be cut out. They had just left the dining house after a dismal meal of porridge and milk and she was starving. She could not go on like this.

The other women were accustomed to living like animals, and there wasn't an ounce of class in the lot of them. Whereas, she had been raised in the lap of luxury and would never acclimate to the harsh realities of incarceration.

Supposedly, her parents were appealing her conviction and she would be going home soon. At least, she had convinced herself of this in a determined effort to survive from one miserable day to the next.

The inmates were allowed visitors for fifteen minutes every three months. Fifteen minutes. That was hardly enough time for a proper greeting. At any rate, today was the big day. Maybe her parents would bring good news.

Would her own mother even recognize her now?

Suzanne ignored the fact that she was filthy, starving, and wearing a tattered dress that was a notch below the attire of any female servant at

Magnolia House. With a grim smile, she made her way to the commons to greet them and spotted her father the minute the guard opened the door.

He mother clutched her husband's hand and all but swooned at the sight of her pitiful daughter as she took a moment to collect herself. With a cheery smile plastered on her face she hurried forward, stopping short when she was close enough to actually see, and smell, her daughter. "Suzanne, darling, you look…"

"Don't bother, Mother." Suzanne rolled her eyes, holding up a hand to stop her. "I know exactly how I look and I am not in the mood, nor do we have time for one of your uplifting speeches built on lies."

"But you have lost so much… weight," Mary cried, as her hand fluttered at her throat. She decided to ignore her daughter's demeaning insult. The poor thing couldn't be blamed for having a short temper in a place like this. "Are they feeding you well?"

Suzanne could only glare at her, wondering how she could possibly be the offspring of someone so incredibly dense. "Yes, Mother. Why, of course they are. We just this minute left the dining hall where we dined on ham so tender it would practically melt in your mouth, buttery creamed potatoes, green beans swimming in fatback grease, and blackberry cobbler that would put the cooks back home to shame."

"Thank goodness," Patricia gushed. "I had no idea they fed prisoners so well."

"Suzanne was being sarcastic, darling." Silas shook his head sadly, glowering at his daughter. "We have traveled for days to see you, Suzanne. We fought tooth and nail to keep you out of prison and stood firmly by your side every day of the trial, and this is the thanks we get? Don't you think you could at least be civil toward us now."

"She didn't mean anything by it." Mary cast pleading eyes toward her daughter. "Did you, dear?" Her husband's words had effectively thrown ice cold water in Mary's face, Still, she wouldn't be allowed another visit for three months and she intended to make the best of this one. But her daughter had changed. How could she turn on her own parents, the two people who loved her most in the world? *Had her mind truly snapped?* "Come then," Mary chirped, forcing a bright smile. "Let us take our seats with the others."

Suzanne slumped down in a chair that gave no promise of supporting her meager weight, hiding her horrid hands in the folds of her skirt. "We had porridge, Mother, which is oatmeal mixed with milk. To go with it, we each get half a cup of warm milk and a biscuit. Our meal never varies. We eat the same thing for breakfast and lunch every day. For dinner we have vegetable soup."

Mary's hand went to her throat as her eyes filled with tears.

"In the three months I have been here, potatoes have been added to the soup twice. It's mostly carrots, onions and lentils." She looked away from her parents, unable to stand the sight of them. "Perhaps that is why I appear malnourished."

"Speaking of food, Jasmine baked a basket of goodies for you." Mary's seemed to choke on the words as she cut her eyes at her daughter. "The guards… confiscated our basket. I'm so sorry, darling."

"You should be." Suzanne imagined that porker Mona inhaling the food that had been sent for her. She had so many people to get even with. She wished she could talk to Amari about a mass spell to curse the lot of them all at once.

"Suzanne," her father warned, in a menacing tone that she had rarely ever heard.

"As should you," Suzanne turned on her father, accusing him with her eyes. "How could you let them send me to this… this pigsty. You have no idea what goes on in here. The degrading things I have been forced to do." She glanced at her mother and tried to calm down. "You wouldn't be able to comprehend the truth even if I told you."

The sight of her mother's stylish traveling suit with a dainty little hat perched on top of her head, and a matching reticule clutched at her side caused a burning rage in Suzanne. She felt the urge to hurt her mother, crush her soul as her own had been crushed. She wanted to wound her.

Make her feel pain.

This woman, who would be returning home to her grand plantation to be waited on hand and foot by doting servants, while *she* slept on a narrow, uncomfortable hammock suspended above a dirt floor.

Suzanne crossed her arms over her chest and nodded toward Maxine sitting in a corner quietly observing. Mary nodded and smiled at the unattractive woman.

"That is Maxine, my roommate," Suzanne informed them.

"She seems like a nice enough... person," Mary whispered.

"Now, imagine being forced to be intimate with her."

Mary's gasp echoed around the room as her face colored an unsightly shade of green. Suddenly, her hand flew to her mouth and she raced toward the exit.

"You only said that to hurt your mother," Silas chided, his own stomach churning at the vivid image his daughter's words had conjured in his mind. "You should be ashamed after all the heartache you've already caused her."

"She needs to hear the truth and stop living in a fairy tale. The rules of etiquette and society don't apply here. Look around you, father. Shouldn't I be the one on the receiving end of your sympathy?" She glanced out the window and noticed her mother, bent over and heaving. "You promised to appeal my conviction. What can you tell me about it?"

"There is nothing yet to tell. While your lawyer is doing all he can, he admits that it's difficult to fight someone as powerful as Nathan Rhodes."

Nathan shouldn't be powerful very much longer. Not with the curse she had laid upon his and Jeremiah Jordan's heads on the morning of her sentencing.

May they both rot in hell for the unbelievable agony they had caused her.

Suzanne watched through the window as her mother tidied herself and smoothed her skirts. Sweat beaded on her brow as she fanned herself with a dainty little fan that was more for appearance than practicality. When her mother took her seat again, Suzanne said, "Tell me all the news from home, Mother."

Mary opened her mouth to say something, but cut her eyes at Silas and clamped her mouth shut. She kept one eye on the door since her stomach was apparently far from settled.

Suzanne knew her mother well, having witnessed this reaction numerous times. "What was she about to say before she thought better of it, father? For heaven's sake, go ahead and tell me. It's not like I can do anything, about whatever she's trying to hide from me, locked away in this squalor."

Never one to mince words, Silas admitted, "Daniel and Malinda Jordan are to wed in the fall."

"What!" Suzanne screeched, momentarily drawing the attention of the guards and everyone else in the room. "My own brother is marrying the sister of the man who sent me to prison for five years? Please, tell me you are joking."

"I wish I was." Silas shook his head despairingly. "I informed Daniel that if he marries into that family not only will he be disowned, but that he is never to bring that... woman on our property."

Suzanne's dull eyes glistened with excitement. "What was his response?"

"He was hurt," Mary answered, as tears shimmered on her lashes. "He told your father, rightly so, that Malinda hadn't done anything against us and should not be held responsible for her brother's actions."

"Don't be so naive, Mother. They are all in cahoots. Every last one of them and don't you forget it," Suzanne snarled. "They have hated me since the day I married their precious son and cuckolded him."

With good reason.

Silas thought it best to keep his opinions to himself on that subject. "The ceremony will be held at Samuel and Beth's annual Harvest Ball."

"For crying out loud," Suzanne jumped to her feet to tower over her parents with her hands planted on her hips. "Surely, you jest. Samuel and that mealy mouthed Beth are throwing that sniveling bitch Malinda Jordan a wedding celebration?"

"I'm sure the party will be given in your brother's honor," Mary was quick to correct her.

"You don't say," Suzanne snapped, sarcastically. "Essentially, what you are telling me is that both my brothers have turned their backs on me."

"They were both terribly upset by the scandal you caused, dear."

"Understandably so," Silas added. "You tried to murder two people, Suzanne. What made you think you could get away with those crimes?" He glanced around the room at the seedy group of unkempt outcasts looking his way, and lowered his voice. "So yes, Samuel and Daniel are both angry with you at the moment. Perhaps they will come around, given time."

"Who cares whether or not they come around? They will both be married to imbeciles and I fully expect you to strike them from your will.

Magnolia House should be mine alone." Suzanne waited for her father's reaction, but got none. "Samuel married into money, and Daniel is about to, so neither of them have need of yours." She sat down and glanced toward the corner of the room where hundreds of rats had left their calling cards.

She hated the nights when rodents came creeping into her room. An ugly infected sore was beginning to swell with pus from a particularly nasty rat bite on her left foot. It was impossible to get a night of undisturbed rest. If you tried, the vermin would be under the cover with you come morning. Maxine's only redeeming quality was keeping the rats shooed away.

Silas could only shake his head. Did Suzanne actually believe he would leave her the plantation, with its thousands of acres that he had worked so hard to build into what it was today? Though he loved his daughter more than life itself, he had no doubt that she would run the plantation into the ground in less than a year's time.

Suzanne assumed that her father's head shake had been directed toward his wayward sons. "My only concern from here on is survival."

"Why Suzanne, honey, whatever do you mean? Why wouldn't you survive?" Mary was appalled by her words. "No one has threatened you have they? Does your father need to speak to the warden on your behalf?"

Suzanne threw back her head and laughed, a perfectly evil sound. "Yes, please. Father, do have a heart to heart with the warden." She wiped tears from her cheeks with the back of her hand. "Oh, mother, you have forever been clueless about the world around you, but not to worry. I have a friend on the inside who is gathering a few supplies as we speak."

"What kind of supplies?" her mother asked.

"Oh," Suzanne simpered, suddenly turning coy. "Just a few goodies to make gifts for some people."

"Like who?" Her words reminded Silas that his daughter now claimed to be a powerful voodoo priestess. "Surely, you wouldn't have it in your mind to harm your own brothers, Suzanne."

Nobody cares that I was left to rot in this hellhole for five years.

But I'm supposed to care what happens to them?

I think not.

"Why, of course not, father. Don't be silly. I cannot believe you would even suggest such a horrible thing." Suzanne smirked, her evil grin telling him otherwise. "At any rate, don't concern yourself with things you know nothing about. Just go home and stay on my lawyer's behind until he gets me an appeal. I have to get out of this place. Do you understand? I will die if I have to stay here five years."

"I will do my best," Silas promised.

"We've already seen that your best wasn't quite good enough, haven't we?" Suzanne didn't seem to care that her cruel words cut her parents to the bone.

Without a word of farewell, she stood and exited the room, totally ignoring her mother's outstretched and waiting arms.

Chapter 4

A huge crescent moon hung over the ship as it slashed through the gentle swells of the calm Caribbean Sea. Lynna strolled the moonlit deck arm in arm with her husband.

Each morning, they secretly feared the harsh morning light would reveal that they were not headed home to join their son, but were still thousands of miles apart with each believing the other dead.

Lynna gazed at Joshua with his finely chiseled jaw, his wavy black hair with one lock that always seemed to fall carelessly across his forehead, white teeth that gleamed brilliantly in the moon's glow, and his broad, muscular frame. He was alive.

So very alive.

All the months of agony, the waiting, the worry, the what ifs, had been for naught. No woman had ever been happier than she was to have her husband by her side, where he belonged. She could finally put the horrors of the past behind her and live the life she had yearned to live, as a wife and mother to her son.

"What has you so deep in thought, my love?"

"Too many questions to name them all, Joshua." Lynna tilted her head and smiled into sparkling sea green eyes. "Why did Suzanne turn so much hatred on us? Is she inherently evil? Is her mind no longer stable?"

"Suzanne seems to have some morbid fascination with me. I should've had the common sense to never get involved with her to begin with."

"Will she ever let you go?" Lynna put voice to the thoughts that troubled her.

"She has no choice, my love. My family has endured enough pain at her hands. I intend for it to end when we return home." Lynna felt the muscles tense in his arm that rested around her waist. "One way or the other."

"I can hardly imagine Suzanne languishing away in a jail cell."

"The courts should concur that she is a danger to society as a whole and keep her locked away for the remainder of her abominable life."

"Do you really believe they will send Silas Fletcher's daughter away for life, with all his money and clout?"

"Stranger things have happened, darling. Silas Fletcher's money and clout don't begin to compare to your father's. We will have to wait and see if the justice system delivers the justice Suzanne deserves. If you ask me, death would be the only suitable punishment for the crimes she committed against you."

"What about you, Joshua? She tried to murder you, and what about Beau? She left our son without a mother or father. I can only imagine the agony our families were forced to live through when we both disappeared. I just want Suzanne safely behind bars where she can never harm any of our loved ones again."

"As do I, my love." Joshua's lips were set in a rigid line. "I can honestly say the world would be a better place without Suzanne Fletcher in it."

He stopped walking and pulled her against him as his hands rubbed her arms briskly in the cool night air. "Since I blame myself for allowing Suzanne to sink her talons into me, it's my responsibility to protect my family from her."

His words carried a disturbing, ominous undertone. "Please, allow the authorities to deal with her, Joshua. I couldn't bear it if I lost you again."

"You won't lose me again, Lynna, nor I you. You have my word on it." His fingers unwittingly bit into her arm with his next words. "Suzanne Fletcher or Sean Devereux will ever come between us again."

"Joshua, Sean…"

"Please, love. Not now." Joshua held her face in his hands, forcing her to take his words seriously. "I'm not in the mood for one of your uplifting pirate turned gentleman planter speeches."

Lynna couldn't be offended by his words when the pain in his eyes was so clear. "I'm sorry, Joshua."

"Sorry that a mangy pirate kidnapped you and did God only knows what…"

His words caused her to inhale sharply. "Did you not believe me when I said Sean never forced me to do anything against my will, Joshua?"

"Of course, I believed you. You would have no reason to lie to me." He peered into her crystal blue eyes for several minutes before changing the subject to a safer topic. "What I find hard to believe is that you are here, in my arms again. So many nights I had gut wrenching, too vivid, nightmares of you being trapped on an island with a man who used your body for his own form of deviant satisfaction. A man who received pleasure from your pain."

Lynna rubbed his forehead with her fingertips, hoping to erase the horrible images from his mind. "Even though I know it's true, it's hard to believe Suzanne hated me enough to send me to such a deranged person. I cannot imagine having such hatred in my soul, for anyone."

"Suzanne doesn't have a soul."

Lynna paused to listen to dolphins calling to each other in the still air as her mind raced across the the Caribbean Sea to Devereux Acres.

Joshua's mind was flooded with memories of long, sleepless nights filled with an almost unbearable pain that refused to be banished into the wind. "You could never imagine the hell I went through each and every night, wondering if you were crying out for me to help you. I thought I was going insane, Lynna."

A dark shadow crossed Joshua's eyes as he rubbed a hand over his face. "It was an indescribable torture that I hope never to live through again. So with that in mind, believe me when I say that I will never allow Suzanne to harm my family again. I will see her dead first."

Lynna knew from the steely glint in his eyes that he meant every word. She also knew just what to say to move his thoughts to a happier subject. "How are Lucille and Clara adjusting to their new surroundings?"

"You would think Clara had lived at Sea Grove all her life." Joshua chuckled, recalling sweet memories of the charming little imp. "She's the darling of the plantation, since to know Clara is to love her."

"And Lucille? Is she adjusting to her new life?"

"Not as quickly as Clara. Lucille was not accustomed to having help with her chores and it's taking some getting used to on her part. When I left, she was still insisting they could cut their own firewood."

"I am continually amazed by the ingenuity of those two."

"Wait until you meet them." Joshua smiled fondly. "You will truly be amazed."

"I look forward to it."

"I's lookin' faward ta meetin' dem myself," Rob announced, strolling across the deck. "An' dis Suzanne. I gots a bone ta pick wit' dat witch."

Lynna crossed her arms over her chest and pursed her lips. "Rob, as I told Joshua, we will allow the authorities to handle the situation with Suzanne. I won't risk either of you spending the rest of your life in a prison cell because of her."

"I ain't gwine ta no prison, but she gone pay. An' dis Amari person. She gone pay too fo' all de pain an' sufferin' dey done cause' you. Dey shoulda nevah messed wit' you, Buttercup."

"Suzanne is already in jail, Rob, so she is receiving punishment for her crimes. Believe me when I say that you don't want a voodoo queen harboring ill feelings toward you."

"I done been 'round voodoo all my life, on evah plan'ation I been on. I knows de harm a voodoo curse can cause, but it a risk I gots ta take. Dis Suzanne an' Amari is gwine pay fo' whut dey done to you."

"Rob, please listen to me and heed my warning," Lynna urged. "Let's put this entire episode behind us and move on with our lives."

Rob almost bent his body double to climb down the narrow hatch and go below, and ignore her. "G'nite Buttercup, Joshua."

"Good night, Rob."

The second he was out of sight, Lynna clutched her husband's arm. "Joshua, you must talk to him. Make him forget this ridiculous notion of seeking revenge on Suzanne and Amari. I can't even imagine what Amari might do to Rob if you can't convince him."

Joshua was of the opinion that Lynna's talk of voodoo was pure nonsense. There was no such thing as an actual voodoo curse. Still, he wasn't about to let her know his true feelings on a subject so close to her heart. In hopes of avoiding the discussion of spells and curses altogether, he turned to meet his wife's eyes. "Can we put Suzanne, Amari and everyone else out of our minds and just enjoy each other?"

Lynna would love nothing better than to close her mind to the tragedies of the past, and the uncertainties of the future. "Yes, darling, we can."

Chapter 5

Charleston, SC
Mid June, 1855

Lynna breathed deeply of the soothing smell of lowcountry plough mud. After eight agonizingly long weeks at sea the *Windjammer* had finally docked in the Charleston Harbor. With the bells of Saint Michaels tolling the noon hour she rested her hand in the crease of her husband's elbow as he escorted her off the ship.

She was a bundle of nerves, realizing that before night fell she would have her son in her arms and could finally put the misery of the past year behind her.

"Would you care to reserve a room in a hotel and enjoy a night on the town before heading to Sea Grove?" Joshua teased, as they headed through the many vendors hawking their wares, each trying to outshout his neighbor and gain the attention of Joshua and his deep pockets.

"You must be joking," Lynna admonished. "I don't wish to spend one minute longer than is absolutely necessary away from my son, and I would certainly never choose to spend a night away from him when I am so close to home."

"Of course you wouldn't, darling." Joshua's sparkling eyes let her in on the joke. "It's for that very reason that I have a carriage waiting. We will have a decent meal and hopefully be home before dark."

The carriage led them away from the hustle and bustle of the docks and across a tree lined cobblestone street to Queen Street. Lynna peered out the window to enjoy the view of the Holy City.

When the driver pulled to a stop in front of the Wayfarer Restaurant Joshua helped Lynna from the carriage and onto the stepping block. His hands lingered on her tiny waist. A brief moment of regret registered in his eyes when he realized how sorely he would miss their night's onboard ship, where he could pass the duties of sailing the vessel to his first mate and spend morning, noon, and night making sweet love to his wife.

After almost two months of around the clock lovemaking, he had no doubt that Lynna was with child. So he had every intention of continuing the pleasurable routine while she still had her slim figure. Not that he didn't enjoy making love to her when she was full with child, he did. There were just so many more options and available positions with a slender frame. "Are you hungry, love?" he queried, with his hands still encircling her waist.

"Famished." In fact, she seemed to wake up and go to bed hungry.

He released her and placed Lynna's hand in the crook of his arm to lead her into the elegant establishment.

"Captain Jordan." The maitre'd beamed, leaving another couple in midsentence as he rushed to greet them. "It has been too long since you dined with us. Come, your corner table is available."

"Thank you, Jacques." Joshua led Lynna through the dimly lit restaurant, pausing to greet several acquaintances before returning his attention to the maitre'd. "We have been at sea for the last eight weeks, actually twenty-one weeks for me, and I have never been so happy to plant my feet on solid ground." He proudly added, with a broad grin, "Jacques, I would like you to meet my wife, Lynna Jordan."

The shock was apparent on Jacques' face. "What do you say? Wife? Why, we must celebrate." Grabbing a passing waiter, he instructed, "Henry, champagne. Bring our finest bottle for the newlyweds." He turned to Lynna and pulled out her chair, waiting until she was seated before taking her hand. "I am honored to meet the woman who has successfully tamed our Captain Jordan."

"I would like to meet her myself," came a sultry feminine voice from behind Lynna.

Lynna glanced up as an extremely curvaceous woman came into view. At the same time, a beaming smile lit Joshua's face, alerting her that he recognized the female voice sight unseen.

"Resa?" Joshua's eyes danced merrily as he hastily removed the napkin from his lap and stood just as the rather voluptuous woman practically fell into his arms. "Aren't you a sight for sore eyes?"

"I heard the *Windjammer* had made port and I knew this is where I would find you, you lusty devil." Resa rose up on her toes to plant a kiss on the curve of his jaw. "You always did fill your belly before coming to my establishment."

A crimson hue flushed Joshua's neck as he cleared his throat, turning his attention to his wife.

"Lynna, this is Resa. A very dear friend of mine since we were… sixteen."

"I remember the day well." Resa grinned a sly grin. "Joshua and I are very good friends." She reached for Lynna's hand and couldn't help but smile when Joshua's wife touched her as timidly as she would a sleeping skunk. "I have heard so much about you, honey. Let's just say I am delighted to see that you won this irresistible rake over that highfalutin' Suzanne Fletcher."

Lynna had no desire to carry on a conversation with this… person. It was clear that any establishment she owned would be located in the red light district. "Are you acquainted with Suzanne?" Lynna asked, pretending indifference as she gazed at a menu.

"While I've never had the displeasure of meeting the ne'er-do-well, your husband visited me several times during their disastrous marriage to… discuss his dreadful predicament."

It was obvious that this odious woman and her husband had been lovers.

Sensing that a storm was brewing between the two women, Jacques winked at Joshua and drew Resa's attention. "Would you care to start with your usual she crab soup, Miss Resa?"

"Yes, please, Jacques." Resa returned her attention to Lynna. "If you've never had it, I urge you to try it. I promise you won't be disappointed."

Lynna glared at the flirtatious woman who she was sure had lain with her husband numerous times. Still, it was impossible not to like her. She turned to Jacques with a radiant smile. "Yes, she crab soup for me as well."

"I'll have the same," Joshua announced.

After the waiter had poured their champagne, Resa gulped her entire glass and held it out for a refill. "Speaking of Suzanne, she certainly got her comeuppance, didn't she?"

Comeuppance?

"I have been at sea for twenty one weeks," Joshua was quick to remind the lady of the evening.

Lynna steepled her fingers under her chin as she had seen Lisbeth do so many times, and leaned across the table eager to hear every word.

"You mean you don't know?" Resa gasped. "Why, I didn't think there was a single person in the entire state who hadn't heard of Suzanne's plight."

"We haven't," Joshua assured her, with a touch of annoyance. "Although, we certainly would like to."

Resa placed her champagne flute on the table and sat back with a wide grin, prolonging the suspense. "I am pleased to announce that Suzanne Fletcher was sentenced to five years of hard labor at the Mississippi Women's Prison Farm."

Joshua and Lynna's simultaneous gasps echoed around the room, causing fellows patrons to cast curious glances their way. "Five years?" Joshua was stunned by the harsh, yet well-deserved sentence. He had heard horrible accountings of what went on behind the closed doors of the prison farm. In truth, he had expected little more than a slap on the wrist for the only daughter of Silas Fletcher.

"Hard labor?" Lynna was completely astonished. She had a fleeting image of the arrogant Suzanne, filthy and tattered, finally locked away in a place where she couldn't harm anyone. "Just where she deserves to be."

"I couldn't agree more." Joshua chuckled. "Mother always said we reap what we sow. I do believe Suzanne's harvest has finally come in."

Resa raised her glass for a toast. "Speaking of harvest, I hope they put her in a cotton field and not in some little vegetable garden picking tomatoes. I hope the deranged twit actually gets five years of hard labor."

"Perhaps Suzanne will be a changed woman by the time she's released." Lynna prayed for the sake of Silas and Mary that their daughter could amend her evil ways.

Resa giggled. "If she survives for the next five years and lives to be released, she will be crazier than she was when she went in. I'm sure the sex fiend will go stark raving mad in a prison full of women, with nary a pecker in sight."

Joshua gasped at her crude words, hastily covering his mouth with a napkin to keep from spewing champagne across the table. Lynna almost choked on a sip of bubbly liquid as Resa giggled behind her hand. "How much would you care to wager that she acquires a taste for... feminine pleasures before they release her?"

Joshua shook his head. "I never bet on a losing proposition."

Lynna was speechless. The soup arrived and she lifted a spoonful of the creamiest, most delicious soup she had ever tasted to her lips. Lost in thought, she didn't say a word until the next course of shrimp and grits was placed before her.

Suzanne?

Being intimate with another woman?

What an absurd notion.

Chapter 6

Suzanne sat in a tin foot tub that was about the size a small child would fit comfortably in, vigorously scrubbing her body from head to toe. Her hair was one huge knot, and lice and several other varieties of creepy crawlies had feasted on her tender scalp until it was raw and bleeding from her constant scratching. Would her hair ever be tangle free again?

She rubbed soap into her hair as best she could to produce a good lather, which only produced more tangles. Oh well, no sense crying over something she had absolutely no control over. She was grateful that Maxine had been able to secure her a meeting with the warden. And a bath.

Alone.

She cut her eyes toward a guard posted by the door, and smiled sweetly. "Would you perhaps have a comb or brush I might borrow?"

The guard snickered, ignoring her.

"Very well, then." Suzanne had to wonder where Maxine was, having expected her to try to squeeze her fat ass into the little foot tub with her. She reached for her dress and, miracle of miracles, discovered that her request for a clean frock had been granted. It was still a shapeless, coarse, and itchy garment, but at least it was clean.

She ran her fingers through her hair as best she could and gathered the tangles into a bun. While the guard had her head turned, she grabbed a quill from a nearby desk and shoved it through the wad of hair to hold it in place. Suzanne had been here long enough to know that if the guard noticed the theft she would snatch it out of her hair. Although, the current snaggle toothed sentry didn't seem to be overly alert to her surroundings.

Suzanne now had a clean dress, her hair was clean and reasonably coiffed, and bare feet.

Who would have thought Suzanne Fletcher Jordan could be so thrilled with so little?

"I'm ready," she announced, to the guard.

The guard glanced up from picking her teeth, apparently annoyed that she had to move her expansive bottom from her seat, and harrumphed. She tossed the toothpick on the floor as she removed her keys to unlock the door.

With the guards back turned Suzanne retrieved the toothpick and stuck it in her pocket. *Finally.* Something to remove the crud from under her fingernails and toenails. She was practically ecstatic over the tiny sliver of wood. As she followed the guard along the corridor, she hastily dug the toothpick under her fingernails to remove specks of dirt and God only knows what else.

They walked down a long hall without seeing any other prisoners. Making a right, then a left, and finally through a locked door, they entered a space that was worlds apart from the dismal prison. They walked into an elegantly furnished hallway with Tiffany lamps, bookcases filled with classics, plush upholstered wingchairs, and a gorgeous Aubusson rug. For the first time since arriving at this dump, Suzanne felt at home with her surroundings.

The guard paused before a door and knocked.

"Come in," came a soft, lilting voice from behind the portal.

The guard opened the door and stepped aside to allow Suzanne to enter, when she paused on the threshold unable to take another step. Who was this woman?

She could not be the warden.

The woman sauntered across the room to take Suzanne's hand. "Come in, dear. Don't be shy. I'm Warden Fontaine."

Suzanne had a feeling that her jaw was hanging open, still, she couldn't help herself. The woman was stunningly beautiful. Dressed in a violet day dress, her shiny black hair was piled atop her head, and her sea green eyes sparkled.

She looked very familiar.

"Don't look so shocked, Suzanne. It isn't written in stone that prison wardens must be old, fat, and cursed with a scattering of warts across their nose." The woman laughed at her own joke, a rather tinkling sound. She turned to the guard and waved a dismissing hand. "You may leave us now."

The guard looked uneasy about leaving the warden alone with a woman who had been convicted of two counts of attempted murder. "I will be outside the door if you need me." Giving Suzanne a contemptuous look, she added, "Just give a holler."

Again the warden waved her hand,

dismissing the guard. "Do come in and have a seat, Suzanne. May I call you Suzanne?"

"Yes, of course."

You are the warden, after all.

"Thank you. Now, before we get down to our little meet and greet, I would ask a small favor."

A favor?

What could the warden possibly want from her? "If I can."

"Oh, you can or I wouldn't bother to ask." Again, her tinkling laughter echoed through the room. "I ask that you not tell Maxine of our meeting. I know how... fond she is of you. I wouldn't want her to think I was going behind her back, since I rely so heavily on her for information on the other inmates."

"Tell her?" A puzzled frown knit Suzanne's brow. "I was under the impression that Maxine had arranged this meeting."

"Heavens, no." The warden waved away her words. "She doesn't know a thing about it."

Now Suzanne really was confused, yet she decided to forego her questions and sit back and let the warden talk.

"Are you hungry, Suzanne?" The warden clapped her hands as though they were about to sit down to afternoon tea.

Suzanne refused to be made the butt of another joke. "I had my ration of soup and bread for dinner."

"I meant to ask if you are hungry for real food?" The warden turned to lift the lid from a platter. When she did the enticing aroma of crispy fried chicken, stewed potatoes, green beans, corn on the cob, and a bowl of peach cobbler filled the air.

Suzanne's mouth and eyes watered at the sight and smell of the tempting food. Of course she didn't dare move toward it. She knew better than to even entertain the notion of actually being permitted to taste the mouthwatering fare spread before her. So why even bother fantasizing about it. It would be jerked from her reach long before she could sample it.

When she remained rooted to the spot the warden's face took on a quizzical expression. "I thought you would be hungry, Suzanne, or I wouldn't have instructed the cook to prepare a meal just for you."

If Suzanne didn't know better she might believe the warden was actually serious, as though she would be allowed to eat the scrumptious feast before her.

She nonchalantly moved toward the table and tentatively reached for a chicken leg. With her back to the warden, and before the woman could even consider reaching out a hand to stop her she shoved the entire drumstick in her mouth and stripped every morsel of meat from the bone.

She glanced around warily, but didn't notice any guards rushing to seize her, or the plate. She grabbed an ear of corn and cleaned the cob in a few swift bites. Forgoing the fork, she shoveled green beans into her mouth with her fingers before sinking her teeth into a flaky buttermilk biscuit that had her sighing with pleasure.

With her belly full, and grateful that her back had been turned and the warden hadn't witnessed her making a hog of herself, Suzanne daintily picked up the bowl of cobbler and a spoon to take small bites, dabbing her mouth with a napkin after each bite. "That was delicious. Thank you."

"I'm glad you enjoyed it. I realize the meals in the dining hall are somewhat less than appetizing and believe me, I am diligently fighting for more funds to provide better meals for the inmates."

Suzanne didn't give a fig about the other inmates. She returned the empty bowl to the tray and covered each dish with a lid. She was clean and had a full stomach. What more surprises could the day possibly hold? From the look on the warden's face, she was about to find out.

"I'm sure you are wondering why I asked you here, Suzanne."

"As a matter of fact, I am."

The warden gazed out the window at the cotton fields blooming with pink flowers. "Those flowers will soon fall off and be replaced…"

Suzanne knew more about cotton than probably everyone else in this prison combined, certainly the warden. For that reason, she wasn't about to sit quietly and be schooled on its growing process.

Clearing her throat, she said, "Because cotton has a long growing season it is best to plant early, as soon as the soil has warmed sufficiently. After planting, seedlings typically appear in about five days. Weeds must be continually removed from the plants due to the fact that they compete with seedlings for water, light and minerals. The first flower buds appear in about six weeks, and in another four weeks the buds will become flowers."

Suzanne motioned toward the window.

"Now, as you said, the flowers fall off after three days, leaving behind a small seed pod known as the boll. Each boll contains about thirty seeds and up to five hundred thousand fibers of cotton. Each fiber grows its full length in three weeks and for the following six weeks each fiber thickens. In about ten weeks after flowering, the boll is mature and splits open and the raw cotton fibers burst out to dry in the sun. As they lose water and die, each fiber collapses into what looks like a twisted ribbon. This is the time for harvesting."

"I forgot you were raised on a cotton plantation." The warden giggled. "Please, forgive my error."

"Not just any cotton plantation," Suzanne corrected, imperiously. "Magnolia House is one of the most productive plantations in the entire South."

"I stand corrected." The warden walked behind her desk and sat down, where a folder lay in front of her. She opened it with a flourish and lifted a sheet of paper from the stack. "It says here that you consider yourself to be skilled in the ancient art of voodoo, Suzanne."

Aha.

So that was it.

The warden wanted her to lay a curse on one of her enemies.

Suzanne shrugged. "I have some practice with voodoo."

"Are you any good?"

"I haven't had any complaints yet."

"Any voodoo dolls?"

"Too many to count."

"Do your curses work?"

"Like a charm."

The warden leaned her elbows on her desk, motioning for Suzanne to take the seat in front of her. "It says here that you were convicted of two counts of attempted murder. Joshua Jordan and his wife Lynna Jordan."

"That's what they tell me."

Surely the woman didn't expect a confession, so they could prolong her sentence by another five years.

The warden propped her chin in her hands. "Correct me if I am wrong, but would a true voodoo priestess have failed at the murders?"

Suzanne didn't know how to respond.

The woman had a good point.

The warden watched Suzanne with keen interest. "Tell me about Joshua Jordan."

Suzanne didn't have to think overlong on her response. "Joshua Jordan is a handsome devil, to be sure, way too handsome for his own good. In fact, women seem to fall at his feet."

Sadness flickered across the warden's features as she turned her chair to gaze out the window. What was that all about?

Had the warden perhaps had a fling with the dashing sea captain in the past?

"Joshua has this finely chiseled jaw, black hair that is so soft to the touch, and a body to… well you get the idea."

The warden made no reply, but Suzanne heard her release the breath she had been holding. When she finally spoke, her words were just above a whisper. "And sea green eyes with the power to take your breath away."

Chapter 7

Lynna was as nervous as a cat in a room full of rocking chairs when the carriage pulled to a halt in front of Sea Grove in a cloud of boiling dust. They needed rain, but judging by the cloudless sky it wouldn't come today. The sun was beginning its daily descent as she gazed across familiar fields.

Not knowing what to do with her hands, she adjusted her bonnet and nervously smoothed her skirt. She couldn't ever remember being more jittery. At long last, the moment she had dreamed of for so long had arrived. She was about to walk up the steps to Sea Grove and finally be a mother to her precious son.

She heard the sounds of a pianoforte drifting through the open window and turned toward the music. That's why the occupants of the house failed to hear the carriage and no one had rushed to greet them. That gave her a few more minutes to compose herself. To prepare for the inevitable heartbreak should her son run screaming at first sight of his long lost mother.

Joshua knew Lynna had no cause to be so nervous. A broad grin played across his impossibly handsome features as he lifted her from the carriage and drew her against his broad chest to still her rising panic. "Take a deep breath, darling," he whispered, against her lilac scented hair. "Everything will be fine, I promise." He took her hand to lead her up the verandah steps. "Are you ready to meet your son, my love?"

"What if he hates me?" Lynna croaked the words, around a hard lump that seemed to swell in her throat.

"Don't be ridiculous." Joshua tilted her chin to meet his loving gaze, touching his soft lips to hers. "Everyone you are about to greet loves you, just remember that and enjoy your homecoming."

"And Beau?"

"He has loved you since the day he was born, Lynna. You are his mother. Don't get disheartened if he's a little shy at first. Give him time to get to know you again, my love."

Joshua opened the door and clutched his wife's hand in case she decided to bolt, as he tugged her toward the parlor. Lynna took a deep breath, squared her shoulders and entered the room.

"Uh… uh…uhh!" Clara squealed. She was the first to notice them. Her eyes lit up and her face broke into a wide grin as she tossed the cloth she had been attempting to embroider to the floor.

Why Patricia insisted that she learn something so extraordinarily foolish was beyond her scope of reasoning to begin with. How is embroidery a useful or necessary life skill?

Startled gasps were heard around the room as Clara leapt into Joshua's outstretched arms.

Joshua lifted the girl clear off her feet to swing her around and around. "Did you miss me, Clara?"

Her rapid head motion, along with the fact

that she still had her arms clutched around his neck, was answer enough.

"As I missed you." Joshua grinned affectionately. "I had grown rather accustomed to having you constantly underfoot."

Clara released her hold on his neck to swat his chest with her small fist.

Joshua returned her feet to the floor as he realized that Lynna was walking toward the toddler sitting on Nathan's lap. Beau chewed vigorously on a ragdoll as his mother approached.

Nathan didn't make a move to greet Lynna. No one did. Everyone watched with bated breath as she knelt down on the floor in front of her father with tears of joy streaming down her cheeks. "Hello, my darling Beau," she murmured, softly. "What do you have there?"

Beau briefly glanced her way before returning his attention to his ragdoll, causing her heart to skip a full beat. His eyes were the exact same shade of sea green as his father's. In fact, he was the spitting image of Joshua.

"I had a ragdoll like that when I was a little girl. It was my favorite toy." Tears streamed down Lynna's cheeks as she realized that her son had no memory of her. She was nothing more than a bothersome visitor to him.

Beau had little use for strangers and turned toward his grandfather to climb up his shoulder as far as he could go, keeping his back to Lynna.

Not to be outdone, Lynna brushed a tear from her cheek and moved around to the back of the chair, gazing into her son's enchanting eyes. She covered her face with her hands and peeked between her fingers. "Peek a boo."

Beau giggled.

Lynna beamed.

She covered her eyes again and quickly released them. "Peek a boo." This time Beau laughed out loud. It was the sweetest sound she had ever heard.

She played the game until he offered her his wet ragdoll, choosing to nibble on his grandfather's shirt instead. Lynna took his cherished doll and clutched it to her breast, wishing she could hold her son there as well.

She reached out her arms for Beau and was crushed when he scooted down to sit in her father's lap, effectively presenting his back to her.

"Let him get to know you, darling," Nathan whispered softly, with tears of happiness shining in his eyes. "It shouldn't take long." He reached out his hand to take hers. "My prayers have finally been answered."

"As have mine, father."

"He will come around in a day or two, you'll see," Patricia said, softly.

Malinda had stood back as long as she could, and raced across the room to embrace Lynna. "You look so well and healthy, when the last time I saw you I was afraid…" She looked her over from head to toe, and finding nothing amiss she moved in for another hug. "Oh, Lynna, I am so happy you're home."

"I second that," Aunt Judith cried, coming up behind Lynna and waiting her turn. "I thought, why… we all thought… oh, it is too horrible for words." She ran her hands down Lynna's arms, peering intently into her eyes. "You are well, Lynna? You have no lingering effects from your… illness?"

"None that I have noticed, Aunt Judith." Lynna took her aunt's hands and kissed her cheek. "I feel wonderful." She turned to meet Joshua's eyes. "I have everything I ever wanted."

"All's well that ends well." Jeremiah chuckled, motioning for Lynna to come to him. She did, and received a bear hug from Joshua's father. "The last time I saw you, I had no hope of ever…"

"Neither did I, father." Joshua followed closely behind Lynna to pump his father's hand. "I have discovered over the years that sometimes… hope is all that sustains this family from one tragedy to the next."

"We have certainly encountered more than our fair share of misfortune over the years." Jeremiah held tight to his son's hand, thankful to have him home safe and sound. "I pray that all the misery is behind us now."

Joshua nodded. "That is my prayer as well."

Everyone in the room had welcomed Lynna, save one. She turned to the young girl. "Hello, Clara. I have heard so much about you."

Clara bobbed her head in agreement.

"I can't wait to get to know you and your grandmother." Lynna held out her arms and Clara rushed headlong into them. She held on tight to the special child, breathing in the scent of Malinda's favorite perfume. "Clara, you saved Joshua's life. I will never be able to repay you for all you have done for my family. But rest assured that I will spend the rest of my life trying, if you will allow me to."

Clara's cheeks blushed a becoming shade of pink as she ducked her head and shook it shyly.

"She says no thanks are necessary," Joshua supplied. "Clara's gift to others is so natural that I'm not even sure she's aware of it."

Lynna caressed Clara's long strawberry blonde curls. "You will forever have my undying love and gratitude."

Joshua moved to where Nathan sat and held out his arms to his son. Beau bounced excitedly and reached for his father, eagerly wrapping his chubby little arms around his neck. "How's my little man?"

Beau responded by sticking his finger in Joshua's ear.

"I understand perfectly." Joshua tickled Beau's belly and had him squealing with laughter.

Lynna sat on the settee watching father and son at play. They were so much alike. "He is a tiny replica of you, Joshua."

"Poor child, to be so cursed." Joshua sighed dramatically. "Faced with an entire lifetime of fending off bothersome females."

"Joshua Jordan, you are simply incorrigible," his mother joked. "You will have people believing you truly are vain."

Lynna found it impossible to focus on their lively banter when she only had eyes for her son. She slowly walked over to Joshua and held out her arms. Beau was having none of it. He buried his face in his father's neck, refusing to budge.

"Just be patient, my love," Joshua urged, witnessing her crestfallen look. "Tomorrow we'll take him on a picnic, just you and me, so he can get to know you again." Joshua noticed Milly standing in the hall just outside the door. "I do believe it's time for your supper, Beau." His son was sound asleep and snoring softly as Joshua lifted the precious bundle and placed him in Milly's waiting arms.

While her son was asleep and couldn't set up a fuss, Lynna placed a light kiss on his silky cheek and inhaled the freshly powdered scent that she remembered so well. She could hardly wait for the sun to rise in the morning so she could spend time alone with her husband and son.

When Milly and Beau left the room Joshua took a seat beside his father's wheeled chair. "Resa tells me that Suzanne received a sentence of five years of hard labor."

"That she did." Jeremiah beamed. "I was concerned when Silas had one character witness after another testifying to Suzanne's almost nun like existence before you entered the picture and promptly led her down the road to ruin."

Joshua lit a cheroot, blowing rings above his head. As he knew she would, Clara rushed over to poke her finger through the rings. "The jury actually fell for that line of malarkey?'

"Hook, line, and sinker. "Jeremiah nodded toward Nathan. "Until he stepped into the courtroom with an entire flock of attorneys. They had their own set of character witnesses, the ones that knew the *real* Suzanne."

"It was a six week spectacle." Jeremiah scrubbed his hands through his hair. "This town had never seen anything like it and probably never will again."

"I wish I could have been there to see it."

"I wish you could have too, son, especially when they dragged Suzanne out of the courtroom in chains. Oh, but you can believe she went kicking and screaming every step of the way, while issuing all manner of voodoo curses on mine and Nathan's head."

"That she did," Nathan agreed with a hearty laugh. "I shall have frogs living and breeding in my stomach until they come out my eyes, ears, nose and mouth."

"Oh, father," Lynna cried, rushing to his side.

Suzanne had cursed her father?

She, unlike the others in the room, knew all too well that voodoo was no laughing matter and was to be taken deadly seriously. "Have you been ill?"

"Not in the least." Nathan chuckled. "I could not be better, especially now that my only daughter has been returned to me. Don't let such foolishness bother your pretty little head, darling."

"Voodoo is real, father. The curse Suzanne put on me almost killed me. I would be dead now if not for…"

"Who Lynna?" Nathan urged, eager to hear his daughter's accounting of the last several months. "Who do I reward for saving your life?

"Sean Devereux." Joshua's tone sounded more harsh than he had intended. He found it almost impossible to act in a rational manner where the pirate was concerned. "The pirate has Lynna convinced that he stole her away to Trinidad, only to protect her from Suzanne's evil curse."

"Has me convinced?" Lynna lifted a confused brow before turning an icy glare on her husband. "Joshua, exactly what do you mean when you say Sean has me convinced? Are you saying that perhaps I imagined the entire ordeal on the ship? Or the fact that I was so near death was only a dream? Are you suggesting that the intense pain and suffering I endured was but a figment of an overactive imagination?"

"Trinidad?" Nathan interrupted. "Why Trinidad, darling?"

"Sean's grandmother lives there, on a cocoa plantation."

"Well, I'll be damned," Nathan said. "I never would have guessed Trinidad in a million years.

"Did you by chance go to Carnival while you were on the island, Lynna?" Joshua asked, irritated beyond measure for no apparent reason other than hearing the man's name. "I hear they celebrate with a grand party."

"As a matter of fact, we did."

"We, meaning you and Sean?"

"Yes, Joshua. Sean is my friend."

"You actually have the audacity to stand there and say that Sean Devereux is your friend?"

"Yes."

"Then perhaps you should have remained on the island with your friend."

"Perhaps I should have."

No one in the room moved or made a sound. This was not the homecoming they had expected.

Joshua couldn't let it rest. The wound was too fresh. "I find it hard to believe that I'm married to a woman who calls the most notorious pirate to roam the Caribbean in recent years her friend. A man completely devoid of morals."

"Come down off your pompous high horse, Joshua." Lynna was unable to suppress the anger she felt. "He hasn't been a pirate for years. He traded his ship for a cargo vessel and has been in legal trade since."

"So?" Nathan queried. "Are you saying the man did *not* kidnap you?"

"That is exactly what I am saying, father. He took me to prevent Suzanne from carrying out her plot to *murder* me."

"Surely, you aren't naive enough to believe that," Joshua stated, as calmly as possible. "He took you away to have his way with you. To convince you that I was dead, hoping you would fall into his waiting arms." No one in the room missed the quick flash of rage in Joshua's eyes. "Tell me, Lynna. Was his ploy successful?"

Lynna's outraged gasp echoed around the room, appalled that her husband would speak to her so in front of both their families. "Sean was always a gentleman to me, Joshua. Which is more than I can say for you."

"So, now I am being compared, and found lacking, to a man who rapes innocent women for sport, steals from any and all without remorse, and kills anyone who stands in his way?"

"I told you, Joshua. Sean is no longer a pirate." Lynna crossed her arms over her chest, shooting daggers with her eyes. "He lives a respectable life now."

"Bully for him," Joshua sneered.

"I don't care for your snide comments. You have no way of knowing how near death I was after Beau's birth, but I thank God every night for sending Sean to rescue me. While on his ship I prayed for death to release me from my unbearable torment. After Suzanne cursed me a second time, he never once left my side, holding my head as I vomited into a bucket, bathing me…"

"He… bathed you?" Joshua clutched the back of a chair when he felt the almost overpowering urge to shake some sense into her, make her see the pirate's intentions were far from noble.

"Yes, he did, while I lay in a pool of my own vomit and urine."

"Oh, you poor darling," Judith cried.

"He also forced me to eat when I would have starved, changed my soiled bedclothes, rubbed ointment on the horrible sores that riddled my face, and even went to the shaman on the island to purchase a spell to remove the curse."

She turned to face her husband, disappointment glistening in her eyes. "Sean did all that for me, while you stand here trying to convince everyone that I must be crazy and that voodoo is something to be scoffed at."

"I never insinuated that you were crazy, Lynna." Joshua massaging his temples. "Please, don't put words in my mouth."

Too angry to say more to her husband, Lynna moved to her father's chair. "Father, please, do not take this curse lightly. I beg you." She dropped to her knees and laid her head in his lap as hot tears soaked his breeches. "I cannot lose you again."

"Of course, I will do as you ask, my darling." Nathan stood, pulling Lynna to her feet and drawing her close. "Tomorrow, we will visit Amari and she what she would advise us to do."

"When is the next full moon?" Lynna sniffled, and blew her nose. "Most spells have to be performed when the moon is full."

"In three days." Nathan turned to Jeremiah. "Since Suzanne cast a spell on your head as well, would you care to join us?"

Jeremiah winked at Nathan when Lynna's head was turned. "If you don't mind, purchase a curse removal spell for me while you're there."

Joshua wanted to laugh out loud at such nonsense, but thought better of it. He had already allowed his jealousy of Sean Devereux to get the better of him. He should have known Lynna would defend the pirate. He was exhausted and wanted nothing more than to lie down with Lynna in his arms. "Shall we retire for the evening, love."

"You go ahead, Joshua." He was surprised by the harshness in her voice as he held her angry gaze. "I have been away from Aunt Judith for too long, and we have so much catching up to do. I will sleep in her room tonight."

"As you wish," Joshua muttered, before turning to stalk up the stairs to his room.

Voodoo.

Hah.

What balderdash.

Chapter 4

Lynna sat in a rocking chair beside Beau's bed and listened to his steady breathing. She smelled his sweet baby scent and caressed his soft midnight curls for over an hour. When she had her fill, for tonight, she gave him one last good night kiss and nodded to Milly as she slipped out the door and went to her aunt's room.

She found Judith sitting on her balcony, as fireflies danced around the beards of Spanish moss that dripped from the trees and frogs tried to out croak each other. The steady drone of cicadas reminded Lynna that she was finally home.

Why didn't she feel at home?

She wondered if Sean and Lisbeth were sitting on the verandah at Devereux Acres enjoying another breathtaking sunset, Lisbeth sipping from a glass of wine. She missed the sound of palm fronds clicking in the gentle breeze, the waves crashing against the shore, and the smell of sweet cocoa scenting the evening air.

"Talk to me, Lynna." Judith moved to the edge of her seat to take her niece's hand. "Tell me what is troubling you. You try to hide it, but I know you too well."

"You always did." Lynna laughed uneasily. She would like nothing better than to unburden her soul to her aunt. Let someone else carry the weight for a short while. She drew her legs underneath her and leaned back to get comfortable. "I wouldn't even know where to begin, Aunt Judith."

"I find it's best to start at the beginning, dear."

So she did. Telling her every detail that had led up to the night of the Hammond's Masquerade Ball. Her sickness, Suzanne's curse, Sean's tender care, Trinidad, Lisbeth, Doc Buzzard, and finally, the day on the beach when she had felt an almost uncontrollable urge to feel Sean's naked, sweaty body pressed against her own.

"I was willing to go to any means necessary to get home to Beau, Aunt Judith." Lynna covered her face with her hands, ashamed to meet her aunt's eyes.

"You have nothing to be ashamed of, Lynna. Any mother in your position would have done the same thing. There is no disgrace in doing what is best for your child."

"After months of being together, going to Port of Spain, attending Carnival, performing the curse removal spell, things started to… change between us."

"How do you mean?" Judith knew exactly what she was saying, yet she wanted Lynna to admit it to herself. "In what way?"

"I began to develop feelings…"

"You were attracted to him?"

"Yes. I mean… no. Not at first. He had been by my side through it all, and we were always together, and we enjoyed being together, and… oh, Aunt Judith. What am I going to do?"

Judith stood, drawing her trembling niece into her arms. "About what, Lynna? Why are you so upset? Just be honest with me, darling. I only want to help."

Lynna held on to her aunt for several minutes as she rocked her gently and rubbed her back, just as she always had. After her tears were spent and she felt like she could breathe easier after a good cry, she drew a cleansing breath. "The night of the Hammond's Ball was so unbelievably…"

She stopped herself from saying more and left her aunt's arms to stand at the rail, peering into the dark night. "I almost fainted from shock when I realized I was dancing with Joshua. You must understand that I thought he was dead, Aunt Judith. I never once imagined him to still be alive."

"We all thought he was dead, darling." Judith stood beside her, inhaling the fragrances of jasmine and honeysuckle on the night air. "No one could blame you for moving on with your life after what you had been through. You are lucky to be alive." She smoothed Lynna's hair from her face. "When you believed that your husband was dead, were you happy on the island?"

"As happy as I could be, without Beau. The island is so beautiful, Aunt Judith. You would love it."

"I'm sure I would." Judith refused to allow her to change the subject. "Tell me about Sean."

"Sean is… was… very good to me. As I said earlier, he alone nursed me back to health. That's why I get so infuriated with Joshua. He was so grateful to Clara and Lucille for saving his life that he brought them here to the plantation to live, and I'm happy that he did. Yet, he wants to kill Sean for extending the same courtesy to me."

"The pirate had already attempted to kidnap you to his island you once before, Lynna. When Joshua found out that he had taken you again, did you really expect your husband to feel generous toward him?"

Lynna dropped her head wearily in her hands. "Why can't I make anyone understand that Sean saved my life and should therefore be praised, rather than constantly scorned?"

"We do understand."

"No, you don't. None of us would have arrived at the conclusion that Suzanne had cursed me in time to save me. With everyone thinking I suffered from childbed fever, I would have died, Aunt Judith. I would have lain in that bed across the hall and died a slow and agonizing death if not for Sean."

"I agree, my darling. You wouldn't have lived more than a few days at most."

"Thank God, Sean was able to foil Suzanne's devious plot to kill me. He took me away because it was the only way to save my life. Why can't Joshua see that? How can he be so blind?"

"He sees it, Lynna. He sees it in your eyes whenever you mention Sean's name. Jealousy is a powerful emotion. Not knowing the truth, and the constant worry of not knowing, is even worse. Only you and Sean know what really happened on that island. Joshua only knows what you tell him."

Lynna could not have this discussion tonight. She went into her aunt's room to undress and pull a soft cotton nightgown over her head.

"I'm afraid Joshua is planning to seek revenge on Sean. If he does I will never forgive him, Aunt Judith. He should be thankful that Sean was there to rescue me, just as Clara rescued him."

Judith took Lynna's hand. "Your words are true. Yet, you have to admit that Joshua's situation was vastly different from the one you found yourself in."

"Of course, I would," Lynna replied, exasperated. "You must also realize that I didn't choose my circumstances any more than Joshua did."

"Neither of you did. Fate can be a cruel mistress. But everything that happened is in the past. It's time for you both to put the last year behind you and move forward with your life. You have a son to raise."

For the first time, Lynna smiled a brilliant smile. "I can hardly wait to be a mother to Beau."

"Do you love Joshua, Lynna?"

"With my heart and soul."

"Then, please, give me an honest answer to my next question, darling."

"If I can."

"Do you love Sean?"

Lynna's sharp intake of breath echoed through the still night. "Aunt Judith, how can you ask me that?"

"Just answer me truthfully, Lynna."

"I can't answer your question because I don't... know the answer. I have feelings for Sean, but I can't put into words exactly what they are. If I am..."

"If you are what, darling?"

Lynna was quiet for several minutes, forcing a smile she was far from feeling. "If we don't get some sleep I won't be able to keep up with my little toddling angel tomorrow. Joshua and I are taking him on a picnic, and I intend for him to adore his mother by the time we return home."

Judith had never known Lynna to withhold the truth from her. Yet, she was doing so now.

Whatever was troubling her, she wasn't ready to share it.

Chapter 8

Suzanne's fingers had rough calluses along the entire length of them. She had picked enough cotton and filled enough sacks to supply the entire female population of Mississippi with sufficient cotton for a year's worth of frilly dresses.

Having left her hammock at 4:00am, she and the other inmates had arrived in the field by 5:00am and would be forced to work until dark.

She slung a scratchy burlap pick sack over her head. The sack had been reinforced on the bottom with heavy cloth to prevent it from wearing out as it was dragged along the ground. A shoulder strap on front of the sack rested on her shoulders so it could be pulled along behind her, leaving her hands free to remove the cotton from the bolls. The sack measured about six feet in length.

Suzanne hated picking cotton in the early morning hours since the dew made the threads stick to her fingers. Her hands, fingers and wrists were hideously scarred from the dried bristles of the plants, but that wasn't the worst part. It was the constant stooping and bending to pluck the cotton once it had blossomed. Some of the inmates were forced to get on their knees and crawl when their backs simply gave out from years of stooping.

Suzanne gathered as much cotton as she

could hold in each hand before tossing it into her sack. She had long since learned the secret was to pluck the cotton out of the boll without getting stuck by the sharp burr surrounding it. She had developed her own rhythm to get her from one hour to the next and averaged picking one hundred pounds of cotton a day.

With each fluffy white boll she picked, she imagined it to be one of her enemy's eyes she was gouging out. Mainly Lynna's, but sometimes Joshua's, Clara's, her parent's, or one of her brothers. She intended to get even with the lot of them.

She was eagerly awaiting her parents' next visit to hear all about Nathan and Jeremiah's graveside rites. How she would love to be in attendance at their funerals.

Sweat streamed down her face in rivulets and into her eyes as the sun scorched her skin. In all honesty, she hardly felt the sun anymore. Her skin had been charred to the point that heat rarely bothered her. She lifted a hand to touch her face, but the skin on her fingers was so tough she couldn't feel the leather like texture of her once porcelain skin.

She had a farmer's tan. Her face, neck, and hands were as dark as some of the workers on her father's plantation, while the rest of her body was still lily white. Her back, arms, and legs were crisscrossed with whip marks and riddled with bites and festered sores. She was a disgusting mess.

Would any man ever want her again?

As a diversion from the monotony of picking cotton she allowed her mind to wander to happier times. Her nipples hardened and an ache settled between her thighs as she recalled the many nights she and Joshua had made sweet, passionate love in the pond, or on the soft carpet of grass beside it. She smiled, remembering their wedding day. *The happiest day of her life.* They would still be married if not for Lynna. She was the root cause of each and *every* one of her problems.

"Quit woolgathering and get back to work," Mona shouted, from several rows over. "Don't even waste your time thinking about a man." The guard laughed heartily. "Have you taken a good look at yourself lately?" Giving Maxine a wink, she added, "Just be thankful Maxine still has a hankerin' for you."

Suzanne glanced down the row at Maxine as she winked and licked her lips, and felt her stomach churn.

Chapter 9

The occupants of Sea Grove were surprised to see Clara willingly hand Beau over to Joshua and grab her straw bonnet. With a bow tied neatly under her chin, she stood by the door, waiting impatiently.

Joshua eyed her with keen interest, wondering why Clara felt so strongly that she should accompany Lynna on her visit to Amari. Now *he* was concerned. Clara had been born with a veil. The older she got, Joshua noticed that she could sense things others could not. What was she sensing now? He would have to call on this ridiculous voodoo person with his wife, if for no other reason than to keep her safe.

Clara leaned against the doorframe, tapping the toe of her soft kid slipper on the floor. Until recently, she had never even heard the word voodoo. She and her grandmother had stayed up late into the night as Lucille explained the ancient religion. Now, after being told what little her grandmother knew on the subject of curses, spells, zombies and voodoo rituals, Clara didn't like the thoughts of Lynna visiting Amari one bit.

"Lynna, darling," Joshua began, as he sauntered to the mantle to take down his bandalore. He tossed it a few times, laughing as Beau's head moved up and down as he watched the toy travel along the string.

Lynna longed for a way to freeze that moment in time.

"I really wish you wouldn't insist upon sneaking onto Samuel's land to get to the conjure woman's cabin. Are you aware that you could be prosecuted for trespassing? We are both smart enough to realize that we won't be welcomed with open arms, after that unpleasant incident with his sister?"

Lynna paused, watching father and son. Beau had one arm around his father's neck and was leaning his head against Joshua's chin as he reached for the bandalore. "Honestly, Joshua? Do you really think my father's team of lawyers couldn't get a simple trespassing charge dismissed?"

"She has a good point. Let her go, son," Jeremiah advised. "I can't say whether Lynna suffered from a voodoo curse or childbed fever, but whichever it was it was the worst sickness I have ever encountered. If there is even a possibility that Nathan or I could be struck down with that, or a similar illness, I say let us take whatever precautions necessary to prevent it."

"Thank you, Jeremiah." Lynna hurried over to plant a soft kiss on his forehead. "For always being the voice of reason."

"What can it hurt?" Nathan agreed.

Joshua could only shake his head at the amount of nonsense coming from a room full of adults. "Shall we go then?"

"Are *you* going with us?" Lynna queried, in disbelief.

"Of course." Joshua gave Beau the

bandalore to puzzle over. While the child was thoroughly engrossed with the new toy, he handed him to Malinda after a kiss on his rosy cheek. "If my darling wife insists on visiting this…" luckily he had stopped before saying the word fraud… "this champion of the nether world, then I suppose I am going as well." He pulled Clara against him for a quick hug. "It would appear as though Clara has every intention of joining us as well."

"It certainly looks that way." Nathan chuckled.

Joshua drove the buggy with Lynna and Nathan on the seat beside him. Clara sat in the back as they traveled through the forest and down the back road between Sea Grove and Cedar Hill. The seldom used and heavily rutted road had knee high grass and weeds growing in the center, making for a slow and bumpy passage.

They had been traveling for half an hour when Joshua pulled the horses to a halt to gaze across the road at the remains of a rotting tree. "This is where my father lost his legs."

Lynna squeezed Joshua's hand, realizing how painful the sight must be for him.

"After his accident the tree was never cut for firewood because the superstitious workers refused to go near what they referred to as the *voodoo woods*. They would not go within an inch of the Cedar Hill border for fear of the conjure woman and her curses." Joshua could only shake his head. "They still talk about the ghost of the little girl who led my father into the path of the falling tree. I remember Big Jim telling me it was a bad omen if you saw the little girl. It meant bad juju was headed your way."

Lynna glanced toward the dead tree and the dark woods surrounding it, fully convinced that they could indeed be haunted.

Joshua shook the reins and prodded the horse forward. "I remember as a child hearing Big Jim whisper about Amari, when he allowed me to go hunting with him."

"Amari?" Lynna asked.

"The voodoo woman who reigns over these woods, supposedly very powerful. Big Jim often warned me to never take this road because it leads straight to the devil woman's door."

"Are you nervous?" Lynna whispered, softly.

Joshua chuckled, taking her hand to rest on his rock hard thigh. "When the workers refer to this area as the voodoo woods it is nothing more than superstitious nonsense, darling."

Lynna stared into the quiet woods, painfully aware that voodoo was far more than superstitious nonsense.

They were silent for the remainder of the ride, each deep in thought until the woods ended and they came to a small clearing.

While the house was a typical workers cabin, there was something different about Amari's. For one thing, it was set far apart from the others. You could barely see the next house in the distance when, as a rule, cabins were practically built on top of one another.

A rocker with a cushioned seat sat on the porch and marigolds grew in a well kept bed on either side. There were curtains at the window and a rag rug to wipe your feet before entering the dwelling, both unusual luxuries.

Nathan climbed the steps to the cabin, knocked on the door and waited.

After several minutes had passed, they heard shuffling feet on the other side and presently the door opened. Amari looked past Nathan at Lynna, and she immediately saw the recognition and surprise in the old woman's eyes.

"You should be dead," Amari mumbled, apparently not at all pleased that one of her curses had failed. "You must know a powerful root worker to still be alive." Her eyes searched Lynna from head to toe for any signs of illness.

"A shaman on the island of Trinidad, evidently one considerable more formidable than you, prepared a curse removal spell. As you can see, it worked like a charm." Lynna sauntered into the room, uninvited. Amari moved out of the way for the others to enter, eying Lynna with disdain. When Clara passed, Amari gasped and moved back a few steps.

It was all Lynna could do to keep the laughter that bubbled in her throat from erupting to the surface.

The great and powerful Amari felt threatened by sweet Clara.

Amari moved to the fireplace to sit in her rocker, motioning for Lynna to take the seat beside her and the others to sit at the table. "Now I understand why you still walk with the living. A shaman is a powerful juju man. I didn't think anyone in this country had the power to uncross one of my curses." She glanced at the rich white man standing with Mister Jordan's wife. "Who are you?"

"I am Lynna's father," he announced, proudly.

"Would you care to state your business?" Amari didn't care for white men, especially rich ones.

"Before I do," Nathan replied, "would you be so kind as to answer a few questions for me."

Amari knew what was coming.

"What did Suzanne offer you in exchange for murdering my daughter?"

"A year's worth of supplies," Amari didn't sound the least ashamed of her unscrupulous behavior. "Blankets, food, material to make a new set of clothes, coffee, sugar, flour and a sack of hard candy."

"So, in essence, you will do whatever anyone asks as long as the person doing the asking can pay your fee. Would that be an accurate assessment?"

"Yes, sir, that about sums it up." Amari waved her hand in the air. "Look around you. My childhood was spent in New Orleans where my mother was a quadroon ladies' maid. I was reared in the big house at her skirt, therefore, I was never around the working class." Dancing flames reflected the firelight in the voodoo woman's eyes. "When the mistress passed, her only son separated mother and I by selling us to different owners."

Amari huffed out a deep sigh. "While this life was foreign to me, I have learned to make the best of a bad situation. Have you ever been poor, sir?"

"Yes." Nathan shuffled his feet and leaned back to cross his ankle over his knee. "As a child."

"Then you should understand." Amari pointed a gnarled finger at Clara. "Who are you, young lady?"

"Her name is Clara," Lynna answered.

"Why do you answer for her?"

"Clara does not speak."

Amari held out her wrinkled hands to Clara. When the young girl took her hands, Amari shuddered as a jolt of current sizzled up her arms. She gazed intently into Clara's eyes. "Would you like to speak?"

"I won't allow you to fill her head with rubbish," Joshua warned, not about to let this sham artist get Clara's hopes up only to have them brutally crushed. He took Clara's arm and pulled her away from the woman, leading her out the open door to stand on the porch.

Clara's eyes were riveted on Amari as she pondered her words.

Would you like to speak?

"We didn't come here for you to make promises to an innocent child, when you have no possible means to deliver on your promises," Joshua gritted. "We are here to purchase a curse removal spell."

Amari was silent for a moment, unable to pull her eyes away from Clara. "Just ask your wife if I can deliver on my promises." She picked up a bowl and pestle from the hearth and began crushing what appeared to be dried frog legs into a powder.

Lynna smiled. "I'm afraid that I must agree with my husband. You placed a wasting spell on me, did you not?" For emphasis she lifted her skirt and twirled around in front of the old woman. "I could not be healthier."

Amari didn't especially care for being the butt of Lynna's joke, nor the suggestion that her curses were anything less than effective. "Can you tell me you did not suffer such unbelievable pain that you prayed for death to release you from the agony?"

Noticing a shadow darken his daughter's eyes as they filled with the remembrance of excruciating pain, Nathan stepped forward. "Can you just make the curse removal spell, so we can be on our way?"

Amari lifted a lid to stir a pot on the stove and judging from the smell, the contents were anything but edible. "Which of you has been cursed? I will need as much information as you can give me before I give you an answer."

"Both my father and Lynna's father were supposedly cursed," Joshua answered from the doorway, unable to hide a smirk. He found it hard to believe he was actually having this discussion.

"Can you tell me who cast the spell?" Amari knew she could uncross most spells, with the exception of curses cast by her own teacher.

"Suzanne Fletcher."

Amari's hands stilled as she glanced up from underneath her lashes. No one in the room missed the surprise that briefly registered in her eyes. She herself had taught Suzanne the ancient art of voodoo, so her work would not be easily reversed. "What spell did she cast?"

"Something about frogs coming out of our

ears, nose, and throat." Nathan almost laughed out loud, while Lynna didn't seem to find the discussion humorous at all.

Nor did Amari. Her eyes grew wide. "How long ago?"

"Roughly three months." The laughter died in Nathan's throat when he saw the look of alarm in the old woman's eyes.

Amari had no doubt that frogs were coming to life in his stomach as they spoke. The spell normally took at least three months to come to fruition. She knew one thing for certain, after Suzanne had placed the curse she had to find a way to make the victims ingest the blood of a frog.

She had to wonder how Suzanne was able to accomplish that while sitting in the town jail. Apparently, she had become bosom buddies with one of the servants at Sea Grove.

Lynna was growing impatient. She wanted to purchase the curse removal spells and get as far away from this detestable woman as she could. "The shaman in Trinidad gave me a powder that I released into running water, and a rose quartz to wear close to my heart for nine days. Can you duplicate that spell."

Appearing somewhat insulted, Amari was quick to inform her, "I do not duplicate spells. I perform my own, but these things take time."

"And your payment?"

"Two wagon loads of firewood."

"It will be delivered today," Joshua assured her, stepping into the room to prod his wife out the door. "Now, we will bid you good day."

Joshua ushered Lynna and Nathan in front

of him and turned back to see Amari pilfering through an old wardrobe in the corner. "When will the spell be ready?"

"It will take a few days," she answered, still rummaging in the wardrobe. "I will send word when you are to return."

"Very well then." Joshua closed the door behind him, grateful to be leaving the loathsome woman's presence.

When everyone was loaded in the buggy, Joshua turned to Lynna, happy that the charade was over. "There now, are you feeling better about the curses that were placed on our fathers?"

"Not in the least. In fact, I won't rest easy until we have performed the curse removal spell." She tried to cheer up for her husband's benefit and turned smiling eyes toward him, hoping to forget the cross words from the night before. "Let's take our son on that picnic when we get home."

"Uh. Uh. Uh." Clara grunted behind them.

They glanced at each other sideways, wondering who was going to tell her.

When they arrived home, Malinda occupied Clara with a fitting for a new dress while Lynna, Joshua and Beau slipped away from the plantation.

After a short ride Lynna spread a blanket under the same tree that she and Joshua had their last picnic under. She smiled, recalling how irate Joshua had been when Suzanne came charging up and almost ran them over. Lynna shook her head and breathed a relieved sigh. Suzanne wouldn't be a threat to her happiness again for a long, long time.

She was distraught when she attempted to lift Beau from the buggy and he was having none of it.

"Easy does it, darling." Joshua urged. "Don't rush him."

Easy for him to say.

Beau adored his father.

The day was glorious. Blue skies, a warm breeze causing the wild flowers in the fields to sway, and bright sunlight streaking through the leaves of a shade tree. Joshua sat Beau on the seat, then climbed down and reached up for him.

The child jumped, landing in his father's arms with a squeal of delight. He immediately turned around and reached for the seat to do it again. Joshua allowed him to jump several more times. "That's enough for now. Let's see if Milly packed you a chicken leg."

She had, along with potatoes cooked in green beans, still warm buttermilk biscuits, and chocolate pound cake. Lynna watched as Joshua took a plate and pulled chicken off the bone, breaking it into tiny pieces. He handed Beau a biscuit to nibble on while he cut the potatoes and green beans into bite sized pieces.

Joshua was already a wonderful parent. She had a lot of catching up to do.

Beau went straight for the potatoes, sitting down to savor his meal. Joshua poured a cup of lemonade and would occasionally offer Beau a sip. She watched quietly as long as she could before motioning for Joshua to hand her the cup. The next time Beau was thirsty she held it to his lips.

The child grunted and turned his head,

pointing to his father with a greasy finger. Joshua only grinned, refusing to intervene. Lynna again held the cup to his lips and this time he drank, emptying it. She sat, patiently waiting for him to get thirsty again. When he did, he allowed Lynna to hold the cup without reservation, causing her to beam with happiness.

One small step.

With his belly full, Beau glanced around for a soft spot to lay his tired head. Lynna's fully rounded chest appeared to be the softest spot available, so he climbed toward her and reached out his arms. When she lifted him Beau snuggled against her and she closed her eyes, completely content with her world. He laid his head on her shoulder with his bottom stuck out and his hands clasped between them.

"I told you he would come around," Joshua whispered.

Lynna's face glowed brighter than the noonday sun. She leaned against the trunk of a tree and held her son close, vowing to never let him out of her sight again.

With their picnic reduced to chicken bones and empty containers, Joshua lay down on the blanket with his hands behind his head. To Lynna, he looked like one of the Greek gods she had read about, so handsome he could take her breath away. He turned just in time to catch her staring.

"I know," he teased. "I only get better with age."

"And more conceited." She giggled. "You always were too self assured of your dashing good looks, certain that any female you passed would fall at your feet."

"You fell didn't you?"

She had to grin. "I suppose I did."

"As I fell for you, my love. The proof of that love is nestled in your arms."

Lynna dropped her head to place a soft kiss on Beau's silky curls and gaze at her husband with adoring eyes. She was completely content for the first time in her life. "We are a family at last."

Chapter 10

Clara saddled Jezebel to go for a ride as she often did in the afternoon while Beau was taking a nap. Only today, she wasn't headed toward the river for a swim, she had a much more important destination in mind. Her mind was churning with questions when she brought Jezebel to a halt in front of the conjure woman's cabin.

Amari looked up from watering her marigolds with a sly grin. Clara already had the gift of healing.

What other talents did she possess?

"Come up on the porch and I'll get you a cold drink." Amari stood slowly, carefully straightening her arthritic spine. "You must be thirsty on such a hot day."

Clara tethered Jezebel and ambled up the steps. She was hesitant to drink anything a voodoo queen offered her, no matter how thirsty she was.

As she took her seat, she noticed the makings of a little doll in a basket beside the rocking chair. Strange. The doll wore a dress almost identical to the one she was wearing, with thread almost the exact color as her own hair sewn on the doll's head.

Before she could ponder overlong on why the old woman had a doll made to her likeness,

Amari returned with two tall glasses of lemonade and handed one to Clara.

The instant both their hands were on the glass Amari jerked, having felt a current of lightning streak through the glass and into her hand.

What powers did this strange young girl possess?

She had never felt anything like the surge that rushed up her arm at the girl's touch

The jolt traveled to every part of her body and caused the hair on the back of her neck to rise. She quickly released the glass, though her arm still tingled with a pins and needle feeling, as if her arm had gone numb and the blood was slowly returning. Amari massaged her arm, glancing at Clara from under her lashes to see if she'd had a similar reaction.

Clara was busy watching the condensation stream down the outside of her glass and licking her lips. She was thirsty.

"Go ahead and drink it, Clara. I have no cause to put a curse on you. It wouldn't take anyway."

Clara looked at her with a baffled expression.

Why wouldn't a spell take on her?

What was wrong with her?

Amari took a seat in her rocker. "You have no idea of the power you possess, do you, girl?"

Clara shook her head as confusion wrinkled her brow.

What power?

Amari released an irritated sigh. "By all rights, Nathan Rhodes and Jeremiah Jordan should have been dead and in their graves long before I removed the curse. The spell Suzanne placed on them should have been fatal. In all my years, I've never known anyone to survive it, but it is my understanding that they are both still alive and well." She looked at Clara with a certain amount of admiration. "They would not have survived if you hadn't been near them."

Clara was even more confused, patting her foot impatiently as she waited for the old conjure woman to explain.

She hadn't done anything to save their lives.

"You have the power to block a curse, Clara," the woman finally said. "You are the only person I have ever known with such an ability."

Amari watched Clara with keen interest as she talked. While she had mixed enough sleeping powder in Clara's drink to knock out a mule, for several hours, the young girl sat before her sipping lemonade as bright eyed and bushy tailed as when she arrived.

Amazing.

Yet, disturbing at the same time.

At a dear friend's request, Amari had promised to cast a spell on Lynna Jordan that would ruin the holiday season at Sea Grove for the entire family.

Clara would prevent the spell from working.

So Amari had been instructed to take Clara out of the picture.

But how?

None of her spells would work on someone as gifted as Clara. While she pondered on an effective spell to get rid of the bothersome child once and for all, she would need to come up with a scenario to temporarily get her out of the house. That way, whatever curse she concocted could take effect.

Perhaps she would send Clara to Cedar Hill for a few days to help the pregnant Beth. Surely, Samuel's wife would rejoice at the notion of having someone to help keep her rambunctious daughter entertained for a few weeks.

Especially if Beth was suddenly inflicted with a severe case of morning sickness.

They sipped their lemonade in silence as Clara swatted at persistent gnats that buzzed around her head and watched a lizard run across the porch rail. Chickens scratched and turned their heads sideways as they dug for worms in the freshly turned earth of the flowerbeds.

Amari chuckled. "That lizard used to be the overseer here."

Clara glared at Amari as if she had taken leave of her senses, before returning a jaundiced eye to the lizard.

Amari's face was deadly serious. "I turned him into a lizard. Now he comes to my porch each day and sits on the rail, watching me. Always pleading with those sad eyes for me to change him back."

The conjure woman leaned forward in her chair and put her face in front of the lizard. "You're just wasting your time when you should be off catching bugs. I warned you what would happen if you kept parceling out your evil to the workers, but you wouldn't listen." She threw back her head and cackled. "You are listening now, aren't you?"

The lizard didn't move or bat an eye.

Nor did Clara. Was the old woman crazy?

Could she really turn a man into a lizard?

While the lizard had Clara's rapt attention, Amari reached into the basket and retrieved a long, sharp pin. With one swift motion she jabbed it clear through the head of Clara's voodoo doll.

Clara scratched her head at the site where the pin had entered, and the other side of her head where it had exited, as if she had been bitten by mosquitoes. She remained riveted on the lizard, showing no evidence of pain.

Amari leaned back in her chair, astonished. Never in her life had she witnessed anyone completely immune to one of her dolls. Neither her powders, nor her voodoo dolls worked on Clara. She would be forced to prepare her strongest curse yet, and she would need a few strands of Clara's hair to concoct it.

She rose slowly from her chair and stretched her back, walking behind Clara. She took handfuls of her shining strawberry curls and lifted them on top of her head. "Do you ever wear your hair up, Clara?"

Clara shook her head.

Malinda said she wasn't old enough yet.

"You really should try it sometime. It would be a most becoming style for you, especially at the Harvest Ball where there will most likely be several local boys your age attending." When Amari knew that Clara's head was filled with dancing and Balls, she dropped her hair. As if by accident the old conjure woman lifted several strands, twisted them around her finger and pulled.

"Uh!" Clara jerked away.

"I'm sorry, dear. My hand got caught in a tangle." Amari returned to her chair, dropping the hair in the basket on top of the doll for later use.

Still curious about the lizard, Clara placed the glass on the floor at her feet and pointed to the lizard with one hand while rubbing her head with the other.

"Oh, as far as lizards go, he's fairly content." Amari laughed. "He suns himself all day and has all the bugs he can eat. He just has to stay alert for predators."

Clara made a turning motion with her hand.

"Will I turn him back?" Amari asked.

Clara nodded.

"I don't think so." She shook her finger at the lizard. "He's too evil. He enjoys seeing other people in pain. The workers are better off without him."

When the conjure woman finished speaking the lizard promptly presented them with his back and scurried down the porch rail.

"Now he's all in a dither." Amari laughed until tears rolled down her cheek. "He'll run off and pout but he'll be back, unless a bird has him for lunch."

Clara puzzled over the lizard for a few more minutes before turning to Amari. She pointed to her mouth, then to Amari, then back to her mouth.

"You want to know if I can give you back your speech, don't you?"

Clara nodded eagerly.

Amari leaned forward in her chair for emphasis. "If you really wanted to speak, you could. You have always had the power to do so."

The old woman was talking crazy talk.

Of course, she wanted to talk like everyone else. Clara exhaled an annoyed breath and glared at Amari, shaking her head with annoyance.

"To answer your question, yes. I can give your speech back to you. But be warned, it will not be fast, nor will it be easy. It will require some effort on both our parts." She gazed into Clara's eyes, hesitant to touch her. "Most importantly of all, it must be our secret. No one else can know."

Clara made the motion of buttoning her lips. She jumped up from her rocker and grabbed a stick, writing one word in the dirt.

How?

"I'm afraid that is a secret as well." Amari made a motion of buttoning her own lips. "You just trust me, Clara. All your questions will be answered in due time. Now you must return home before you are missed. Come back one week from today at this same time and we will get started."

Clara nodded to let Amari know that she understood. At the bottom of the steps she glanced toward the flowerbed and noticed the lizard sunning on a rock, ever alert for predators.

She climbed on Jezebel's back and waved timidly to Amari. Clara didn't believe for a minute that the voodoo woman had the power to give her speech back to her, but one thing was crystal clear. The old woman held ill feelings toward Lynna.

And probably Beau.

It was Clara's intention to find out what those intentions were, and put a stop to them before any harm came to her loved ones.

Amari watched the young girl's horse gallop down the road until she was out of sight before picking up the basket with the doll and strands of Clara's hair. She placed the glass Clara had used in the basket and walked around the yard until she had added five black crow feathers.

She now had all of the ingredients she needed for her curse.

Chapter 11

Beau was finally coming around. He and his mother took long walks through the garden or saddled up Lynna's horse and rode to the river to watch minnows swimming near the water's edge. He was learning to pick flowers and grinned from ear to ear as he presented them to his beaming mother. He was a such beautiful child, the image of his father, and doted on by every member of the household.

They had just returned home with his hands overflowing with wildflowers to present to his grandmother, when a young boy arrived. He didn't say a word as he cautiously looked Lynna over from head to toe. Coming to a hard fought decision, he reached into his pocket and withdrew a crumpled piece of paper. The lady had hair the color of the sun and she was very pretty, so hopefully she was the one the conjure woman told him to give the message to. "Is you Miz Lynna?"

"Yes."

"Den dis fo' you."

The boy jerked the horse's reins and galloped away in a cloud of dust before Lynna could even thank him. She adjusted Beau on her hip and read the note.

Your request is complete.

You may come now.
Amari.

Come now? Why, Joshua would be livid if she visited Amari without him. However, Jeremiah and her father were accompanying him to another meeting and they wouldn't be home until late.

What could it hurt?

After taking Beau inside for his nap, Lynna slipped out of the house and returned to the saddle.

The forest was cool and quiet except for birds calling to one another that there was a visitor in their midst, and the occasional deer leaping into her path. Lynna was enjoying the scenery and a cooling breeze, when she suddenly felt so exhausted she could hardly hold herself upright in the saddle. She tired so easily now. Dismounting, she tethered her horse and sat on the ground against the trunk of a tree, enjoying the peace and quiet.

After some time, her aching bottom reminded her that she had been sitting in one spot too long. As she was getting to her feet she heard what sounded like a child's playful giggling.

Where was the sound coming from?

She glanced across the road toward the dead tree and realized that she was in the exact spot where Jeremiah had lost his legs. She would forever swear that she saw a little girl standing on top of the fallen tree, smiling at her. Big Jim's warning echoed in her head.

It's a bad omen if you see the little girl.
Bad times are headed your way.

Lynna closed her eyes for a moment, rubbing them with her fists. When she opened them the girl was gone. An uneasy feeling settled over her as she mounted her horse. Surely, it had been nothing more than her imagination.

Her nerves were on edge when she entered the clearing to find Amari sitting in a rocking chair on the porch talking to a… lizard? Nonsense, the old woman was probably just mumbling to herself.

"I'm glad you came alone," the conjure woman said.

Lynna had to wonder how Amari knew who she was when she hadn't looked up from her work once. "Why are you glad?"

She set aside the bowl of green beans she was snapping and flexed her stiff fingers. "Your husband is not a believer, and that weakens the spell. When you release the salt in flowing water do not allow him to go to the river with you."

"Anything else?" Lynna found it hard to keep the hostility she felt for the evil woman from seeping into her voice.

Amari laughed softly, meeting Lynna's eyes for the first time. "You should not hold such animosity toward me, dear. It was nothing personal."

Lynna could only glare at the woman. "Call me crazy, but I tend to take it personally whenever someone tries to kill me. You didn't know anything about me. Nor, did you try to find out. You just set out to murder me without a care for the innocent child I carried."

"In my own defense, I had no idea you were carrying a child at the time of Suzanne's visit."

"Would it have mattered?"

"Probably not," Amari admitted.

"I didn't think so. You don't strike me as being a woman who would lose sleep over something as trivial as the death of an unborn child. Now, if you will give me the curse removal I can be on my way."

Lynna felt sick to her stomach and motioned to the wood stacked neatly between two trees. "I trust your payment is satisfactory."

"Yes, thank you." Amari put her bowl on the floor and stood slowly. She went in the house and called over her shoulder, "I will only be a minute."

Still tired, even after her short nap, Lynna had been considering a brief rest in one of the inviting rocking chairs when she found herself clutching the porch rail as a powerful wave of nausea swept over her. She rushed up the steps and took a seat, gripping the arms of the chair until her knuckles whitened. She forced slow, calming breaths, and waited for the sickness to pass.

When the nausea finally eased she leaned her head back, wiping at the beads of perspiration that dotted her forehead with a trembling hand.

Amari returned and offered her two salt packets, identical to the ones Doc had made.

Lynna accepted the packets and stood on shaky legs. She had started toward the steps when Amari grabbed her arm with her crippled fingers. "Do you want me to fix you a potion to get rid of it?"

Lynna was dumbfounded, gaping at the old conjure woman with her mouth hanging open. "Get rid of what?"

Amari reached out and rubbed a gnarled hand over Lynna's stomach, mumbling some unintelligible words.

Jerking away from her hand, Lynna cried out and hurried down the steps. At the bottom she stopped and turned to peer into Amari's eyes. "What did you say?"

Ignoring her, Amari asked a question of her own. "You are not happy to be bringing a new life into the world," she stated, in an ominous voice. "Why is this, when you should be overjoyed?"

"Your words are crazy?" Lynna again felt nausea bubbling in her throat. "You have no idea what you're talking about?"

Amari shook her head as she turned to go inside. When she closed the door behind her, the conjure woman was still chanting strange, incoherent words.

Chapter 12

Lynna was in the kitchen cleaning Beau's face and hands after a messy meal of mashed sweet potatoes and black-eyed peas when she heard the butler greet a visitor at the door. She lifted her toddler and grinned when he adamantly refused to release his biscuit and continued to gnaw on it. "You seem to be wearing as much food as you ate, mister. Let's go see who our visitor is."

Settling Beau on her hip, she hurried down the hall and turned into the parlor, stopping dead in her tracks. "Beth?"

"Hello, Lynna," Beth's gaze fell to Beau as she beamed at the adorable child. "Would you just look at the little darling? Isn't he the most precious thing you ever laid your eyes on?"

Lynna couldn't help but smile. "He and I are slowly getting reacquainted, but yes, he is rather adorable. Why didn't you bring Bethany with you to play with Beau?"

"My daughter was too busy playing hide and seek with Clara to gallivant across the countryside with her mother." Beth laughed. "My daughter is absolutely thrilled to have a playmate. I'm so happy you thought to suggest it. You can't imagine what a great help Clara has been."

Suggest it?

Lynna thought Beth and Samuel had requested that Clara visit for a few weeks.

Oh well, it wasn't important, as long as both families were happy with the outcome.

"I'm so glad we could help, and Clara adores Bethany."

Beth hung her head with shame, fidgeting with her reticule. "Besides, I wasn't sure how I would be... received after all that... happened." The smile left Beth's face as she turned serious. "Lynna, I came to apologize."

"Whatever for, Beth?" Lynna was astonished that dear, sweet Beth would feel the need to apologize. "You've done nothing wrong."

"I'm here to apologize for Suzanne's atrocious behavior." Beth turned to the window, gazing toward the pond and the lattice work gazebo, ashamed to face Lynna. "It was reprehensible, and I still can't believe Samuel's own sister was capable of something so... heinous."

"Are you saying that you and Samuel aren't mad at us for having Suzanne convicted and sent to prison?"

"Mad? Dearest, Lynna, of course not." Beth turned from the window, covering a smile with a gloved hand. "I personally think it was the best possible outcome for the situation."

"The best outcome?" Lynna was astounded. "Come sit with us, this little man is heavy." Beau immediately scrambled out of her arms and pulled up on the back of the settee in an attempt to gnaw on the wood trim. Lynna tugged him back to her lap and offered him a noisy rattle filled with seeds that Rob had made. "Does the rest of the family share your sentiment?"

Beth exhaled a ragged sigh. "Samuel, Daniel and I are of the same mindset, while Silas and Mary are rather upset, as you might expect. They even threatened to disown Daniel if he marries Malinda."

Lynna shook her head sadly, feeling responsible for the grief of so many people. "How terrible for Daniel."

"What did they expect?" Beth was on her feet again, too agitated to sit still. "For you and Joshua to sit back and do nothing after their daughter hired men to murder Joshua, and then tried to kill you with a voodoo curse? It's insane. They should count their blessings that Suzanne is locked away where she can't cause harm to anyone else."

Beth threw up her hands and paced the floor. "I can't imagine why they fought so hard to keep her out of prison when Samuel and Daniel both agreed that she should be made to pay for her crimes."

"You don't know what a relief it is to hear you say that, Beth." As Lynna stood to give her friend a heartfelt hug, Beau wrapped his arms around her neck to lay his head on her shoulder. "Your coming here means so much to me."

Beth grinned. "Well, I did have a specific reason for coming today."

"And what was that?"

"To invite you and the family to the Harvest Ball, and the wedding, of course."

Completely taken aback by the invitation, Lynna was unsure of just how wise it would be to attend a ball given by Suzanne's brother. "Will Silas and Mary be there?"

"When I told them we were celebrating Daniel and Malinda's wedding at the Harvest Ball, they refused to come. Which is fine by me. All they ever talk about is winning an appeal for Suzanne and getting her sentence reversed, so they can send her to some asylum for treatment, God forbid."

In Lynna's opinion there was little danger of that happening. "Father's lawyers have assured us that her sentence will not be overturned."

Beth looked over her shoulder to make sure no one was listening. "Lynna, did Suzanne really put a voodoo curse on you? I always thought voodoo was hocus pocus nonsense, not to be taken seriously."

Lynna grasped her hand with an urgent plea. "Please, believe me when I tell you that voodoo is not nonsense. It is very real. Suzanne wanted me dead, Beth."

"From what I hear she almost succeeded."

Lynna rubbed her eyes, refusing to allow her mind to return to those terrible days on Sean's ship during the peak of her illness. "I thank God daily that Sean rescued me when he did."

"Rescued you?" Beth noticed how her friend's features softened when she mentioned the pirate. "I thought he abducted you?"

"It's complicated, Beth." No one had understood the circumstances behind her abduction thus far, why would Beth be any different? "Sean took me away to prevent Suzanne from killing me."

Beth forced a smile she was far from feeling. "Then I am eternally grateful to the dear man."

"I wish my husband felt that way."

Beth was certain that he never would. Not after her husband's recent talk with Joshua. In fact, he had informed Samuel that he was counting off the days until he could return to Trinidad and rid the earth of the pirate scum.

Beth watched as Lynna absently sat in a rocker by the window and cuddled her sleepy son close to her breast, deep in thought. Her friend obviously had things on her mind that she wasn't ready to share.

Beau yawned, snuggling closer against his mother as she stared out the window. He was asleep in seconds. "This is my favorite part of the day. I get to hold him for over an hour without him wiggling out of my arms to explore what's around the next corner." Lynna sighed, her heart swelling with happiness as she rocked her son. "I never knew the love that existed between a mother and child could be so strong."

"Neither did I, until Bethany Breanne came along. Soon I will have another child to love." Feeling like she was interrupting a mother and son moment, Beth stood to take her leave. "Can I expect to see you and Joshua at the wedding?"

"Of course." Lynna spoke softly so as not to wake her sleeping child. She held out her hand to take Beth's hand and squeeze it. "We wouldn't miss it."

Chapter 13

Nathan passed the creamed corn down the table and reached for a platter of crispy butter fried pork chops. After stacking building blocks all afternoon so his grandson could take great joy in watching them topple to the floor, he was starving. At the same time his stomach felt oddly full, as though he had already consumed a five-course meal.

He sipped his sweet tea and decided to wait a few minutes and allow his stomach to settle before attempting to eat.

As he did, his insides rumbled. *Loudly.* Not your typical *feed me* rumble, but a loud and insistent growling that echoed through the room as though a volcano was about to erupt in his stomach. "Please, excuse me." He glanced up from his plate with a flaming face, embarrassed beyond words.

Lynna smiled sympathetically at her discomfited father. "Did you miss lunch, Father."

"No, actually, I had a rather hearty meal." Before the words were out, his stomach rumbled ominously. Only this time it was accompanied by what felt like a sharp knife to his gut. He gasped for breath when his bowels seized, squeezing his insides until he bent double in the throes of excruciating pain. The intense agony gripped his midsection, ripping from back to front until he was unable to hold back an anguished groan.

"Father?" Lynna cried, standing so fast that her chair clattered to the floor. She rushed to his side to wipe his heavily perspiring forehead with her napkin. "Is it the curse? Perhaps the curse removal spell we performed last night hasn't had time to take effect. We will return to Amari at once and get you the help you need. I promise."

Nathan put his hands on the table to rise and return to his room. When he strained to stand, the action caused the most humiliating experience of his entire life.

His bowels... exploded.

As if that act alone was not the epitome of degradation, not only did his bowels erupt, but the defecation was followed by the most ghastly odor anyone in the room had ever encountered. It was a bowel movement with a chemical odor and death smell combined.

No one in the room could stomach a bite of food and hastily fled the table. Actually, they fled the house entirely and moved to the verandah.

Servants coughed and gagged as they rushed to open windows and doors. Still, the nauseating scent lingered, infiltrating the walls and floors. One of the kitchen servants was heard to mumble, "Sumphin' done crawl' up his ass an' died."

Only Lynna remained with her father, holding several cloth napkins to her nose while feeling a strong urge to rush to the window and relieve her stomach of its contents. The others had left for the promise of fresh air, but also because they knew Nathan wouldn't want them to witness his humiliation.

"Father, what can I do?" Lynna mumbled, through several layers of cotton. The intensity of the smell caused her eyes to burn until tears streamed down her cheeks.

When Nathan was finally able to straighten up, his drawers... squished. "Go outside with the others, darling. The pain has passed. I will go upstairs to take a bath and change. I don't know what happened, nor when I will be able to show my face again."

"Don't be ridiculous, father," Lynna insisted. "We know... this... did not come from you, but from Suzanne's curse."

"Be that as it may, darling, I have nonetheless shat myself in front of a room full of people, at the dinner table no less. It's hard to look someone in the eye and carry on a casual dinner conversation after that." Nathan stood, his drawers drooping heavily as though they were filled with hot, slippery mud. *He wished.* "Now run along while I attend to my own disgrace."

"Are you sure?" While Lynna craved fresh air above all else, she was reluctant to desert her father in his hour of need. "I would be glad to..."

"Please, darling, just go outside with the others and leave me to my shame."

When he reached the bottom of the stairs Nathan looked through the hall and into the kitchen. Empty. The servants had raced out the back door after throwing open every window in the house.

He slowly and carefully made his way up the stairs, leaning heavily on the rail. His drawers were filled to capacity. His every step was planned, so as not to disrupt whatever his breeches held and send it oozing down his leg and to the floor.

By the time he made it to his room, with his backside rubbing against the contents of his breeches, his behind was raw and burning like fire. He went to stand in front of the open window and peeled down his breeches and drawers. The sight he exposed made him cry out and drop sharply to his knees, feeling faint.

A nasty wad of green, slimy dead frogs lay in a puddle in his breeches. Their eyes were wide open and their arms and legs were wrapped around each other in a tight huddle. With a horrified shriek, he kicked out of his pants legs. Those living... creatures could not have been inside him all this time.

He stuck his head out the window and took a deep breath, which was a dire mistake as he commenced to dry heaving. When he gathered the courage for one more look he was grateful to see that the frogs were indeed dead. Still the atrocious smell emanating from the hideous pile singed every last hair in his nose.

He held his breath as best he could and moved to the washstand to cleanse himself. He would do what he could, then get dressed and go downstairs to call for a bath to be drawn.

When he was dressed, and feeling almost human again, Nathan was making his way down the stairs when he heard a familiar screech of agony. He arrived on the verandah to find Jeremiah bent double with pain. Nathan hurried to his side. "Just hold on. The pain will pass shortly."

Jeremiah was red as a beet in the face with

sweat leaving a trail down his temples as he strained to rid his bowels of their nemesis.

Nathan turned to Joshua. "Call for Big Jim. He will need to carry your father to his room shortly." He pitied the poor man, having to hold what was about to come out of Jeremiah in his arms.

Joshua went to the edge of the verandah and shouted for Big Jim, the caregiver who had rarely left Jeremiah's side since the day of the accident. He ran around the side of the house with a look of stark terror, having already heard the news from the servants. He had the feeling that whatever was going on here was not natural, and he wanted no part of it. He was wholly convinced that the smell coming from these men's behinds was not of this earth.

Finally, after a loud explosion and a look of immense relief, Jeremiah was able to lean back in his chair, pain free, and wipe the sweat from his brow. The smell was even worse this time, if possible. Everyone hurried down the steps to mill around on the lawn.

Secretly, Nathan was relieved that he would not be forced to carry the shame of this debacle alone.

Big Jim removed his shirt to tie around his nose before reaching for Jeremiah. It didn't stop him from gagging when he bent over him, turning his head to vomit his lunch over the verandah rail. "I's sorry Mist'…"

"Don't talk, Big Jim…" Jeremiah urged. "Try to hold your breath as much as you can."

"Yassuh," Big Jim said, gagging.

"Call for a bar of strong lye soap and take me to the river. Get some matches too. We will need to burn these clothes."

Nathan raced upstairs to gather his own bundle of ruined clothes and met them at the buggy. "I need a good soaking as well."

"What happened to us?" Jeremiah asked, as Big Jim lifted him into the buggy.

"Frogs," Nathan whispered. "You are not going to believe this, but we were full of frogs. Just like Suzanne said we would be. I must warn you ahead of time to be prepared for what is waiting when you pull down your breeches. It will not be a pretty sight."

Big Jim leaned over the side of the buggy and vomited again.

He would be the one to pull down Mist' Jeremiah's pants.

Sally, the cook, shook her head as the buggy pulled away. "I ain't knowin' whut dem white folks gwine eat fo' supper. All de food in dat house gots to be throwed out."

Juanita the upstairs maid agreed, "An' weah have ta warsh evah stitch of clothes in dat house fo' deys kin wear dem again."

Flora, the downstairs maid, tisked tisked and chided them, "You gals got it easy. Weah have ta warsh evah wall, flo', winder, an' stick of furniture in dat house fo' de white folks will come back in." With a sorrowful shake of her head, she motioned for her helpers to follow her. "Come on, le's jus' git it ovah wit', den we kin take a bar of lye soap an' head down to de rivah."

Chapter 14

Suzanne moved to the window in the warden's office to watch as several convicts worked in a large vegetable garden. She saw staked up tomato vines loaded with ripe tomatoes, cucumber and green bean vines snaking around tall corn stalks, onions, pepper plants, watermelons, and cantaloupes.

What really caught her eye was a huge nearby oak tree where the inmates could seek shade on the scorching summer days. Lucky devils. She had slaved under a blazing sun all summer without a tree in sight.

She watched an old woman stooping to pick beans, remembering the warden's words from their last meeting.

Sea green eyes with the power to take your breath away?

She had to be acquainted with either Joshua or Jeremiah Jordan to know the color of their eyes. "If I may ask a question, there is something that has puzzled me since our last meeting."

"What would that be?" the warden queried.

"How you knew the color of Joshua Jordan's eyes?"

The warden closed the folder and leaned her elbows on the desk, almost bristling with nervous energy. "From what I hear Joshua's eyes are identical to his father's."

"Yes, he did inherit Jeremiah's green eyes, as did Beau." Suzanne still wore a confused frown. "Are you acquainted with Jeremiah Jordan then?"

"My mother was." The warden glanced up from her desk with a look of pure malice. "I was forced to listen as my mother cried herself to sleep over him. One night, she held me on her lap as her tears fell on my cheek. I heard her whisper, 'Jeremiah could take my breath away with his sea green eyes."

The warden didn't seem at all pleased with the memory and glanced up at Suzanne with a calculating gleam in her eyes. "To answer your question, no. I have never had the pleasure of meeting my dear, sweet father."

"Your... father?" Suzanne stammered, falling down in a chair as she eyed the warden with stunned disbelief. "You cannot be serious. Jeremiah Jordan is your father?" Although, now that she really looked at the warden, it was true that she could be Joshua's twin.

"From what I have been told."

Suzanne could almost hear the warden grinding her teeth. "Were your parents married?"

She drummed her fingers on the desk and scowled. "Jeremiah Jordan would never risk his impeccable bloodline, or his reputation, by marrying a quadroon."

"Your mother is a quadroon?"

Dear sweet Lord in heaven.

The Jordan reputation is about to suffer a blow that it will be impossible to recover from.

"Are you telling me that Joshua and Malinda Jordan have an illegitimate sister with more than a few drops of Negro blood flowing through her veins?"

"That would be an accurate assessment."

"Oh." Suzanne clapped her hands together and laughed gleefully. "This is wonderful. Why, I have never heard anything so completely scandalous in all my born days." She couldn't sit still, bouncing in her seat and grinning uncharitably. "Won't this news bring the high and mighty Jordan family down a few pegs. Why, they will be shunned. Social outcasts. They will no longer be welcomed in the finer homes." With a beaming smile, she breathed, "I cannot wait to spread this bit of juicy gossip."

The warden flinched, bending to brush invisible lint from her skirt in an attempt to hide her flushed face. Suzanne was describing her daily life with all of its humiliation and shame, until the day she left home and moved to a new town where no one knew of her family tree. "You will not be spreading this gossip, Suzanne."

"Why ever not?" Suzanne's eyes gleamed wickedly.

She would like to see the warden try to stop her.

"Why, one letter to a certain gossipmonger in Charleston and it will make the rounds of the entire county in less than a fortnight."

The warden shook her head firmly. "We wouldn't want Jeremiah to find out about the curse. At least not until we decide to enlighten the poor man as to who has been the cause of his suffering all of these years."

Suzanne was shocked clear down to her toes. "Jeremiah Jordan was cursed?"

"By my mother," the warden announced, proudly.

"If I may ask, who is your mother?"

The warden glanced at Suzanne from underneath long, sooty lashes. "Larue Fontaine."

Suzanne placed a hand to her hammering heart as a slow smile curved her lips. "Your mother is... Larue Fontaine? *The* Larue Fontaine of Savannah? The most famous voodoo queen to ever live?"

"As well as the once cherished lover of Jeremiah Jordan of Charleston, South Carolina." The eyes she turned toward Suzanne snapped with green fire. "That was before he decided to toss my mother aside for the wealthier Patricia Middleton, which was probably the worst mistake of his life."

The warden went to the sideboard, her eyes burning brightly as she poured two shots of whiskey. "Mother never was one to take betrayal lying down." She tossed one shot back and handed the other to Suzanne. "Jeremiah didn't wait around long enough to discover that my mother was carrying his child."

"You?" Suzanne gasped, raising a once finely arched brow. Actually, she felt almost faint by these new stunning revelations.

"Yes, me. As payment for leaving her... ruined, my mother placed a curse on Jeremiah that would affect not only him, but his offspring, as well as their offspring."

"The entire Jordan family has been cursed?"

Could this day possibly get any better?

"Suzanne, dear, I must ask you a question."

"Go ahead."

"Did you honestly believe Jeremiah Jordan lost his legs in an accident?"

"Well, yes. He was felling trees when he saw a young girl in the path of a tree. He pushed her to safety, but he didn't make it out of the way in time...." The warden's tinkling laughter caused Suzanne to snap her mouth shut. "Are you saying that your mother caused Jeremiah's accident?"

The warden nodded. "And what of your decision to have Joshua shot? Did you honestly believe you came up with that idea on your own?"

Suzanne's startled gasp echoed around the otherwise quiet room.

"Amari planted the idea in your head."

"Wait... you know Amari?" Suzanne was baffled.

"She is an old family friend." The warden poured herself another drink and went to sit behind her desk. "By all rights, Joshua should be dead now. But according to Amari, he is being shielded by someone with an aura much stronger than hers." She gave her words a moment to sink in before adding, "A girl named Clara."

"Joshua was nursed back to health by a young mute girl named Clara and her grandmother. Neither of them seem very powerful, although I did hear a rumor that Clara was born with a veil."

Suzanne was quiet as the warden stood. Her shoes made soft whispers as she paced back and forth across the floor. "The girl was born with a caul? That explains everything. I will need to send this new information to my mother as soon as possible." She turned a beaming countenance on Suzanne. "You have already proven to be a valuable asset, just as I knew you would be. That's why I had you brought to Mississippi to serve out your sentence."

"*You* are the reason I'm rotting in this hellhole?"

"Yes, but with good reason. At one point during the trial your father's lawyer was winning over the jury. We couldn't allow that to happen, since we needed you here to gather as much information as we could. So Amari lay a few curses on the judge in the trial."

Suzanne was incredulous. "Why would Amari do that to me?"

"Oh, honey, we must all occasionally suffer for the greater good, or in Mother's case the greater evil." The warden's tinkling laughter pierced the air. "I promise to make it up to you."

"When?" Suzanne questioned. "How?"

"Soon, that is all I can tell you. Very soon."

Suzanne was still pondering the warden's stunning revelations. "Was your mother the cause of any other delightful mishaps?"

"Mother knew the best way to hurt Jeremiah would be through his children. And the best way to hurt Joshua would be through the one he loved most, which is Lynna. Even though I know this is difficult for you to hear, Suzanne, Joshua has loved Lynna since the moment he first laid eyes on her."

Suzanne grew pale, but didn't speak.

"Mother caused a ship that Lynna was sailing on to sink, but somehow she lived to see another day. Whatever mother threw at her the girl seemed to dodge and come through it unscathed. Even Amari's wasting spell was reversed. To this day, mother has trouble believing that Lynna found someone capable of uncrossing one of her spells."

"Your mother caused all of those wonderful tragedies to happen?" Suzanne whispered, in complete awe of Larue Fontaine.

"Actually, Amari cast the spells for mother. As I said, they have been dear friends for years. I recall many late night visits to her cabin in the woods when I was a child, as they thought up new and exciting ways to make Jeremiah's life miserable."

"Are you telling me that I trained under a dear friend of Larue Fontaine?"

"Yes, and since my mother trained Amari it could be said that you learned from a master."

Suzanne could only stare at her with her mouth hanging open.

"Now, Mother has decided to focus on Jeremiah's grandchildren as a new and entertaining source of amusement. Amari tells us that Lynna Jordan is expecting another baby."

"I hadn't heard the... joyous news." Suzanne wondered why her mother would feel the need to withhold this information from her. Then, she took a second to wonder who the father of the slut's second child might be. Perhaps someone on a Caribbean island? "Mother didn't mention it during her last visit."

The warden breathed a heavy sigh, walking around the desk to stand in front of Suzanne. "Amari has already placed a curse on Lynna's baby while still in the womb. I do hope the Jordan family enjoys our Christmas present this year."

"Magnificent!" Suzanne giggled. "I just wish I could be there to witness the drama unfold. I would dearly love to watch Lynna suffer."

"I imagine there was quite a bit of suffering involved with Amari's wasting spell."

"While Lynna is well acquainted with misery, I assure you, it hasn't been nearly enough." Suzanne couldn't stop smiling. "My head is spinning with all this new and wonderful information."

"Go back to your cell, Suzanne. I will keep you informed of any updates." The warden grinned. "Who knows, we may have need of your services in the not too distant future."

Chapter 15

Lucille and Rob sat in rocking chairs on the porch of Lucille's cabin, shucking corn and discussing the best way to keep deer and other aggravating varmints out of their vegetables. They were both proud owners of new homes built in a clearing set away from the other cabins, with a shared garden between them. Hearing a horse approach, they looked up to see Joshua's steed galloping around the corner with Beau grinning from ear to ear and holding tight to the reins.

"You done brung our lil' man ta see us, ain't you?" Rob was immediately on his feet, reaching up to take Beau.

Beau bounced happily and gurgled some jumbled words, reaching out his arms and causing Rob to beam with pleasure. "We sho' has miss dis lil' feller. Ain't we, Lucille?"

Lucille wiped her hands clean on her apron and reached for Beau. He wasn't at all pleased to be leaving Rob's arms. Still, he allowed her to plant noisy kisses on his cheek and neck and cuddle him against her expansive bosom for several minutes without a fuss. "This baby always smells so good, and look here. He's done got another tooth."

"That makes four." Joshua beamed, proudly. "According to Milly, he's giving her a fit with those teeth."

"I don't doubt that." Lucille grinned. "He's nine months old. I guess it's time to wean him from the teat."

Beau seemed almost resigned to the attention he was receiving and appeared to be waiting it out. Joshua couldn't help but grin as his son patiently submitted to Lucille's affectionate embrace for a reasonable amount of time before reaching his chubby arms out to Rob. He already knew how to keep the women happy.

"How did you get the baby away from Clara?" Lucille continued to rub Beau's back as Rob held him.

"Clara heads down to the river for a swim every day about this time. Beau and I decided to sneak out the back door when she wasn't looking."

Rob knew Joshua well enough to know when something was on his mind. In fact, he had been expecting a visit from him for a few days now. "You re'd' ta put de *Windjammer* in de wind an' head fo' Trinidad, ain't you?"

Joshua's eyes shone with excitement. "Are you with me?"

"You know I is," Rob grinned. "I gots a sco' ta settle wit' dat pi'ate. Ain't no man gwine mess wid Buttercup an' live ta brag 'bout it."

"Buttercup." Joshua shook his head, not quite sure of what to make of his wife lately.

She was… different somehow since her stay in Trinidad.

"Lynna is going to be a problem, Rob. You know how protective she is of the cretin."

"I still ain't understandin' why." Rob tossed

Beau in the air causing him to squeal with delight. "Is you?"

Joshua shook his head, clearly puzzled. "It's a question that keeps me awake at night. I don't understand it any more than you do, and there is something else that I can't for the life of me understand."

"Whut's dat?" Rob sat in a rocking chair, crossing his legs and placing Beau on his foot to *ride a hawsy*.

"Lynna is expecting another child, and for some reason she's determined to keep it a secret."

This caused Rob to pause, giving Joshua a questioning glance. "Whut fo'?"

Joshua looked to Lucille for help. "Lucille, as a female, why would a woman attempt to keep something like this from her husband?"

Lucille thought a moment before answering. "Well, she knows good and well that's one secret she won't be able to hide for long. Maybe she's waiting for just the right time to tell you." She pointed her finger at Joshua, and chided, "Don't go reading more into this than you need to. Just give her some time."

Joshua glanced at Rob, still happily bouncing Beau. "As much as I would enjoy putting my hands around his neck and squeezing the life out of Sean Devereux, I missed Beau's birth. I would like to be around to share in the arrival of the new baby."

"We kin wait til spring. Dat pi'ate ain't gwine nowhere."

Rob was right. "It's settled then. As soon as my daughter is born we set sail for Trinidad."

Lucille laughed. "You seem convinced that it's a girl this time around."

"It is, Lucille. I feel it in my soul." Joshua reached for Beau as he latched his arms around Rob's neck and scrambled up his shoulder, refusing to leave.

Rob chuckled. "You jus' go on 'bout yo' bizness an' let dis lil feller stay heah fo' awhile. He likes ta go wit' me ta feed de chickens an' hawgs."

Joshua watched the happiness spread across both Beau and Rob's features as they headed toward the chicken pen.

"Rob surely does love him some Beau." Lucille picked up an ear of corn and commenced her shucking. "Almost as much as he loves Lynna."

"Tell me about you, Lucille." Joshua turned back to her with a smile. "Are you happy in your new home? Do you need anything?"

"I ain't never knowed such leisure in all my born days. My woodpile is always replenished, my smokehouse is full of meat, my garden is free of weeds, and the vegetables would be picked if I hadn't insisted on doing it myself. This cabin is so tight critters can't crawl between the floorboards and you ask me if I'm happy, when I'm living like a queen?"

"As you should be, Lucille. As you should be." Joshua looked to the chicken pen where Beau would bend over to pull up a single stem of grass and toss it to the chickens. Rob laughed, grabbing a handful so the chickens would come right up to Beau, causing the child to jabber to the poultry. "What about Rob, is he happy here?"

"Sometimes when we sit out here in the

evening after supper, I can tell he misses his island. He wouldn't be able to leave Beau now though. I just wish he could find him a good woman."

"It's not like there aren't plenty of suitable women on the plantation." Joshua could count off at least a dozen without even thinking too hard. "Surely one of them could meet his high standards."

"All I can say is she best not be the jealous sort, cause ain't no woman ever going to replace Lynna in Rob's eyes."

"Those two have a bond that I envy."

"Now it extends to Beau as well. Rob would break a person in half if either of them were threatened."

"Very true, Lucille," Joshua clicked the reins to back his horse away from the porch. "I'll ride out to the fields and talk to the overseer."

"Take your time." Lucille chuckled. "You'll have to pry those two apart when you get back anyway."

Chapter 16

Clara watched as Amari added a pinch of this, a teaspoon of that, and some vile smelling powder to a glass of water. The conjure woman stirred intently as she mixed the powder into the liquid.

What was this smelly concoction?

And did the woman really expect her to drink it?

"Gargle with this, Clara." Amari instructed.

That wouldn't be so terrible.

She would gargle, but she was not about to swallow the noxious liquid. Taking a tiny sip, she tilted her head back and gargled as she walked out the front door and to the edge of the porch. After what she thought was sufficient time, she spat the fizzy liquid into the flowerbed, and felt no different than when she arrived. She was quick to let the voodoo queen know her spell hadn't worked. "Uh."

Amari shook her head, breathing an impatient sigh. "If you will recall, I warned you that it would take some time, Clara. I realize that patience is hard to come by in one so young, but give it some time. I promise you it will work."

Clara spit the foul taste out of her mouth again, and sat down in one of the rockers. She didn't mind playing along with Amari's little game of *let's give Clara her speech back*, but gargling in vile liquid was taking the game a bit too far.

She leaned over the porch rail to spit again and noticed that her spittle had landed on a marigold. Her heart did a flip flop when she saw the once beautiful flower turning brown and shriveling. So her visits were no longer a *game* to Amari either.

The old woman was playing for keeps.

The little doll with the dress like hers was still in the basket. Only now it had what looked to be real hair sewn in, the same color as her own.

She took a seat in the rocker beside Amari and smiled. "Do you like my doll, Clara? I'm making it for you."

Clara perked up immediately. She loved dolls. She was too old to play with them of course, but she liked having them in her room to look at. She remembered what her grandmother had told her about voodoo dolls. Most of them were made specifically with the sole intent of bringing pain and suffering.

Amara patted the doll's hair in place and held it out in front of her proudly. Even to Clara, it was obvious the doll was made to her likeness.

"Here's what I need you to do in order to restore your speech, Clara."

She watched and waited.

Amari reached into her basket and handed her several straight pins. "I need you to pin the doll to the bottom of your mattress so it will be hidden, and leave it there."

Clara shrugged, holding out her hands in the age old symbol for why?

Amari frowned, unaccustomed to having her

instructions questioned. "Because the doll has magical healing powers. If you ever want to talk you must do exactly as I say."

Clara nodded and took the doll.

"Before I forget, don't bother to come tomorrow. I have a guest coming this afternoon to visit overnight."

Guest?

Who could it be?

"In fact, I must cut todays visit short because I have so much to do before my company arrives. Sit a spell if you like, but I need to get busy."

Clara walked down the steps, glancing over her shoulder to see Amari already entering the house. Whoever was coming had the old woman almost giddy with anticipation.

She would slip back tonight and see who was the cause of so much excitement.

Beau climbed up on Rob's shoulders as happy as a clam. They had fed the chickens, hogs, goats and cow, or rather Beau had fed them. The lad had grown more attached to Rob than ever, and Rob couldn't have loved the child more if he was his own son.

After the animals were fed and Beau, Lucille, and Rob had sat down to supper, Beau and Rob headed to their favorite fishing spot on the river. They had only been there a few minutes and were watching the cork bob when Rob noticed a woman walking toward them. A beautiful woman. She had light toffee skin and shiny black hair that fell down her back in cascading ringlets. "Evenin',

Ma'am."

The woman hurried to Rob's side, beaming at Beau. "What a beautiful child."

"Thank you, ma'am. Me an' my lil' buddy jus' come down ta de rivah ta catch a mess of crappie."

"I see." Judging from the stringer of fish hanging from Rob's belt buckle, it had been a productive trip. "Fried crappie is one of my favorite meals."

Rob eyed the woman curiously. "I ain't tryin' ta git in yo' binness, but whut you doin' out heah in dese woods alone?"

"Oh, I was visiting a friend across the way and decided to go for a walk. Lucky for me that I did, because I met two new friends." She squeezed Beau's chubby leg. "Aren't you just the cutest thing?"

Beau grinned, reaching into a can to hand her a muddy, wiggling worm.

"He mus' like you, cause Beau don't usually cotton ta strangers. Heah he is givin' you a worm."

"Thank you kindly for the present, Beau." The woman accepted the gift and smiled at the beautiful child. "I've always had a way with children."

While Beau and Rob fished, Clara was in the big house listening to Patricia drone on and on about adding and subtracting, without doubt the most boring subject ever. She had already been taught to read and write, although numbers were still a puzzle.

Patricia noticed. "Judging from the glazed

look in your eyes I would guess that you are in need of a short break."

Clara nodded eagerly. *Or a long break.* Either worked for her.

"Very well, rest your eyes for a few minutes while I get us a cool drink."

Clara smiled her appreciation. She was tired after her morning with Amari, and deciphering columns of numbers until her head ached. She leaned her head back on the settee and closed her eyes, allowing her thoughts to drift.

In her mind, she saw the river as if she were standing in front of it. Leaves swirled past as a fish jumped and noisily plopped back down and a turtle bobbed his head out of the water. Rob was there, as was Beau.

They were fishing with cane poles. She watched Rob put a worm on a hook and toss it in the water with one hand, with his other firmly around Beau's waist to keep him from the water's edge. She saw Rob glance up with surprise when a woman walked out of the woods. The woman's back was to Clara and she couldn't see her face.

Something didn't feel right.

The hairs on Clara's arms and the back of her neck stood up. A loud buzzing noise filled her head and sharp pains began shooting from one side to the other. She cried out when the pain reached a crescendo. She tried to ignore the intense agony and placed her hands on her head, forcing herself to concentrate.

Rob and the woman talked and laughed until Rob's cork began to bob in the water. Clara watched as he pulled a large crappie onto the bank.

When he released Beau and had his back turned, the woman put her hands on the little boy's back and gave him a shove hard enough to send him headfirst into the rushing water.

Beau would drown!

Clara took off out the front door like a bullet as she watched Beau's head quickly disappear beneath the surface of the swiftly moving current.

She instinctively knew which way to run, exactly which river bend they were at. She ran until her sides ached and her breath was coming in gasps, but she didn't slow down.

Please, don't let me be too late.

Just when she was sure she would collapse from exhaustion she saw Rob, Beau, and the strange woman standing on the riverbank, talking. She watched as Rob's cork began to bob in the water. In slow motion, she watched Rob remove his hands from around Beau's waist.

If only she could scream a warning to Rob.

She opened her mouth, but no words would come. Instead, she picked up a dirt clot from the field and flung it with deadly precision to bounce off Rob's head.

"Whut de..." Rob lifted Beau in his arms and turned to see Clara breathing heavily and red faced from exertion. "Whutchu you hit me upside de head fo', gal?"

Clara squatted on her knees to rest, too exhausted to try to explain. She cast an evil eye toward the woman and started moving toward her.

"Hello, Clara, dear?"

How did this woman know her name?

She gave Rob a beaming smile as she turned

to leave. "While I have enjoyed spending time with you and Beau this afternoon, I really must be going. We will meet again, soon."

"Yas'sam, dat be jus' fine."

Clara cuddled Beau in her arms and motioned to Rob that the child would be returning home with her. It would be a long time before he was allowed out of her sight again. Rob could visit the contemptible woman all he wanted, but Beau would not step a foot near her.

"Whut was dat all about, gal?" Rob questioned Clara when the beautiful woman was out of sight.

Clara stood Beau on the ground and held him firmly by the hand as she pretended to push him into the river.

Rob gasped as his heart beat triple time. "Dat woman tried to push dis baby in de rivah?"

Clara nodded.

"Was dat Amari?"

Clara shook her head no.

"You know who de woman is?"

Again, Clara shook her head.

"Den I gots ta fine out who she is fo she try to hurt dis baby again." Rob shook his head sorrowfully. "Po' Buttercup. How many enemies do she got?"

Chapter 17

Lynna and Malinda traveled to Charleston for a dual purpose, to purchase material for them each to have a fabulous new gown for the Harvest Ball, and for a beaming Malinda to have the final fitting for her wedding gown. On a whim, Lynna decided to stop by the post office.

With sweating palms and a racing pulse she folded a much abused letter with suddenly trembling hands and slipped it into the pocket of her skirt. The envelope looked as if it had been carried in someone's pocket for weeks before finally being posted.

There was no return address, only Lynna's name and instructions for the missive to be delivered to Sea Grove. Not much for the casual observer to go on.

Yet, she recognized the handwriting immediately.

The realization of who the missive was from caused her heart to slam against her chest.

The mail hadn't been called for in weeks so she couldn't be sure when the letter had arrived. That didn't concern her at the moment. Of utmost importance now was finding a few moments alone, away from Malinda, to read the letter and get rid of it.

The suspense was killing her. It would be impossible for the letter to remain in her pocket, unread, until they returned home.

What if something had happened to Lisbeth?

She cleared her throat, and with her hand clutching the letter inside her pocket she turned to Malinda. "While you're being fitted I'll just look at material and try to decide on a color for my new gown. It's… difficult with so many to choose from."

Malinda was so busy twirling in front of the cheval glass and giving final instructions to the seamstress that she only glanced up and nodded.

With a weak smile Lynna hurried around a corner, hiding behind several bolts of cloth in every hue of the rainbow. When no one was looking she broke the seal and tore open the envelope with trembling hands.

My dearest Lynna,

I hope this letter finds you well and happy. Grandmama sends her love and best wishes for your continued happiness. I don't know where to start, so I will speak from my heart. I love you, Lynna. Just when I was ready to say those three words to you, I stood at my window and watched you sail out of my life.

Just as I had begun to dream of spending the rest of my life with you, here on the island, and raising Beau alongside our children on Devereux Acres, you successfully crushed all of my dreams. It feels as though a part of my soul is missing. I can't accept that I might never see your beautiful smiling face again.

For my own peace of mind, I must ask a question of you. Are you happy? If you are, although it will be the hardest thing I have ever been forced to do, I will move on with my life, somehow.

Since we battled Suzanne's curse together, your happiness has been my top priority. You said once that you could never be happy without Beau. Hopefully, he is in your arms now and your life is complete. If not, and you feel as if a part of you is missing, as I do, then you know where to find me. I will always be here for you, waiting, with open arms.

Yours Always,
Sean

"Oh, my sweet Jesus." The letter slipped from Lynna's numb fingers and fluttered to the floor as she leaned against a wall of cloth, unable to support her own weight. "Sean, what have I done?" she whispered, sinking to the floor as long buried memories surfaced.

It was all so clear.

She was back in her bedroom at Devereux Acres and…

It was time to get dressed for the masquerade ball and her gown was, in a word, exquisite. She was dressed as a fairy princess with yards and yards of pale green gauzy material, and dozens of appliquéd ferns and flower blossoms flowing from the tight fitting waist.

The top of the gown was snug and caused her breasts to nearly overflow the tiny seed pearls and embroidered daisies that embellished the bodice. Her hair would be dressed with real leaves and daisies and a simply darling little mask would cover her eyes.

When her bath was ready, she dismissed the maid and slipped into the enveloping warmth of the water, eagerly anticipating her first masquerade ball. In truth, was she really anticipating the ball? Or at long last fulfilling her promise to Sean?

Before she had time to answer her own questions, she heard the door to her bedroom click shut, causing her to scoot deeper under the water until only her head was visible. Apparently, one of the maids had forgotten to put out one of the pieces to her costume.

"Good evening, beautiful lady." Sean smiled lazily, peeking around the door. "I'm sorry if I caught you at a bad... well, no need to lie. I'm not sorry at all that I caught you... in your current state." Lynna hadn't touched the bar of soap to lather up yet, so the water was crystal clear, leaving nothing to Sean's increasingly erotic imagination.

Moving to the edge of the copper hip tub, he kneeled down and grinned. "If you recall, I have had much experience at bathing you and am more than willing to offer my assistance now should you be agreeable."

Lynna gazed deeply into his dancing hazel eyes as he flashed her a broad smile, feeling her stomach clench into a tight fist of desire. What did this man do to her? How could a mere glance cause her body to react so?

Striving to hide the effect that his nearness was having, she murmured, "Thank you kindly for the offer, Sean. But, unlike when I was on your ship,

I am not ill and am quite capable of bathing myself."

"Pity," Sean murmured.

"A pity that I'm not ill?"

"A pity that I won't be allowed to rub a bar of soap across every square inch of your body." Reaching his hand over the edge of the tub, he allowed his fingers to trail along the top of the water, extremely close to the edge of her breast. Lynna knew that if he were to touch her, she would simply melt into the water. She tensed as her need for this man almost overwhelmed her.

Sean didn't fail to notice her reaction. The time for talk had passed. He watched her eyes glaze with lust and knew she would offer no more resistance to his advances.

He stood to remove his shirt, exposing the hard muscles of his chest and abdomen. The mere sight of him shirtless always did strange things to Lynna's nether region. Now was no exception.

Her mouth watered and her tongue shot out to moisten dry lips, causing a tremor to rush through Sean's flanks. He placed one arm under her legs and the other under her back, lifting her out of the water.

"What are you doing?" Lynna protested, feebly. "You are making a terrible mess, and if you recall, I promised to come to your room after the Masquerade Ball."

"Before, after, what difference does a few hours make?" Sean's lips descended to hers and she didn't even attempt a reply. His mouth on hers was all that mattered now. His soft, moist lips that melded with hers as their tongues mingled, his

hands molding Lynna's slippery body to his.

Sean placed her lovingly on the bed and bent to remove his breeches. Lynna watched his every move with unabashed desire until he moved his hard, naked body atop hers. Suddenly, the last several months of misery seemed far, far away. She was living in the present now and she wanted this man, desperately.

Almost an hour later, Sean gathered her close, holding her until their pounding hearts had slowed and they both could breath normally.

He rose up on his elbow and gazed into her clear blue eyes. "That was..."

"Amazing," Lynna finished his sentence for him. "All that I thought it would be, and more. Do we have to go to the Ball?"

"Do you have another suggestion?"

"I would be content to remain here. With you."

Before he could respond a sharp rap came at the door. "Lynna, darling," Lisbeth called. "Are you dressed? It's almost time to leave for the Ball."

"Um... yes, yes, almost," she called. "Just a few more minutes."

"I will be waiting downstairs."

As Lynna gently shoved Sean to her side, he grinned. "Why the sudden change of heart? I thought we were going to skip the Ball?"

"I can't disappoint your grandmother." She sighed, bending over to kiss his irresistible lips. "And we have the entire night ahead of us."

"We have the rest of our lives ahead of us," Sean corrected,

Lynna stretched her legs and pressed her full length against him. Sated, she wanted only to linger in the aftermath of their passion for a few more minutes.

"Lynna, dear, we are already fashionably late," Lisbeth called. "Do you intend to miss the Ball entirely?"

Lynna was off the bed in a flash. "Five minutes, Lisbeth. I promise I will be down in five minutes."

"Sean, quick," she whispered, "help me get dressed."

"Lynna, darling, whatever is wrong?" Malinda asked, bending to retrieve the letter. Thankfully, Lynna snatched it out of her hand before she could bring it close enough to read.

She glanced up to find Malinda towering above her with a bewildered frown. "Did I hear you correctly?"

"Probably not." Lynna dismissed Malinda's words with a wave of her hand, smoothing her skirt to have something to keep her hands busy. Her heart pounded as if she was still in her bedroom at Devereux Acres with Sean. "What did you think you heard?"

"It sounded like you said, 'Oh, my God, Sean. What have I done?'"

Lynna laughed shakily, a hysterical sound. "I don't really remember what I said." She folded the letter and slipped it back in the envelope to tuck in her pocket. "It's not important."

Dear God above.

If only she had waited a few more hours on

that fateful day in Trinidad before giving herself to Sean. If only she had held out until after the ball as she had originally planned, she would have known her husband was alive and never given herself to another man.

"I see," Malinda said, although she really didn't. She had heard Lynna say the words plainly. Why would a letter from Sean Devereux cause her such distress? "Did you choose a color for your gown?"

"No… um… not yet." Lynna was grateful that Malinda chose not to pursue the subject of the letter. "I'm still… debating over a few choices."

"This color would go perfectly with your skin tone." Malinda held a bolt of lavender silk under Lynna's chin. "Perfect."

Lynna all but snatched the cloth from her hand and tossed it back on the table. "Any color except lavender."

"Why ever not?" Malinda cried. Why on earth was Lynna behaving so peculiar today? "What has gotten into you, Lynna? Lavender has always been one of your favorite colors."

"Not anymore," Lynna whispered, forlornly, lifting a bolt of bright yellow silk and holding it to her chest. "I think yellow is my new favorite color."

"I have to admit that it does make your blue eyes sparkle." Malinda smiled. "I still don't know what you suddenly have against lavender though."

"Now, what color for you, Malinda?"

"Definitely blue. It's Daniel's favorite color, you know."

"Blue it is." Lynna randomly lifted a bolt of baby blue material . "This is the one."

"It's lovely," Malinda agreed. "Daniel will simply adore it."

"I'm sure he will." Lynna hugged the darling girl, hoping to make her forget the letter tucked safely away in her pocket. "Oh, Malinda, I am so happy you're marrying Daniel. I just wish it could be under happier circumstances."

"Don't be sad, Lynna. We aren't." Malinda carried both bolts of material to the counter since Lynna's mind seemed to be a thousand miles from the milliner's shop. "Daniel is convinced that his parents will come around in time. If not, it will be their loss, not ours. We will be happy with or without them. Now, let us go to the Wayfarer Restaurant for lunch. Spending money always makes me hungry."

Jacques seated them at Joshua's corner table. "Good evening, my exquisite Jordan ladies. What can I bring you to drink on this unpleasantly warm day?"

"Iced tea for me." Malinda daintily patted her forehead with a lace handkerchief.

Lynna used her napkin to dab at her décolleté. "I'll have tea as well."

Jacques bowed gallantly. "Would you ladies care to begin with a shrimp cocktail?"

"That sounds lovely, Jacques." Lynna flashed a beaming smile that left the man stunned by her unique beauty. "Thank you."

"And for you, Miss Malinda?"

"The same please."

Just as tall glasses of iced tea were being served a bundle of curvaceous energy bustled through the door in the form of Resa. "I heard you were in town, Lynna."

"Hello, Resa."

Did the woman know the comings and goings of everyone in town?

Or just Joshua, and anyone related to him?

"Would you care to join us?"

"Why, yes, thank you. I would." Resa chose not to wait for Jacques and seated herself, causing every part of her body to jiggle in the process. "The humidity today is simply awful, isn't it? Why, I feel positively wilted."

Lynna glanced at Resa, then at Malinda. "Have you ladies met?"

"No, I don't believe we have," was Malinda's lukewarm response.

Lynna made the introductions. "Resa, this is Malinda Jordan, Joshua's sister."

"It's very nice to meet you, Malinda," Resa warmly clasped Malinda's hand in hers. "I've been friends with your brother for many years."

Malinda looked to Lynna for a reaction, but got none. How strange that Lynna was being so nice, even cordial, to this woman who from all appearances was not entirely respectable.

Resa lowered her voice a notch. "I have some news that I have been just dying to tell you, Lynna." She leaned her elbows on the table as her eyes danced with mischief. "I am... friendly... with one of Suzanne's lawyers and he told me just this week that Suzanne Fletcher is practically unrecognizable these days."

"What do you mean by unrecognizable?"

"I mean the girl spends her days, from sunup

to sundown, working in a cotton field." Resa fanned herself vigorously as though just repeating the words made her lightheaded. "In a cotton field I tell you. Can you credit that? My, my, my, how the mighty have fallen."

Jacques placed a glass of wine in front of Resa, who took a sip before continuing, "My friend visited her at *the farm* recently after her parents had complained of the poor treatment their daughter was receiving in the facility. According to him, her hands were a mass of calluses, she was barefoot, and her entire body was just crusty with dirt."

"Crusty?" Malinda finally found her voice and repeated the word.

Resa nodded rapidly. "He claims that not only was she constantly clawing at her lice infested head, but that her legs, feet, arms and every other exposed part of skin was covered with… get this… rat bites."

"Rat bites," Malinda squealed.

"Yes. My God, can you even imagine? Rat bites? Oh, and he swears that she can't weigh more than one hundred pounds soaking wet."

"How awful it sounds," Lynna murmured.

"Yes, the   place sounds just awful." Resa giggled. "And exactly where that evil, conniving bitch needs to be."

Chapter 18

Suzanne sat across from the warden sipping a mint julep. This was the second time in a month she had been called to the warden's office. What had she done to deserve such an esteemed honor. She swallowed the last of her drink and placed the mint sprigged glass on the desk before her.

"I send for you as often as I can without raising too many eyebrows, Suzanne." The warden rearranged her paper, quill, and ink bottle for the third time in the last few minutes. Keeping her surroundings orderly seemed to be a compulsion with her. "Inmates love to spread gossip, especially when they imagine the warden to be showing favoritism."

Suzanne didn't really care one way or the other. "I imagine it can be a bother."

"While it certainly stirs up a hornet's nest, it's so nice to invite you in and have an occasional civilized conversation. The other women are rather… uncouth to say the least."

Suzanne's eyes rolled as she bit into a delicious sweet roll dripping with powdered sugar icing. "Tell me about it."

The warden laughed at the look on Suzanne's face. "I'm sure I don't have to tell you of the rather disgusting habits of some of the inmates.

Why, I never even knew such atrocities existed until I came here."

"Disgusting is a gross understatement for some of the things I have been forced to do behind the bars of our cell." A delicate shiver passed over Suzanne as she recalled her most recent atrocity.

The warden put her hand to her neck as her stomach threatened to revolt. "I called you here today for a reason."

Suzanne wiped the remnants of the sticky bun from her fingers with a napkin. When that wasn't effective, she licked them clean. "What would that be?"

The warden went to gaze out the window, then peered over her shoulder with a twinkle in her stunning green eyes. "I received a notice in the post this morning that might be of some interest to you."

"Please, continue."

"It seems that prisons, especially in the South, are becoming overcrowded. Who knew women could be such sinful creatures." The warden laughed her tinkling laugh. "It seems that our facility exceeds the limit as well. As such, the commissioner of prisons has mandated that three of my prisoners be released."

Suzanne was utterly flabbergasted.

Released?

As in free to go home?

The warden wiggled a finger in Suzanne's face. "Before you go packing your scant belongings, I must advise you that there are certain conditions that must be met by the three fortunate women who are to receive this pardon."

"Such as?" Suzanne knew there would be a

catch.

The warden picked up the notice and read.

"The inmate must be a model prisoner. The inmate must have served at least one year of hard labor. The inmate must have the written recommendation of three upstanding members of society, such as a warden, a pastor, and a volunteer in the prison system. Finally, the inmate must show remorse for the crime committed."

She tossed the papers on her desk and smiled at Suzanne. "It appears that the warden of Mississippi Women's Prison Farm, me, is to choose ten such commendable inmates. A committee will then pick three prisoners to be released back into society for good behavior."

Suzanne watched in stunned disbelief as the shocking words fell from the warden's luscious red lips. When she had gathered her wits about her, she asked, "Can I rely on you to write a letter of recommendation for me?"

The warden peered at her from under dark lashes. "That depends on a number of things, Suzanne. First and foremost, are you remorseful for the crimes you attempted to commit? Attempt being the key word here. Had you succeeded in the endeavors you would have been sentenced to two life terms, rather than standing before me discussing the stipulations for an early release."

"Warden, I can assure you with all honesty that I am not happy with the way I handled the situation with Joshua and Lynna. Actually, I am very sorry that things turned out as they did."

I wish they were both dead.

The warden winked slyly. "Since you seem sincere and have satisfied all my concerns, then of course, dear."

Suzanne tapped her temple with a jagged and dirty fingernail. "I also need letters from a pastor and a volunteer. How can I manage that?"

"You will be allowed to take a bath early in the morning."

While Suzanne longed to soak in a hot tub for hours, she feared that a clean body would only give Maxine ideas.

What did a clean body have to do with what they were discussing anyway?

At any rate, while they were on the subject Suzanne had a few points to make. "I don't understand why I still have to work in the fields," she whined. "You *are* the warden of this facility and a simple word from you could put me in the vegetable garden, or the kitchen, or even the infirmary. Please, I beg you to put me anywhere except the cotton fields. I simply cannot go back there."

Her heartfelt plea failed to elicit an ounce of sympathy from the stoic warden.

"I'm afraid you have little choice in the matter, dear. There are rules that even the warden cannot break. All well and healthy inmates must work in the field for the first year of their imprisonment." Turning a page in her rulebook, she read, "*A prison should be an unpleasant place, so as to deter people from committing crimes. Once inside, prisoners must be made to face up to their own faults by being forced to do hard, boring work.* "

She closed the book and steepled her fingers as she gazed at Suzanne. "Just be thankful that you weren't sent here a few years ago, when inmates were forced to sleep on wooden beds and wooden pillows during their first thirty days of confinement."

Suzanne hissed a defeated sigh. "In a nutshell, what you're saying is that I have no hope but to return to the fields."

"I'm afraid so. However, we seem to have gotten off topic."

If you had to work in the fields for one hour you wouldn't be quite so chipper.

"I haven't told you about our visitor tomorrow."

"Please, tell me it's a pastor, or a volunteer."

"You are in luck. It's a circuit pastor. He's traveling through our area and has kindly agreed to conduct a service for this congregation of wicked sinners."

Suzanne ears immediately perked up.

A man?

Coming to the prison?

Even if he was a man of the cloth, he still possessed the equipment her body yearned for. Why, she hadn't seen a member of the opposite sex in months. Suzanne had little doubt that before he left the prison chapel, the dear man would enthusiastically pen her second recommendation. "I will certainly attend church services in the morning."

"I thought you might." The warden pretended interest in her fingernails, offhandedly adding, "Just some food for thought, Suzanne. We also have volunteers coming in a few weeks to teach some of the more illiterate inmates to read. How are your reading skills?"

"Atrocious." Suzanne smiled, the lie coming easily. "Simply atrocious."

"Then I will add your name to the list of inmates requiring assistance in that area."

Sensing that her time was up, Suzanne glanced over her shoulder as she pulled the door open. "By the way, can I ask your name?"

"Jerica Jordan Fontaine." She said the middle name with utter distaste. "You may call me Jerica, in private of course."

Church service the following day was as boring as Suzanne could have expected. The visiting preacher was a homely soul, although he appeared to still be in his prime. That was always a plus when stamina was the desired outcome. Tall, lanky, good teeth, and no prevailing body odor, she wondered if what she had heard about tall, lanky men was true. Glancing toward his crotch, she saw no noticeable evidence of it. Little wonder, as he was presently harping on fire and brimstone.

When he removed a small container of holy water from his pocket and asked if anyone needed an anointing, Suzanne was first in line.

The neck of her dress rose all the way up to her chin, making it impossible to show him an enticing display of cleavage and have him drooling.

What could she do to gain his attention?

As she made to bow down in front of him she pretended to fall, and just before she caught herself she buried her face in his crotch. Miraculously, she fell in a perfect position to press her lips against his shriveled member.

She heard several of the inmates gasp and twisted to see Maxine's face flushed angry red. As Suzanne lifted herself up the pastor rubbed his hand briskly over the front of his breeches.

"Please, forgive me, Reverend," she purred, licking her lips. "Clumsy me."

"That's… quite alright, my dear," the good man almost choked on the words. "No harm… done."

"I was wondering if I could ask a favor of you?" she whispered, "After the others have returned to their cells, and we are alone?"

"Any… anything," he mumbled.

"It's a secret, but I will be waiting in the broom closet if you would care to join me there."

"I… I… yes… I will be happy to pray for you in the broom closet if you would rather do it in private."

"Yes, it's much easier for me to… pray… in private," she whispered, as she headed toward the closet. "Could you please bring a paper and quill when you come?"

Although the good reverend wore a puzzled expression, after the last prisoner had left the chapel he grabbed his satchel and hurried after her.

Chapter 19

Charleston, SC
Late September, 1855

The morning of the Harvest Ball dawned bright and clear. Clara was beside herself with excitement and could hardly sit still for breakfast. Even Beau was having trouble gaining her full attention and didn't quite know what to make of this sudden lack of interest on her part.

Judith had insisted on making her a simply gorgeous pale green frock and she was ready to attend her first barbecue. Granted, she wouldn't be allowed to stay for the ball, but that was of little consequence. She had the entire day ahead of her to… maybe… perhaps… meet a boy her own age.

Lynna's peach colored muslin day dress was spread out on the bed along with her delicate chemise, whalebone hoop, corset, and several petticoats. She tugged on her bottom lip as she peered at the ensemble, worrying if the fasteners would meet to close the back of the dress.

Could she be five months already?

"You seem to be in a quandary, my love." Joshua's smooth voice startled her.

Lynna's breath caught in her throat as it always did on first sight of him in the morning.

Clean shaven, hair still wet and slicked back, and dressed for the barbecue he looked every bit the part of a dashing rogue. *Her rogue.* "I guess you could say that."

He glanced toward the bed with distaste. "I would prefer that you not lace yourself into one of those ridiculous corsets in your present condition. For the sake of vanity, females go about for an entire day so tightly laced you can barely draw a decent breath. It's an absurd notion, and I would be eternally grateful if you didn't confine my daughter so."

Lynna snatched up the chemise with suddenly trembling fingers and clutched it to her midsection, trying to hide the swelling there.

He knew.

She took a deep breath and turned to face her husband. "I should have told you earlier, but I... wanted to be... sure."

"You can be sure, darling." He was still unsure as to why she chose to keep her pregnancy a secret. "The proof is there for all to see."

He closed the space between them and removed the chemise from her hands, dropping it to the bed. "Come, my love," he teased. "Let me hold you while I can still reach my arms around you."

"Oh, you rascal," she shrieked, with mock outrage. "You could always reach around me. I was never that big."

Joshua pulled her naked body against his with laughter dancing in his sea green eyes, as he allowed his hands to roam freely down her back and over the swell of her plump buttocks. To have such a petite body she was well blessed with breasts and buttocks.

Perfect handfuls.

He grabbed a handful of each. "Please, don't take what I am about to say the wrong way."

"What would that be?" As his lips closed over hers, Lynna purred softly. Her breasts were tender, yet Joshua's ministrations didn't cause pain, only a warmth that spread throughout her quaking body.

"Your soft curves are quite delectable and drive a man to distraction, yet when you are with child there is a new lushness, a fullness to your curves that keep you in mind even when you are not in sight." His tongue ravished her mouth, drawing her bottom lip in to suckle like a nursing infant, while his hand never stopped caressing her silken skin.

"Then I have no cause for concern the next time Resa crushes her voluptuous and ever overflowing bosom against you?"

"Never, my love."

Eager to feel his skin against hers, Lynna swiftly undid the buttons on his shirt, slipping it over his broad shoulders. She had a strong desire to taste him and leaned forward to kiss the jagged scar on his chest, raking her tongue against his skin, stopping to lick his nipple and gently nip it with her teeth.

He nudged her gently down to the bed and slid inside her as she locked her legs around his waist. After only a few strokes, Joshua felt her deep contractions squeezing him and buried deep inside her.

Lynna's positively divine yellow watered silk ballgown edged with delicate ecru lace was carefully packed in a box for the short ride to Cedar Hill.

They arrived to find Beth still in bed. Lynna stood outside her door, sympathizing with her dear friend as she heard her retching violently into a slop pot. She was having an awful pregnancy this go round. Having recently passed her own bouts of morning sickness, she knew Beth had no desire for company and headed downstairs to wait. She passed Samuel on the way down. "Oh, Samuel. The poor thing sounds just awful. Is there anything I can do to help?"

"I'm afraid not, darling. However, I must confess that since Clara returned home, Bethany has missed her dearly. Please, allow her to visit as often as she can to keep our rambunctious little sprite occupied until her mother feels well enough to chase after her."

"Of course, we will, and if you need anything else all you need to do is ask."

Samuel hung his head, apparently exhausted. "It's the strangest thing. While Beth wasn't sick a day with Bethany, she has been sick every single day with this baby. I just wish there was something I could do for her." He looked up the stairs toward his wife's room and shook his head sadly. "I hope she feels well enough to attend the wedding."

"I pray that she will." Lynna could hear the band tuning their instruments on the lawn as she hurried down the hall to help the bride dress. "Beth would feel just awful if she missed it."

Malinda was radiant in a gown made from creamy silk organza, cut low with tiny off the shoulder cap sleeves. Row upon row of billowing lace festooned the wide skirt with matching lace around the bodice. Her hair had been pinned atop her head with ringlets falling to frame her beaming face.

The bride peered at her reflection in the cheval glass as she imagined one horrible scenario after the next. "Lynna, what if there is a gopher hole in the garden and I trip while walking down the aisle? What a clumsy country bumpkin Daniel would think me."

Lynna couldn't help but laugh at her dismayed expression as she recalled her own similar fears of a wedding day disaster. "That is highly unlikely, Malinda. You are positively stunning and you will walk down the aisle and into the arms of your future husband without a hitch. Why, I have never once known you to be clumsy."

Lynna removed her shoe and reached inside to remove a dried four leaf clover. "I found this one morning when Beau and I were playing in the grass. Put it in your shoe and it will bring you luck, not that you need it. After the wedding, you will dance the night away in the arms of your dashing husband."

"It's what comes after the dancing that has my stomach tied in knots." Malinda's cheeks brightened as she gave Lynna a timid look.

"Relax, darling." Lynna looked around to be sure none of the older women were listening. "That will be the best part of the entire day."

"Are you sure?" Malinda couldn't have been more shocked by Lynna's surprising words. "Why, one of my dear friends who recently married warned me not to expect too much in the bedroom. In fact, I was basically told to just grin and bear it."

A shiver rushed over Lynna as she recalled her first time with Joshua and her last time a few hours ago. "Oh, you will be grinning when you return from your month abroad, that's for sure. I can't wait to hear your opinion of the honeymoon."

"Thank you for easing my mind." Malinda took a deep breath and smoothed her skirt. "Now, I can put that worry aside and enjoy my wedding."

"As you should."

Patricia bustled into the room carrying a bouquet of roses. "Here you are, darling. The guests are seated and the pastor is ready to begin. Are you ready to become the wife of Daniel Fletcher?"

"Yes, mother." Malinda turned toward Lynna and smiled. "I am."

"Come with me, Lynna." Patricia sniffled and blew her nose on a delicate handkerchief. "Let us take our seats. Malinda, your father is waiting for you at the bottom of the stairs. Be kind to him, he is not taking the loss of his baby girl well."

Her words caused Malinda to tear up all over again.

The wedding of Daniel Fletcher and Malinda Jordan was a splendid affair and went off without a hitch.

After the ceremony, a feast was spread on long tables under the shade of huge oak trees. Ham, steak, chicken, turkey, quail, venison, fish, lobster, shrimp and every vegetable available was waiting to be consumed, alongside a table loaded down with desserts.

Clara sat under a shade tree with a plate filled to overflowing with barbecued chicken and all the fixings. Ethan Stokes sat beside her. His father owned Willow Springs, three plantations over.

She was trying so hard to remember the rules of conversing with the opposite sex that Malinda had so diligently taught her.

Don't talk with your mouth full.
Eat like a bird.
Laugh at everything he says.

She tried to seem interested in his talk of war and killing and how his fondest wish was to wear a Confederate uniform and fight against the abolitionists in the North, she really did, but her mind kept drifting.

"You see, Clara, honey," he droned on and on, "Southern secessionists believe, rightfully so, that the Declaration of Independence gives us the right to change our government when it no longer serves us. So, like my father, I believe the South should secede and become our own territory. If the damned Yankees don't like it, let them come down here and get their tails whipped."

Clara leaned against the trunk of the tree and closed her eyes as he rambled on and on about cannons, uniforms, and the thrill of victory.

She must have dozed off for a second, for when she opened her eyes, Ethan was... *dead.*

His head had fallen back against the tree and his eyes were glazed and staring straight ahead. Blood dribbled from his mouth and nose, and gushed from a gaping hole in his chest.

Since Clara was unable to scream, she put her hands over her mouth and touched him lightly to see if he really was dead, or if she was in the midst of a horrible nightmare. Her slight nudge pushed him to the ground so forcefully that his blood splattered her dress.

She jumped to her feet, searching the lawn for Joshua. To her absolute horror, when she gazed across the lawn the attendees of the barbecue were all dead. Slaughtered, lying in pools of their own blood.

Blood spilled from gaping wounds to run across arms, chests, legs, and faces. Looking closer, she shuddered upon noticing several detached limbs scattered at random around her and across the field. She lurched to her feet to find Joshua and tripped over a... severed hand.

She scanned the sea of dead bodies, crying with relief when none of the faces were recognizable.

Joshua and Lynna couldn't be dead.

But she didn't see them anywhere.

Then slowly, she understood why.

It wasn't the attendees of the barbecue that had been massacred and left to die on the ground, but rather men in uniform. Soldiers, some in blue uniforms and some in grey wool with swords and muskets at their sides, had fallen. The tables laden with food had been replaced by an open field of butchery and carnage.

She heard shouts and looked into the distance to see men in blue galloping away on horseback, laughing as they celebrated their kill.

One man shouted, "Death to the confederacy!"

The bloodbath was too horrible to comprehend. Clara clutched her stomach and closed her eyes as she fell back against the tree.

"So you see, Clara." When she opened her eyes Ethan was saying, "The South will never allow those fools in the North to take away our way of life."

Thank God.

He was alive!

As the buzzing in her ears died away she heard laughter and talking. She relaxed back against the tree and watched happy families milling about on the lawn, either filling their plates for a second time or heading toward the desert table.

What had just happened to her?

Joshua held Lynna close as he spun her around the glittering ballroom. "You were with child at last year's ball. I seem to be doing a decent job of keeping you barefoot and pregnant, don't I?"

"That old saying is terribly outdated and needs to be put to rest. My swollen feet can attest to the fact that I am definitely wearing shoes."

He dropped his hands from her expanding waist and immediately led her toward a row of seats set against the wall. "You should have told me your feet were swelling, darling. It's a good thing Jasmine's not here."

"Why are your feet swelling, Lynna?" Beth appeared beside her, looking radiant and showing no signs of her earlier round of sickness.

The cat was now officially out of the bag.

"I am also with child, Beth."

Beth's squeal of delight could be heard over the sound of the band's lively reel. "Our babies will grow up to be best friends."

Lynna returned Beth's hug and noticed that her friend was turning quite pale. "Is there anything I can do for you, Beth?"

"I just need to lie down." Beth shook her head and hurried toward the stairs with her hand over her mouth. "You stay right here and enjoy the Ball."

Poor thing.

"I will be so happy when Beth delivers her child and her horrible morning sickness ends."

"As will I, my love," Joshua agreed.

"Last year at the ball you were so worried that Jasmine would catch us dancing that we did little more than move in place." She giggled at the memory.

Joshua held her at arms length, smiling fondly. "Jasmine is a force to be reckoned with."

"I would love to see her." Lynna sighed wistfully.

"As a matter of fact, you will. Samuel tells me that since Beth's morning sickness seems to be lasting through her entire pregnancy, he has asked his parents to send Jasmine to help with the running of the household. Much to his surprise, given the disaster that is Suzanne, they agreed. She should be arriving next week."

Lynna was elated by both Joshua's news and the fact that Beth was feeling well enough to spin around the dance floor on her husband's arm. "I cannot wait to see Jasmine."

"You know who I cannot wait to see?"

"Who?"

"My adorable daughter." Joshua's eyes twinkled merrily.

"If my memory serves, you were convinced that Beau would also be a girl."

"I'm positive this time," he stated, with confidence. "I will get my girl."

As he held Lynna with one hand, Joshua massaged his temples with the other where a persistent ache had formed. He couldn't remember the last time he'd had a headache, but this one promised to be memorable.

"What is it, Joshua?" Lynna placed her hands on each side of his face. "What's wrong?"

"My… head is throbbing."

"Sit down." She led him to a chair in the corner and motioned for a waiter. "Here, lean your head back and rest while I get you a cool drink. Perhaps you got overheated while dancing."

"Thank you. Maybe I will just rest my eyes for a few minutes." Closing his eyes did nothing to ease the pounding. In fact, the pain intensified with each heartbeat until he lost all sense of time and space. Nothing mattered except the intense pounding that radiated behind his eyes.

Clara had been sent home after the barbecue and lay in bed tossing and turning. She heard her grandmother snoring in the other room.

Something didn't feel right.

She didn't understand how she knew it, but *Joshua needed her.*

He was at Cedar Hill attending the ball. She slipped out of bed and pulled on her dress and shoes, then raced to the stables to saddle Jezebel.

Joshua's head dropped to Lynna's shoulder as every ounce of energy drained from his suddenly weak body. He no longer had the strength to sip from the drink she held to his lips.

"Joshua, I don't know how to help you," Lynna worried. "If only Jasmine was here."

Samuel noticed that all was not well with his friend. "What's wrong, Joshua?"

When her husband could mumble only a few incoherent words in response, Samuel witnessed the panic in Lynna's eyes. He motioned for Daniel to help carry Joshua into the parlor.

As they lay him on the settee Joshua's hand flew to his forehead, crying out with pain at being jostled so. He would have sworn someone had an axe and was repeatedly bashing his skull with the blunt end. The pain was unbearable.

Just when he came to the conclusion that he would rather be dead than suffer through another minute of the excruciating pain, Clara burst through the parlor doors.

Immediately, Joshua's headache eased.

While he was finally able to focus on the group gathered around him, his head was so sore he could barely move it. "Forgive me for causing such a commotion, but never have I encountered a pain of that magnitude before."

"Has the pain eased, darling?"

"Yes, love, it has." Joshua was able to wipe the sweat from his brow with a trembling hand as Clara rushed to his side, lifting his head to hold in her lap. She murmured soothing words as she caressed his forehead, pushing his damp hair back.

Lynna and everyone else in the room watched as the color slowly returned to Joshua's face and he began to breathe easier under Clara's soothing ministrations.

Clara looked up, flinching slightly when she felt what could only be described as tiny pin pricks bouncing off her skin. She glanced toward the open parlor doors and saw the shadowy figure of the evil woman from the river glaring back at her.

Her first thought was Beau. He was at Sea Grove, safe for now. If he wasn't, she would… feel it. But she was beside herself with worry over the fact that she couldn't protect both Joshua *and* Beau when they were so far apart.

She closed her eyes and drew in a deep breath to concentrate, focusing her anger directly on the woman.

She opened her eyes and smiled when the evil woman jerked, before dropping to her knees and clutching her head. Their eyes met, as the woman's malicious gaze filled with alarm, and awe, at the powers the young girl possessed. She recognized the revenge in Clara's eyes for *anyone* who sought to bring harm to Joshua Jordan.

Clara breathed a sigh of relief as the woman slithered away into the darkness. She had no idea who the beautiful woman was.

But she had messed with the wrong man.

Joshua was alert and talking now, so he didn't need her, but Clara was distraught with worry that Beau might.

She was greatly relieved when Joshua found the strength to stand on his own and announce they would be returning home early.

When they arrived at Sea Grove, Clara was through the front door and racing up the stairs two at a time before the others had even departed the carriage. She shoved open the door to Beau's room, thankful to find the toddler sleeping peacefully. She ran her fingers through his soft silky curls and closed her eyes to listen to the sound of his soft, steady breathing.

"Why were you so concerned for Beau, Clara?" She turned to find Lynna standing beside her with worry clouding her tired eyes. "Were you worried that Beau was in danger?"

Clara nodded.

"Was Joshua's headache caused by a voodoo spell?"

Again, Clara nodded.

Lynna glanced down at her sleeping son as hatred hardened her heart for anyone who might try to harm him. "Beau will be fine, Clara. Milly is here, and I will either sleep here with him tonight or take him to bed with me. I promise you that Beau will not be alone, so you get some rest. You have already had a busy night."

If Clara didn't have urgent plans tonight, no one could have persuaded her to leave Beau's side.

But she did.

As soon as Clara could slip out of the house without being noticed, she quietly pulled open the back door. She closed the squeaky portal gently so as not to disturb the kitchen maids who slept in the room off the pantry.

The night was cool and the dew had fallen, soaking her shoes and the hem of her dress. She tugged her shawl closer around her shoulders to ward off the night chill and moved as silently as possible as she slipped into the stables and saddled Jezebel.

It was a dark night with only a melon slice moon to guide her as Jezebel trotted down the road toward Amari's cabin. Coyotes howled, owls hooted, and other night creatures scurried in the woods in search of their evening meal. The deeper Clara rode into the forest the more her heart pounded in her chest.

How wise was it to come out here alone?

She tethered Jezebel to a tree deep in the forest and walked until she came to the cabin in the woods. She quietly crossed the yard until she could peer into an open window without being seen.

Amari and the beautiful woman sat at the table sipping coffee. Amari said as casually as though she were discussing the material for a new frock, "I think poison would be the easiest way to be rid of the child. I could cast a spell on one of the kitchen helpers at Sea Grove to lace his food with it."

Clara leaned against the trunk of a tree for support, her head spinning wildly.

Poison Beau?

The beautiful woman grinned. "Make it a slow acting poison so he will vomit blood for a few days. His parents need to watch him suffer before he dies."

Clara slid down the trunk of a tree as the loud buzzing roar returned to her head.

"Once you take the child out of the way it will be easier to dispose of his parents," Clara heard Amari say.

Clara found the energy to stand, and without even realizing what she was doing her arms moved up and both her index fingers pointed toward the window.

She saw the color red.

Her skin tingled and she could feel... fire rushing through her veins to gather in her arms.

Then... fire shot form her fingertips.

Amari jerked.

"Is something wrong?" the beautiful woman questioned.

"I feel like I was hit by a sledgehammer." Amari glanced toward the window.

"Perhaps someone has cast a spell on you," the beautiful woman teased.

"While it may be true that I get weaker with each passing year," Amari scoffed, "I still have enough strength to kill the Jordan baby for you. Tomorrow will be the last day the boy will ever open his eyes."

Clara moved to stand just outside the window. As she did, the wind that blew across the land as a gentle breeze picked up by degrees, until it was howling like a banshee. The fierce wind sent rocking chairs sailing across the yard, along with tree limbs, flower pots, buckets, garden tools and anything else that wasn't tethered to the ground.

The stars disappeared behind black clouds that rolled across the sky. Crashing thunder that sounded like cannons blasting rumbled overhead as brilliant flashes of lightning split the night sky, giving Amari a clear glimpse of who stood outside her window.

Amari sighed, accepting the fact that she was powerless against Clara.

Clara's dress whipped around her legs and her hair blew around her head as an eerie glow seemed to emanate from her body. She was a terrifying sight. With her feet braced apart and her arms extended toward the house, she felt the fire shoot through her arms and out her fingertips, and didn't try to stop it.

She watched silently as Amari slid from her chair and onto the floor.

Unmoving.

Not speaking.

Bloody drool oozed from the corner of her mouth. Bright red blood dribbled from her ear and trickled from her nose.

The conjure woman lay completely still.

Nothing on her body worked, except her lungs and eyelids.

She stared out the window at Clara as the beautiful woman from the river hovered over her, calling her name over and over and pleading with Amari to get up.

Chapter 20

Suzanne watched the volunteers lug their boxes of books into the commons, four selfless women who set aside their family chores one evening each month to teach the dregs of society to read. It would be the only book the majority of the incarcerated women would ever pick up.

She must pretend to be one of them.

The group consisted of two obese middle aged women, one elderly white haired grandmotherly type, and one reasonably attractive, yet disheveled, woman who looked to be in her late twenties. Suzanne hoped to be appointed to the younger lady.

She simply didn't have the patience to deal with elderly women and their talk of weather, how the bugs were taking over their green bean vines, and their long list of complaints consisting of everything from gout to those irritating heat rashes that formed under their pendulous breasts.

She, and three *truly* ignorant inmates, were seated at tables. Suzanne had no problem with lying or fakery, but pretending to be illiterate? That could present a problem if she slipped up.

When she noticed the elderly woman headed her way Suzanne jumped up and rushed to the younger lady's side to assist her with a heavy box of books. "Here, let me carry that for you. You must be exhausted after lugging all these books from the carriage."

"It's not really that heavy," the younger lady said, as sweat beaded on her brow and upper lip from exertion.

Suzanne led her to the farthest table and pulled her down beside her. "I am so excited to learn to read. It will open up an entire new world for me, I'm sure."

The woman mopped her face with a handkerchief before holding it to her nose, hoping it might filter the stench of Suzanne's atrocious body odor. "With books you can travel the world without ever leaving home."

"Where do we start?" Suzanne decided that she must be destined for the stage, for she actually sounded excited.

"I need to speak with the other ladies," the young woman hedged. "We normally decide, together, which student would benefit most from our individual skills."

"I have such a strong desire to learn to read, and I can relate better to someone closer to my own age. Can't you teach me, please?" Suzanne pleaded. "Why, I have been fluttering around on pins and needles all day just waiting for this moment to arrive."

The volunteer put her hand on Suzanne's hand and squeezed. "In that case, of course I can." She motioned to the other ladies and pointed to Suzanne as she mouthed, "I'll take this one." She opened one of her readers and smiled at Suzanne. "My name is Naomi, what's yours?"

"Suzanne Jordan."

"Very well, Suzanne. Let us learn your weaknesses, so that we can devise a study plan to get you up and reading." Naomi placed her finger at the beginning of the first page, and instructed, "Please, begin reading and don't be shy. Remember, I'm here to help you. It doesn't matter if you can't pronounce most of the words. Just do the best you can."

Suzanne plodded along painfully, intentionally mispronouncing any word with more than three letters.

"Well, you certainly do need my help, don't you?" Naomi mumbled, sadly, shocked by Suzanne's appalling lack of rudimentary skills. "Don't you worry. I will have you reading in no time."

As Naomi's hand moved across the page, Suzanne noticed a white ring around her otherwise tanned finger where a wedding band had recently resided. "Did you lose your wedding band?"

"What?" Naomi's sharp intake of breath startled Suzanne. "No, I didn't lose it. I just no longer… wear it."

Suzanne knew a scorned woman when she saw one. "I wore my wedding band until the guards snatched it from me the minute I arrived at this stinking hovel." As a tear fell from her watery eyes, she whispered, "You see, my husband left me for a harlot some time ago. That's why I am in this horrid place to begin with."

"Why?" Naomi asked, excitedly. She was intrigued to have a scandalous bit of gossip from this bunch of pitiful miscreants to share at her next quilting circle.

Suzanne shrugged. "For seeking revenge."

"For seeking revenge on your husband, or his harlot?"

"Both."

With growing interest, Naomi closed the book and leaned toward Suzanne. "Did you get your revenge on the harlot?"

"Absolutely." Suzanne swiped at her eyes and glanced down at the book, pretending to concentrate. "The tramp suffered immensely for the pain she caused me."

"How?"

"It was rather simple, really. I visited a voodoo queen on my brother's plantation and she taught me how to cast a spell. I was then able to place a curse on my husband's whore."

"Did the curse work?" Naomi cried, almost beside herself with excitement. This was certainly turning out to be an interesting day, when her visits with the smelly, filthy prisoners normally bored her to tears.

"Like a charm. The strumpet wasted away to practically nothing and suffered terrible agony for months on end."

Naomi gazed off into space with a dreamy look. "How I would love to see my husband's slut suffer."

Suzanne hid a smile behind her hand. There wasn't a spurned woman alive who didn't want to see the other woman suffer. "I could cast a spell to not only bring your husband back to you, but also a revenge spell to cause your husband's mistress a little pain and… suffering.

"Are your spells terribly expensive." Naomi was barely keeping food on the table and a roof over her children's heads. She had precious few coins to spare.

"They can be." Suzanne placed her hand softly on Naomi's and smiled a benevolent smile. "Since you are kind enough to teach me to read, I will cast your spells for free. You only need to supply the materials."

Naomi beamed from ear to ear as she pretended to read to Suzanne. "What supplies will I need?"

"That depends on which spell you would prefer to cast first." Suzanne's eyes twinkled merrily. She was anxious to practice her craft again. "The spell to return your loved one, or the revenge spell?"

"The revenge spell," Naomi answered, without hesitation. "I want to see the homewrecker suffer."

Every woman Suzanne had ever concocted a revenge spell for, had the same answer.

Pay back first.

"I need you to write down what you would like to see happen to your husband's strumpet," Suzanne instructed.

After removing a quill and ink from her bag Naomi snatched a piece of parchment and began hastily scribbling. She was obviously concentrating hard on the woman who had stolen her husband as she wrote:

Let her be hit by a runaway carriage.
Let her be bitten by a rattlesnake.

Let her suddenly develop consumption.
Let her fall in a well.
Let her be shot by a jealous lover.
Let her house burn to the ground with her in
it.

Suzanne wrote detailed directions as to how to conduct the spell and handed Naomi the slip of paper. "If you follow my instructions to the letter, your husband's lover will begin to suffer within seven days."

Naomi folded the paper and stuffed it in her bag. "I hope this works."

"Trust me," Suzanne promised, with a satisfied smirk. "It will."

Naomi left the prison with a dreamy smile and her arms filled with unread books.

The following month, Naomi appeared much happier. Her hair was smoothed back, she had dressed with care, and she carried herself straighter, prouder. She practically glowed with the joy of life.

She opened a book, and whispered, "Three days after I performed the spell, the temptress was hanging clothes on the line and got struck by lightning. The hussy fell dead on the spot. Can you believe it?"

Naomi hid a smile behind her hand as she reached into her bag for a paper and quill. "Can you give me the spell to make my husband return while no one is looking?"

"Of course, but be advised that the Black Cat Bone Spell is the most powerful voodoo reconciliation spell there is," Suzanne warned.

"Your husband will return, but it's by no means a... pleasant spell."

"Just tell me what to do." Naomi giggled.

"First, you will need the corpse of a black cat. Every black cat has within its body one bone that can be used to bring back a lost lover. You must toss the animal into a cauldron of boiling water at midnight and boil the carcass until the meat falls off the bone. The bone you are looking for will eventually float to the top. This bone must be carried on your person for the next nine days."

Naomi glared at her, speechless.

"Can you do this?" Suzanne prompted.

"I... I suppose. If I must."

"You must. Now, after the two of you have reconciled, you will want to keep him tied to you forever." She noticed that Naomi's face had lost most of its color. "Relax, this is a much less repugnant spell."

The woman visibly relaxed.

"To keep your lover forever, you will need one of your husband's shirts. It must be one that he has worn all day and sweated in. You will also need some of his hair since you are going to make a doll."

Naomi breathed a sigh of relief that no animals were involved.

"Cut the doll's clothes out of your husband's shirt, then glue his hair on the head of the doll. Now, this is the most important part of the spell. While your husband is asleep, you will need to gather a speck of lint from his bellybutton to glue on as the facial features of this doll. When the doll is complete, pin it under your bed and he will never leave you for another woman again."

"I will gather the ingredients tonight. Tomorrow, I will insist on giving my husband a haircut and perform the spell while he sleeps. Thank you, Suzanne. I am so thankful that we met. It's almost like destiny."

"I'm always happy to help a woman in need. But you must remember that I have also been badly mistreated by a man. So, I have one simple favor to ask of you in return."

"Anything." Naomi would hang the moon for her new friend. "Just name it."

"I would ask you to write a letter of recommendation so that I may be considered for an early release program here at the prison. Since I have been a model prisoner and have shown such great remorse, I have been chosen to go before the committee after having served one year of hard labor."

"I would be honored to write the letter." Naomi turned toward the door and motioned for fat Mona to join them. "Would you please show me to the warden's office? I have a letter to write."

A wicked grin curved Suzanne's lips. She had her three letters of recommendation. Now, she only had to serve four more months in the backbreaking cotton fields and she would be free.

Won't everyone back home be surprised.

Chapter 21

Charleston, SC
December 1856

A scrumptious feast overflowed the table at Sea Grove on Christmas Eve. Of course, Rob and Lucille had been invited, but they had both confessed that the fancy silverware, china, and crystal glasses were entirely too rich for their blood. Lucille was cooking collard greens and chitlins for Rob in her cabin.

Beth and Samuel were unable to attend since Beth's morning sickness had only gotten worse, and Clara was again visiting Cedar Hill to help keep little Bethany occupied.

"How is my grandchild faring?" Nathan asked Lynna, stabbing a mouthwatering slice of ham to add to a mound of potato salad. "Is she as active as Beau was?"

"Actually, no. The baby has been unusually calm this morning. In fact, I was telling Joshua earlier that I slept uninterrupted for the entire night, which is most unusual. Come to think of it, I don't recall her kicking me this morning either." Lynna looked to Joshua with worry clouding her vision. "Do you think something is wrong with the baby?"

"Not at all, my love." Joshua smiled patiently. "I think the little darling has simply worn herself out over the last few weeks and is resting up for her big day."

"He's right, darling," Judith agreed with a reassuring tone. "Babies often settle into the birth canal as time draws near. I don't think there is cause for alarm."

"Beau didn't settle down." Lynna couldn't help but worry as she nibbled on a deviled egg, having lost her appetite. "Our son was rarely still."

"Yes, I remember." Patricia squeezed a slice of lemon into her sweet tea. "Still, no two babies are alike. But if it will make you feel better I can send for the doctor tomorrow."

"Thank you, Patricia. It would ease my mind,"

Lynna rubbed her stomach and worried.
Something wasn't right.

She hadn't felt her baby move in twenty four hours.
What if?

No. She wouldn't allow herself to even think such morbid thoughts. Aunt Judith and Patricia were more experienced with these matters and fully believed there was no cause for alarm.

Later that night, as Lynna curled her tired body against Joshua's, she couldn't help but share what was troubling her. "Joshua, I'm concerned about the baby. Why has she suddenly stopped moving? What if..."

Joshua shushed her with a finger to her lips. "The baby is fine, Lynna. You'll see."

Please, God, let the child be well.
Lynna has already suffered more than her

share of pain.

"Just wait until tomorrow." Joshua sought to ease her mind, even though his own was plagued with worry. "You'll be complaining about how hard our daughter is kicking you."

"Do you really think so?" Lynna whispered, with a tremulous voice as fear coiled around her heart like a viper.

"Of course, I do. Now try to get some sleep. You will feel better tomorrow. I promise."

Joshua was unable to keep his promise.

After a sleepless night Lynna was pacing back and forth across the verandah, too nervous to sit still as she waited for the doctor to arrive.

"Lynna, darling, sit down and rest," Joshua urged. "You'll wear blisters on your feet."

"Surely, you can't expect me to just sit still and twiddle my thumbs. Don't you understand? Something is wrong with my baby." She dropped her head in her hands and apologized for her outburst. "I'm sorry. It's just that I'm so worried?"

Before Joshua could answer they heard a horse approaching. Lynna rushed to the verandah railing to wait patiently for the doctor to dismount. "Doctor Raymond, I'm so glad to see you." Moving as fast as her swollen body would allow she walked to the top of the steps to greet him. "Something is wrong with my baby."

"What seems to be the trouble, dear?" the kindly old bespeckled man asked.

"My baby has been extremely active for months. Yet, for the past forty eight hours she has not moved once." Lynna's eyes glistened with unshed tears as she reached for the doctor's hands, unconsciously clutching them to her stomach. "She wouldn't just... stop moving would she? What could this mean?"

"Well, it could be any number of things. For one, in the ninth month the baby has gotten so big there is much less room to move around, and remember your child is residing in some rather cramped quarters. For another, perhaps your time is near and the child is head down in the birth position. Of course, I will need to examine you to be sure. If you will excuse us, Joshua." Thus said, he steered Lynna through the door and up the stairs to her room.

Joshua waited none too patiently on the verandah, pacing back and forth until the doctor returned. "Is the baby well, Doctor?"

"As far as I can tell." The doctor paused, as if choosing his words carefully. "While the child has a strong heartbeat, he or she has not turned, nor has your wife begun to dilate. In my opinion, she has a few weeks to go." The good doctor took the time to stuff his pipe and light it, scenting the air with fragrant smoke. "As for why the infant is not moving, that presents a quandary that I will need to discuss with a colleague. I personally have never come across a situation such as this. As I told your wife, let's give it three more days. That will be five days total. If the child hasn't moved by then, I will need to be informed."

"Then what?" Joshua needed to be aware of his options.

"We will cross that bridge when we come to it. For now, go upstairs and try to keep your wife as calm as possible. Lynna may have cause for concern, but she doesn't need to know it, yet."

On the fifth day, Lynna was beside herself with worry, unable to sit, sleep, eat, or focus on anything other than the life she carried inside her.

Something was wrong with her baby.

Not a single movement in five days. "Is the heartbeat still strong?" she asked, once the doctor had completed his examination.

"As strong as it was three days ago." The doctor looked out the window and across the plowed and furrowed fields, obviously deep in thought.

"What is your diagnosis?" Nathan asked. He would bring in the finest specialist from around the world when he knew what they were up against.

"My guess would be that the babe has contracted an illness that makes it impossible to move, or perhaps the child has slipped into a coma, or any number of other ailments. It has all the makings of an impending stillborn birth, except for the fact that the child has such a strong heartbeat. To be totally honest, I am flummoxed. Since I have never experienced anything like it, I suppose we will have to wait until the child makes his or her appearance to discover the problem."

"A coma?" Lynna cried. "An illness? But how? Why would that happen? If my baby has contracted an illness, shouldn't I also be sick."

"It stands to reason that you should," the doctor agreed, nodding his head.

"I want the baby out," Lynna stated, adamantly. "Now. Something is wrong and I want her out."

"While I understand your concern, dear, we cannot just deliver a baby at will. These things follow a natural progression."

"Don't give me that," Lynna snapped, teetering on the very edge of her breaking point. "I've heard women speak of taking... potions... to start their labor."

"Surely, you don't mean to compare yourself to those women," the doctor spluttered, clearly appalled by such a notion. "Those remedies are hardly fit for a woman of quality, such as yourself."

"What difference does it make?" Lynna insisted. "The child is instilled in our wombs the exact same manner, we carry them to term the exact same way, and we deliver them the exact same way. Please, Doctor Raymond, enlighten me as to one difference in the birthing process between a poor woman and a rich woman." When the puzzled doctor could not supply an answer, she turned to her husband. "Please, send Milly to me at once, Joshua."

Joshua looked to the doctor for help. "If you know of a way to induce her labor, I beg you to do so before she seeks advice from the servants."

"Well, there are... ways," the doctor responded, hesitantly. "Yet, they are not always one hundred percent effective."

"Try them," Lynna urged, with renewed determination in her voice.

Nathan, Judith, and Patricia stood outside her door listening to every word and relaying the information to Jeremiah, who sat in his chair at the foot of the stairs.

Nathan knocked and the trio entered the room. "Tell us the ways to induce labor, doctor."

The doctor noted that he was up against five very determined family members. "Naturally, I would strip the membranes."

"Could you be more specific," Nathan asked, looking considerably paler than he had upon entering the room.

"This is done by inserting two fingers inside the cervix and separating the bag of water from the cervix. It has been my experience that this method brings on labor in about half the cases."

"What are the other methods," Joshua asked, feeling the need to sit down while steadfastly praying that stripping *anything* would be the last alternative. None of it sounded entirely pleasant to him.

"I could rub evening primrose oil on the cervix to help ripen it, but that typically takes a few days to a week to begin working."

"What else?" Lynna asked.

"The final alternative would be a dose of castor oil. That seems to be the favored method among the servants."

"I want all three methods." Lynna insisted. She glanced at her family, expecting no rebuttal. "Will you please leave the room so the doctor can strip my membranes?"

"Lynna, darling, shouldn't we..." Joshua began.

"No, Joshua, we shouldn't. I beg you not to waste your time, nor mine, for I promise you there will be no changing my mind. I intend to give my child a fighting chance and for that to happen, we have to know what is wrong with her." Noticing the stubborn set to her jaw, Joshua joined the others in the hall to wait.

Shortly, Lynna called for Joshua to enter. A wave of pity for his wife washed over him when he noticed sweat beading on her brow as pain lingered in her tired eyes. "Joshua, the doctor does not carry evening primrose oil in his bag. I need you to send your fastest rider into town and to his office. The doctor will send a note to his wife."

"Consider it done," He was grateful to have something to do.

"Aunt Judith, will you please get me something flavorful to drink after I take the castor oil. I remember the horrible taste from my childhood." Lynna shuddered, at the thought of swallowing the loathsome liquid.

"What can I do, darling?" Nathan asked.

She took her father's hand and reached up for a brief hug. "When my labor begins please take Beau to visit Lucille and Rob. I wouldn't want him to hear my cries and become upset, and I may be unable to hold them back, even for Beau."

"I will be happy to, my darling."

Patricia bent to place a soft kiss on Lynna's perspiring brow. "I'll begin preparing the necessary items for the birth, and praying."

"Thank you, Patricia. Please, pray," she whispered. "Pray for God to spare my baby."

By nightfall the following night, Lynna was in labor. Hard labor. Unlike her first childbirth the pains didn't start as uncomfortable aches and gradually build. They began as excruciating pain and only got worse, with barely a second to rest between contractions.

The twenty four hours that followed were a haze of agony. Lynna screamed when it felt like someone had taken a red hot dagger from a blazing fire and twisted it cruelly in her midsection. The pain wrapped around her middle, reaching around to her back and squeezing in a vise of torture. With each contraction her stomach tightened painfully, as hard as rock.

Would she survive this birth?

She drifted in and out of consciousness, occasionally seeing Joshua's haggard face above her as he held a damp cloth to her forehead. She vaguely heard Jasmine whisper soothing words.

Jasmine.

Thank God she was here.

Having pierced the midnight air with her screams until her throat was raw, only scratchy whispers could find a way past Lynna's dry, chapped lips as she begged for water.

As the morning sun peeked through the window she could only moan pitifully as the intense knifing pain continued to stab her midsection.

When the doctor announced that he would need to turn the baby, she tried to prepare herself for the pain.

When it was over, she doubted that anyone could have adequately prepared for the torture that followed. She passed out long before the doctor had completed the task.

She was lying in a pool of sweat, blood, and tears when Doc Raymond finally used forceps to pull her still, quiet daughter from her exhausted body and place the infant in Jasmine's waiting arms.

Jasmine held the still infant. The child didn't move, her eyelids didn't flutter, and she was breathing so softly that Jasmine placed a hand on her chest to assure that she was breathing at all. She was breathtakingly beautiful.

Jasmine had witnessed many white babies being brought into the world, but none to compare to this precious little angel. Shiny black curls fell across her forehead, milky skin like dollops of cream, and rosy red lips with a perfect V in the center of the top lip. Jasmine had to chuckle. Joshua wanted a girl that was the spitting image of Lynna, but he surely didn't get one. In the old servant's opinion, he got even better.

Jasmine was relieved to see Lynna sleeping peacefully, finally. Doc had given her enough laudanum to make her sleep until morning. The poor thing needed it after all she had been through.

"Can I see her, Jasmine," Joshua whispered, softly, leaving Lynna's side for the first time all night. His eyes were red rimmed and he was in need of a hot bath and a shave.

"You sho' can." Jasmine beamed proudly at the darling baby.

"She is so beautiful," he breathed. "And so still. What's wrong with her, Jasmine?"

Tears formed on Jasmine's lashes and ran in a stream down her cheek to fall on the baby's blanket. "I wish I know', Mist' Joshua. I sho' nuff wish I know'." Drying her eyes, she sniffed. "Rat now, let me go give her a bath so Doc can figure it out an' fix it fo' it's too…"

Joshua turned, slowly walking back to his seat by Lynna's side. "Don't say it, Jasmine."

Joshua watched the doctor doing whatever they do to women after childbirth, with troubled eyes. Lynna didn't flinch or move a muscle.

After several minutes had passed the doctor stood and handed a bowl of something bloody to one of the servants as he went to the washstand to wash his hands.

"Is it safe to say that you have never attended a similar birth," Joshua asked, afraid of the answer.

"I dare say it is. The baby didn't make a sound, even when I slapped her bottom." The doctor shook his head wearily. "Highly unusual."

"So in your educated opinion, the child is not well?"

"No, she is not." The doctor glanced at Lynna to make certain she was asleep and wouldn't hear his next words. "I will tell you what worries me most. With the baby in a comatose state, such as she is, how will she eat? She has been receiving nourishment from her mother, and now she's on her own. I'm not at all sure she can even swallow." After washing his hands, he reached into his pocket for his pipe. "I would be remiss if I didn't warn you that a coma is nature's way of relieving the suffering of people who are dying."

Dear God.

Joshua hadn't even thought of his daughter… dying. There had to be a way to feed the baby until she awakened from her coma. "And Lynna? Is she well?"

"She appears to be the picture of health. She will be understandably upset when she awakens, and we both know she's going to require answers that I cannot give her."

"Lynna's father has promised to bring in a specialist to diagnose the problem," Joshua offered.

The doctor turned to Joshua with an air of defeat. "The problem will be keeping the baby alive until a specialist can reach her. Without nourishment, your daughter cannot survive, Joshua."

He sank back in his chair feeling more lost and helpless than ever.

His daughter had to survive.

He watched quietly as the door cracked open and Jasmine, followed closely by his mother, entered the room carrying his still daughter.

"Any noise or movement," the doctor asked.

"Nary a sound," Jasmine pursed her full lips in concentration. "She still breathin' though. An' look at de color in dem plum' cheeks."

"Although the baby appears healthy, looks can be deceiving." He relieved Jasmine of her bundle and moved to a chaise lounge by the window where the morning light was best, and unwrapped the blanket.

After a thorough examination of the seemingly perfect and exquisitely beautiful child, he turned to his associate, who had arrived the hour before. "What do you make of it?"

The puzzled man could only shake his head. "I have no comparison to draw on."

"Neither do I," Doc Raymond wrapped the quiet baby in her blanket before handing her off to Jasmine. "All I can tell you is this. If you can find a way to feed the child, she might live. If not, she will die. In fact, it might be better for all concerned, especially the mother, if you put the baby out of her…"

"Don't even think it," Joshua interrupted. "That is not an option. We will find a way."

Jasmine was paralyzed with fear by the doctor's words.

Put Lynna's baby out of her misery?
Was he crazy?

Why, the adorable baby looked anything but miserable to her. "You jus' stay heah wit' Miz Lynna, Mist' Joshua. Me an' Miz Patricia gwine go see whut we kin do ta git some food in dis lil gal's belly."

When she reached the bottom of the winding staircase, Jasmine instructed, "Miz Patricia, I needs you ta warm some milk an' fetch me a eye drapper."

"Right away, Jasmine."

Lucille and Rob were sitting in the parlor with the others, waiting to hear the news. After a brief explanation, Lucille said, "You need my Clara. She was born with the gift of healing."

"She rite," Rob agreed, leaping to his feet. "I jus' ride ovah ta Sea Grove an' fetch Miz Clara."

Patricia smiled her gratitude. "Thank you, Rob,"

Lucille followed Jasmine and Patricia into the kitchen where Patricia immediately began issuing orders. Jasmine sat in a rocking chair cuddling the achingly still infant to her breast.

Shortly, Patricia was holding a bowl of warm milk and an eyedropper. "Try this, Jasmine."

Mumbling a silent prayer, Jasmine put a dropper of milk to the child's lips. She didn't move. Jasmine tried to gently force the dropper between her rosy red lips, but her gums were held tightly together, leaving the milk to dribble down her chin. The old woman felt the urge to force the dropper into the baby's mouth and squeeze, but if she couldn't swallow, the infant would strangle on the milk.

After several unsuccessful tries Jasmine placed the dropper in the bowl and looked at Patricia with eyes that glistened. "Dis ain't gwine work."

Patricia sank to the floor at Jasmine's feet and laid her head in the old servant's lap. "We have to do something, Jasmine. We just can't let my granddaughter die."

Jasmine looked off into space, searching her mind for any solution. "If'n I was home; Pearlie might be able ta he'p us."

"Who is Pearlie?" Patricia sniffled, drying her eyes.

"She de conja woman back home."

"You mean voodoo?"

"Yas'sum." Jasmine looked lovingly at the comatose baby in her arms. "Dis baby 'mindin' me of sumbody done had a curse put on dem."

"A curse," Patricia cried, rising to her feet.

That must be what was wrong with the baby.

Lynna had repeatedly warned them that voodoo was real and to be taken seriously. Patricia wasn't really sure how she felt about voodoo, but she knew exactly how Lynna felt about it. Lynna would want her to go to any means necessary to save her baby, even if it meant seeking out a root worker. "Amari is the voodoo queen at Cedar Hill. We must take the baby to her."

Jasmine immediately stood. "You call fo' de hoss an' buggy an' I git dis baby another blanket an' meet you out back."

Having overheard their discussion from his chair parked near the door, Jeremiah called for Big Jim. "Take me to the buggy. We are going too."

"Yassuh," Big Jim answered. "I carry you ta de buggy, sir, an' I be waitin' right chere when you gits back ta git you out. Please don't makes me go through dem hainted woods dat done took yo' legs."

"Big Jim, I have told you and told you those woods are not haunted. What happened to me was an accident." Jeremiah stopped, having noticed the look of stark terror on the man's face. He was praying so diligently that his eyes rolled back in his head until only the whites showed. "Very well then, stay here."

"Should we tell Joshua where we're going?" Patricia glanced toward the upstairs room where Lynna slept.

"No," Jeremiah answered. "He might try to stop us. I'm only agreeing to this because I know it's what Lynna would want. We should get going, dear. From the looks of our precious granddaughter, we don't have a second to waste."

Chapter 22

Patricia, Jeremiah, Jasmine, and the baby traveled over the road between the neighboring plantations with the sounds of birds tweeting and forest critters scampering about. Crows as black as midnight perched in the highest branches, cawing a warning as they passed. Jasmine crossed herself and clutched the baby tighter.

The day was hot, and in her haste Patricia had forgotten her bonnet. She wiped the sweat from her brow with a dainty lace handkerchief as her eyes met Jasmine's worried gaze over the quiet baby's head. She remembered Big Jim's superstitious ramblings about these voodoo woods and for the first time ever, she did not scoff at his warning. She was determined to focus on the road before her and clicked the reins, urging the horse to move faster.

Amari's cabin seemed to be a beehive of activity this morning. Two fine carriages were parked to the side of the cabin with four bays munching grass in a shaded, fenced in area.

Patricia glanced around uneasily. "Looks like she has company." She pulled the horse to a halt and removed the wet handkerchief from her bodice to wipe at the beads of sweat trickling down her temples.

Before she could step down from the buggy the door swung open and two women, obviously mother and daughter, came to stand on the porch.

"Larue?" Hearing her husband's breathless whisper, Patricia turned to see the shock and disbelief register on his face.

"You know these women?" Patricia asked.

"I know the older one," he whispered. "And the younger one looks so famil…" his voice trailed off as every ounce of color drained from his face. "Why are you here, Larue?"

"Hello, Jeremiah." Larue Fontaine smiled a serene smile. She was still a beautiful woman with black silky hair pinned atop her head and a slender frame with curves still in all the right places. "It has been a long time."

"Over thirty years," he mumbled.

Larue leaned against the porch rail and breathed deeply. "I just love the smell of fresh country air after being cooped up in the city." When no response came from the startled occupants of the buggy, she flashed a wicked grin. "Now, as for why I am here. Unbeknownst to you, I have been a frequent visitor to my dear friend Amari over the years. I have practically been in your own backyard countless times and you never even knew it, Jeremiah."

"You and Amari are friends?" Jeremiah found it hard to believe that his former mistress could be close friends with the old conjure woman.

"Don't look so surprised, sugah." Larue laughed, a chilling sound. "I taught her everything she knows."

Patricia felt a sinking feeling in the pit of her stomach when she looked at the younger of the two women. She bore more than a striking resemblance to Jeremiah and could be Joshua's twin. She turned to her husband and read the truth in his eyes, as her heart sank.

Jeremiah wondered at Larue's reasoning for waiting until now to reveal this stunning revelation, at this late stage in his life. "What do you want, Larue?"

"Oh, I think you know." With a pasted on smile, she put her arms around her daughter's shoulder to draw her close. "To be truthful, I just came to visit my old... *friend*." Her eyes snapped with anger as her demeanor changed in the blink of an eye. "That's not really true, is it? We were much more than just friends, weren't we, Jeremiah?"

Jeremiah glanced sideways toward the rigid figure of his wife. "Allow me to be more specific, Larue. What do you want from *me*? Money?"

"Hah! I have no need of your pittance. I am wealthy in my own right. Have you not heard of me?" When Jeremiah failed to answer, she continued. "I thought it was time to introduce you to someone." She waved her hand toward the young woman beside her, and proudly announced, "Jeremiah Jordan, meet your daughter Jerica Jordan Fontaine."

Jeremiah glanced at the woman whose eyes were as cold and hard as her mothers.

"Hello, *father*," Jerica sneered. "Since you never cared enough to come and meet me, I came to you. My, my, won't Joshua and Malinda be surprised to discover they have a sister?"

"I never knew you existed." Sweat streamed from Jeremiah's brow as he tried to explain his absence from his daughter's life, casting a reproachful eye toward Larue. "Why didn't you tell me?"

Larue huffed an irritated breath, prompting the occupants of the buggy to wonder at her sanity when she bent down to make eye contact and stroke the back of a lizard perched on the rail. "Jeremiah, darling, you are a man of some intelligence. When you make love to a woman as often as you did with me, there are consequences to be expected. Even though you met Patricia Middleton one hot sultry evening on the streets of Savannah and immediately fell in love with her father's purse, you could have at least waved goodbye when you rode off into the sunset. Had you bothered, you would have noticed me growing heavy with your child."

Jeremiah was speechless.

"Don't look so distraught, darling. After the initial shock of being dumped, penniless, and with a child on the way, I sought out ways to make a living for us. Fortunately, I found part time employment with a kindly old woman who told fortunes and sold voodoo curses from her home around the corner from my tiny apartment."

A shiver tingled along Jeremiah's spine. "Your employer trained you in the art of voodoo?"

"Yes, and not to sound boastful, but I rather excelled at it. As you probably know, I am often referred to as the Voodoo Queen of Savannah."

"So I have heard."

"Then you should know that neither I, nor your daughter, wanted for anything from that day forward."

"You're wrong, mother," Jerica ground out. "I always wanted a father like the other children had, especially at Christmas, birthdays, and father daughter dances."

Larue placed a comforting hand on her daughter's shoulder, eyeing the bundle in Jasmine's arms suspiciously. "What have we here?"

"We came seeking Amari's help," Jeremiah began, meeting Larue's eyes. "Now, I'm guessing it was a waste of time."

"It was, in the sense that Amari can no longer help anyone. You see, the dear woman has been struck down by a stroke and is now paralyzed from the neck down. She has to be cared for as though she were an infant." Larue found no sympathy in any of the eyes glaring at her. "But don't be silly, Jeremiah." She waved a bejeweled hand through the air. "What can *I* do for you?"

"We have reason to believe my grandchild has been cursed…"

"Cursed?" Larue interrupted. "You don't say." She moved down the steps for a better look. "Jerica, do come look at this simply adorable little girl," she called over her shoulder. "Why, I have never seen a more beautiful child."

Jerica moved closer as her eyes shone with hatred for the man in the buggy. "Yes, she is exquisite." She looked directly at Jeremiah with all the malice she felt toward her father clearly evident in her stormy countenance. "A pity she will never open her eyes."

"Never open her eyes?" Patricia gasped, as the meaning of the lovely young woman's words dawned on her. "Why would you say such a horrible thing?"

"Oh, Lawd," Jasmine wailed. "I jus' knowed dis baby done had a hex put on her."

Jeremiah leaned over the side of the buggy to grab Larue's arm. "You put a curse on my granddaughter, Larue?"

Larue shook his hand off as her chilling laughter echoed through the clearing. "If anyone should know the effects of a curse it would be you, Jeremiah."

"What are you talking about?" An icy chill settled over Jeremiah. "You cursed *me*, Larue?"

"Years ago. As a matter of fact, I have been the cause of most of your woes over the years, and you never even suspected me."

"The loss of my legs?" Jeremiah gasped. "It was you?"

"Of course, I put the little spirit in your path. You were simply having too much fun with your wife and family while *my* child suffered because of your selfishness. I had to take away your joy."

"I understand your hatred for me, Larue." Jeremiah's voice shook with a combination of anger and fear. "But how could you curse an innocent child who has never wronged you."

Breathing a bored sigh, Larue peered into the forest. "The answer is simple really. I couldn't allow your son to be happy when my own daughter was being forced to live the life of a bastard."

Patricia immediately jumped from the carriage, rushing to Larue's side. "Larue, please believe me. I knew nothing about what transpired between you and Jeremiah before I met him. He has never once even mentioned your name. Please, I beg you. Don't do this to my innocent granddaughter."

Larue laughed, an entirely malevolent sound. It was obvious that she enjoyed watching the wife of the esteemed Jeremiah Jordan grovel at her feet. "Stop making a fool of yourself, Patricia. I have placed a wasting spell on the baby and there is no one in South Carolina, or the entire country for that matter, with the power to remove one of my spells. I would advise you to go home and begin digging her grave."

Patricia gasped, clutching her chest as she fell back against the buggy, mortified. "How can you be so heartless, so totally devoid of emotion? You would see my son suffer for the sins of his father?"

"Yes, I would. With great joy actually."

Patricia crossed herself as she stumbled to the carriage. "May God punish you for your sins."

Larue smirked as fat teardrops slid down Patricia's cheek. "I can promise you that I will not pay as dearly as your husband has, and *will* in the years to come."

Patricia climbed into the buggy, numb, except for the pain in her heart. No one spoke as she urged the horses toward home.

By the time they returned to Sea Grove the baby still had not moved, nor made a sound. The only difference Jasmine noted was that the rosy color had left the darling little girl's cheeks and she was growing pale.

They were losing her.

"We gots ta find a way to make dis baby eat, Miz Patricia."

Patricia was at her wits end, having no idea who to turn to for help. "How, Jasmine?"

"I gots ta think." Jasmine shook her head, bereft. "Dey gots ta be a way."

When Patricia stopped the buggy at the back door Jeremiah leaned toward her to whisper, "Darling, we need to talk."

"Not now, Jeremiah," she answered in an icy tone, filled with contempt. "My only concern at the moment is my gravely ill granddaughter. We will discuss your… affairs with that odious woman later."

"Very well, dear."

When they entered the kitchen Clara and Rob were sitting at the table, with Clara patting her foot impatiently. The instant they came through the door she was on her feet, reaching for the little girl.

As Clara held the baby to her chest, everyone in the room witnessed a miracle. The little girl moved her finger. It wasn't much and it only lasted a second, yet she had definitely wiggled one tiny finger.

Jasmine and Patricia were ecstatic, hugging each other and dancing around like schoolgirls. "Did you see dat?" Jasmine cried. "Soon as Clara tech dat baby she done move her fanger. Clara girl, you is a gif' straight from de heavens."

"I saw it too, Jasmine." Patricia beamed. "Come, Clara, sit in the rocking chair and get comfortable."

Clara did, clutching her tiny bundle lovingly and smoothing her finger across the porcelain skin of the adorable baby's pert little nose. She was the most beautiful child Clara had ever seen.

Why was she so still?

"Fetch some mo' warm milk an' a drapper, Miz Patricia," Jasmine said.

When the milk was ready, Judith bent down in front of Clara and held out the dropper.

As if she had been feeding comatose babies all of her life Clara brought the child to a sitting position with her head cradled in the crease of her elbow, as her lips moved with silent endearments for the little girl.

Clara put the dropper to the baby's lips.

Nothing happened.

She touched it to her lips, trying to gently nudge her gums apart. Nothing. When she touched the infant's lips for the third time, they parted ever so slightly causing simultaneous gasps to be heard around the room.

Clara was able to squeeze in a drop of milk. Everyone waited, afraid to breathe; terrified the baby would strangle on the milk and be unable to cough to clear her air passage.

Patricia feared her heart was surely about to leap out of her chest.

Jeremiah clutched the arms of his wheeled chair until his knuckles whitened.

Rob stood in the corner, unmoving, his huge hands clenched into fists as he prayed fervently for Buttercup's daughter. He vowed then and there to get even with that voodoo woman if it killed him.

Jasmine reached up to hold the lucky gris gris Pearlie had made to wear around her neck and ward off Suzanne's evil.

When the baby didn't appear to be struggling, Clara used the dropper to place another drop on her tiny pink tongue. Patricia reached out to stop her, afraid the baby would choke, but Jasmine put a staying hand on Patricia's and shook her head.

Clara was their only hope.
Without her, Lynna's baby would die.

As they watched and waited, each of them issuing silent prayers, yet trying to prepare themselves in the event of failure, they all saw when the baby's little neck moved and she swallowed the milk. Patricia and Jasmine's eyes grew big as they clapped their hands over their mouths to prevent their shouts of joy from startling the baby girl.

It was a painstakingly slow process as Clara prompted her to swallow almost four droppers full of milk. "Dat's 'nuff fo' now." Jasmine said, happier than she could ever remember being prior to this day. "Let dis sweet baby res'. Dat cow milk liables ta tear her stomach up. We gots ta squeeze out some of her mama's milk ta feed her."

With the color returning to the baby's cheeks, she resembled any other newborn sleeping peacefully. "She looks like an angel at rest," Nathan whispered, reverently. "Clara, darling, you have saved my granddaughter's life and I will be forever in your debt."

Clara cheeks reddened under the praise as she glanced up to see Joshua standing in the doorway. "She saved my daughter's life, just as she saved mine." He bent to drop a kiss on her strawberry blond curls. "I have never thought much about fate, until now. Recently, I have come to the realization that if I hadn't been shot, I wouldn't have met Clara and Lucille." He met Clara's loving gaze, and smiled. "I feel almost as though we were destined to meet, for I am convinced that only you can save my daughter, Clara."

Jeremiah smiled fondly at his adopted granddaughter. "Who would have thought a twelve year old girl could fight the likes of Larue Fontaine and come out the victor?"

Clara's insistent grunt and firm shake of her head drew everyone's attention.

"What did I say?" Jeremiah queried.

"You said twelve." Joshua's laughter rumbled in his chest. "Clara would like to inform you that she will be thirteen soon."

"And I intend to make it her best birthday ever," Nathan replied, grinning at the young girl.

"As will the rest of us, but what did you mean by your reference to Larue Fontaine, father?" Joshua wondered aloud. "What do you know of the supposed voodoo queen of Savannah?"

Deciding to come clean and tell his son what he had so recently learned, Jeremiah finally admitted, "It had nothing to do with fate, son. It would appear that I have been under a voodoo curse for years, as have you."

"What are you talking about?" Joshua was taken aback by his words. "Don't tell me you have fallen for Amari's voodoo nonsense as well."

"Push me into the parlor, son. I have a rather difficult story to tell you." Jeremiah hung his head. "Afterwards, your opinion of voodoo might be dramatically altered."

Patricia tried to lighten the mood, and called to her son's retreating back. "This baby needs a name, Joshua."

"Makenna Mae Jordan." Joshua glanced at Clara and winked. "Makenna after Lynna's mother, and Mae after my daughter's lifesaver."

Clara's blush deepened under his praise. She settled back in the rocking chair with her precious bundle, gently twirling one of Makenna's silky black curls around her finger. She couldn't help but look to her tiny chest to watch the gentle rise and fall.

Joshua pushed his father's chair into the parlor, taking a seat in a wing chair by the fireplace. "What is this about, father?"

Jeremiah leaned back in his wheeled chair and reached for his pipe, lighting it and taking a long draw before speaking. Joshua could tell this was a story his father wasn't eager to share. "It would appear that you have another sister that none of us were aware of, son."

"A sister?" Joshua fell down in a chair. To say he was shocked would be a gross understatement. "Pray continue, father."

Jeremiah brushed at invisible lint on his sleeve, buying time. "When I was young, about your age, I had a quadroon mistress. A woman by the name of Larue Fontaine. As you know, she is a practitioner of voodoo."

"Voodoo again." Joshua jumped up to pace the floor. "That's all I hear lately, at every turn. I am sick to death of the word."

"As am I." Jeremiah agreed. "At any rate, Larue was already carrying my child when I met your mother and fell in love with her."

"You cannot be serious?"

"I wish I could tell you that it was a horrible misunderstanding, son, but I can't. According to Larue, everything bad that has happened to this family is because of a spell she cast 30 years ago."

Joshua allowed his father's unbelievable words to sink in. "Did she tell you that she carried your child?"

"Not a word. Until today."

"Today?"

"She was at Amari's house when we went seeking help for your daughter. She is evil, Joshua. Nothing at all like the woman I knew. And her daughter, or I suppose I should say... our daughter... is definitely her mother's child. Of course, to hear her tell it, I left them penniless and went on to marry your wealthy mother."

"Did you?"

"Well, yes. Only in my defense, I had no idea that a child was involved. Had I known, I would have never left her. I trust you know me well enough to realize the truth of my words when I say that I would never abandon one of my children."

"Of course, I do, Father." Jeremiah Jordan loved his children above all else. "So is it your intention to make amends with..."

"Jerica." Jeremiah gazed out the window. "Jerica Jordan Fontaine. She didn't appear to be very receptive to the idea. In fact, this is the part I have been dreading telling you." He took a deep breath, before continuing. "Larue has cursed Makenna and she claims that no one in this state, or the entire country, has the power to remove her spell."

Joshua felt rage like never before as his

blood simmered through his veins. "This woman has cursed an innocent child? Is she totally devoid of a heart and soul?"

"My answer would have to be yes," Jeremiah admitted, sadly. "She has the coldest heart of anyone I have ever had the misfortune to meet."

Rob sat on the verandah just outside the open window to the parlor. He heard every word and vowed to make the evil woman pay for the harm she had caused Buttercup and her children.

It was much later when Lynna awakened, feeling as though she were in a long, dark tunnel. She could hear someone calling her name from far, far away and wanted to answer. Yet, at the same time she wanted to stay where she was, and rest. The insistent caller would have none of it and roughly yanked her from a deep sleep. She was so tired. The horrible pain had finally ceased and she wanted only to sleep, for days.

"Miz Lynna, we gots ta squeeze out some of yo' milk." Jasmine continued to shake her.

Lynna was confused. "Just bring my baby to me, Jasmine. I can feed her."

"Naw, you cain. De baby ain't able to suck jus' yet. We gots ta feed her wid a drapper fo' a lil while."

"A dropper?" Why was Jasmine talking such foolishness? "You are making absolutely no sense, Jasmine." Lynna fought to come fully awake and understand what Jasmine was rambling about. "Just bring my daughter to me. Where is she?"

Joshua moved toward the bed with a stoic expression, dreading having to tell Lynna of their daughter's precarious condition. He took her hand to tenderly rub her palm with his thumb. "There are some things I need to tell you, darling. First, please allow Jasmine to collect some breast milk for the baby."

"Joshua, I can feed my own child," Lynna insisted. "What is the meaning of this?"

While Jasmine massaged Lynna's breast until a thick yellowish liquid dropped into a small container, Joshua tried to explain the events of the last few hours. "While I hate to be the bearer of bad news when you have so recently given birth, it would appear that a curse has been placed on Makenna."

Lynna sat up so rapidly the container with the few precious drops of liquid scattered across the bed. "Why would anyone curse my baby?"

Jasmine placed her hands on Lynna's chest to gently ease her back down to the bed. "Dis im'potant, Lynna. Now you jus' lay still an' don't be movin' no mo'."

"Who cursed my daughter, Joshua?" Lynna's voice shook as she closed her eyes in anticipation of the horrors to come.

"Amari, from what I can gather. No, actually it was Amari's teacher, a lady by the name of Larue Fontaine."

Hearing the name, Jasmine crossed herself. As Lynna gazed off into space Joshua told her the entire story as his father had told it to him.

"All this time we have been under a curse?" Lynna had often wondered why her life seemed filled with one tragic event after the other.

It all made sense now.

Suddenly, she was beyond tired of people interfering with the lives of her and her loved ones, and she swore she would see every last one of them pay.

"Yes," Joshua admitted, "from what I can gather."

"And Makenna?" Lynna asked the question, terrified of the answer. "Is she… moving?"

"Yassam," Jasmine interjected, cheerfully. "She did move her lil pinkie fanger when Clara took her. An' Clara was able ta git her ta swallow milk when nobody else could. We been feedin' her wit' a eye drapper. Dat's why I need to git as much of yo' milk as I can."

"Why didn't you say so? Here, let me help you." She pushed up to a sitting position and instructed Jasmine to hold the cup while she massaged her breast until the liquid dripped into it.

"Dat should do fo' now. I jus' take dis down so it be ready fo' Clara."

"I'm not sure what we would have done without Clara's healing touch." Joshua brought his wife's hands to his lips. "To be honest, Makenna could not survive without her."

Lynna couldn't focus on his words, her mind was moving in too many directions at once. "If Amari placed a curse on Makenna, who can remove it?"

"Therein lies the root of the problem, my love. After a long talk with my father, it appears that Larue Fontaine has him convinced that no one in South Carolina, or even this country, is powerful enough to remove one of her curses."

"What will we do?" Lynna cried, brokenly.

"We can't sit around and wait for our daughter to die."

"Your father has already sent for Pearlie, the voodoo priestess at Magnolia House. Silas and Mary probably won't allow her to come to our aid, but your father has issued orders to kidnap the woman if need be."

"So we wait?" Lynna whispered. "Joshua, if anything happens to…"

"It won't, Lynna. We will leave Makenna in Clara's arms, where she seems to be safe for the moment. It's almost like whatever sickness has hold of our daughter loses some of its effectiveness when Clara is near."

"Have my father send men to every plantation in Charleston and bring back every voodoo priestess they can find. I refuse to sit in this bed while my daughter is fighting for her life. If Pearlie can't lift the spell, we must find someone who can."

Chapter 23

Pearlie arrived the following evening, dusty and exhausted from the long ride. Her kidnappers had promised she wouldn't be hurt. Still, one never knew about white folks. They also told her what would be expected upon her arrival.

She entered the room apprehensively, peering around at all the eyes focused on her, waiting for *her* to perform a miracle.

They would have a long wait.

Pearlie sprinkled white powder on the baby and chanted a few verses, all the while anxiously cutting her eyes at Jasmine. She walked around the chair and halfheartedly mumbled some incoherent words, raising her hands over the infant's head and unenthusiastically shaking a gourd filled with seeds. After rubbing a foul smelling concoction on the baby's foot, she announced, "I's done all I can fo dis chile. Now, can you take me back home?"

Makenna lay unmoving.

Her feeble attempt at breaking the curse was like a slap in the face to Jasmine. "You aint' tryin' ta remove no curse from dat baby." Jasmine shook with rage at the thought that Makenna's illness could be scoffed at. "Whut you done come all dis way fo', jus' ta put on a show? Why, dey ought ta take you ta de barn an' take de skin of'n yo' back fo' dis disgrace." Going to the back door, Jasmine hollered, "Big Jim, come on up ta de house an' git dis good fo' nuthin' woman. I gots a job fo' you ta do."

The gourd stopped shaking in mid air. Perhaps she had better come forth with the truth before it was too late. "Jasmine, you know you ain't gwine git nobody ta remove a spell dat Larue Fontaine done cas'. Ain't nobody in dese parts powerful 'nuff ta do dat no how." Pearlie hung her head, shamefully. "An' she done put out word dat she gwine curse anybody who foolish 'nuff ta try, an' make dem suffer sumphin' ter'ble 'til de day dey die."

"So you won't even try to lift the curse?" Patricia asked, astounded by the woman's selfishness.

"Naw, I ain't gwine try. An' she done sont riders to ever town an' slave quawters wit' de message dat if anyone even 'temps ta uncross de curse from de Jordan baby, it gwine brang down her punishment hard an' swift."

Jasmine looked at Pearlie with all the hatred she felt glistening in her cold black eyes. "Git out of my sight, woman, fo' I strangle you wit' my own hands."

Pearlie was only too happy to oblige. Without even a biscuit or a sip of water after her long trip, she happily returned to the carriage. Sinking back on the plush upholstery, she breathed a deep sigh of relief to be out of the presence of the much ballyhooed Jordan gal. Every root worker in the South had been warned against helping her and none of them wanted Larue Fontaine's wrath to come down on their heads.

Throughout the evening, Sea Grove saw a steady stream of voodoo workers at the kitchen door, their pockets jingling with Nathan's coins. Jasmine watched from the corner with a steely eye, noticing their weak efforts. Larue Fontaine's words had reached far and wide.

When Jasmine had ordered the last one out of her sight, she slumped down in a chair and watched as Clara fed the baby another dropper of milk.

Patricia slowly trudged up the stairs, dreading having to break the news to Joshua and Lynna.

She didn't need to speak, Lynna read the defeat in her eyes. "Pearlie was right. No one can lift the spell."

"Either they can't, or they won't. None of them are willing to go against Larue Fontaine."

Lynna reached for Joshua's hand as a gut wrenching sob was torn from her throat. "Our child will die if we don't do something soon."

Joshua could only hang his head, at a loss as to how to help his precious daughter. He would gladly trade his life to spare hers.

Toward dusk, Lynna sat straight up in bed as the answer to her prayers was finally revealed to her.

Why didn't she think of it before?

"Of course." She tossed back the covers and made to rise. "We must take her to Doc."

"Who?" Patricia asked.

"Doc Buzzard, the shaman who freed me from Suzanne's curse. He can do the same for Makenna. We must sail to Trinidad with the next high tide, Joshua."

"I will go to the island and bring him here to you, darling," Joshua insisted, gently pushing her back down as he attempted to pull the covers up to her neck. "You aren't well enough to travel yet."

"That would take too much time." Lynna shook her head as she swung her legs over the side of the bed. "Time we don't have."

"Lynna, you have only just given birth." Patricia was aghast that she would ever consider leaving her bed. It was unheard of. "You must remain in bed for forty days during your confinement and do nothing but rest."

"Like I did after Beau's birth, Patricia?" Lynna gently reminded her. "I will be fine. I assure you."

"But, but, but…"

"No buts, Mother." Joshua took his mother's hands, bringing them to his lips. "We will do as Lynna's wishes. You would be the first to agree that a mother knows what is best for her child."

Lynna had expected resistance from her husband as well, but got none. Joshua was willing to go to any lengths to save his daughter's life, and all other options had been exhausted.

She had never loved him more than at that moment.

"I will send a man to assemble the crew. It will be a miracle if I can pull it off, but hopefully by tomorrow evening at this time we can be ready to sail." He turned to his mother and pulled her close.

"Mother, will you see to the packing for Lynna, Clara, and Makenna?" He looked toward Lynna. "What about Beau?"

Patricia moved to the side of the bed, smoothing the damp hair from Lynna's perspiring brow. "You are going to have your hands full with Makenna. Why not leave Beau here, with us?"

Lynna shook her head. "Thank you for the offer, Patricia, but I will never intentionally be parted from my son again. Beau will go with us."

"I understand, darling." Patricia smiled lovingly. "I will see to the packing."

As Lynna drifted into a fitful sleep, on the other side of the voodoo woods Rob pulled his cart to a halt in front of Amari's cabin. It was a neglected and run down cabin from all appearances. Dead flowers lay wilted amid briar bushes and weeds, in what appeared to have once been a thriving flowerbed. As if she could hear his quiet footsteps, the door opened and the famous voodoo woman stepped onto the porch.

"Evenin' ma'am."

"A good evening to you, sir." Larue was thrilled to finally have a visitor in these back woods. "Come sit a spell. I'll get you a cool drink."

"Thank you, ma'am." Rob retrieved a stringer of crappie from the cart, the product of his afternoon fishing trip. "I brung you a mess of crappie."

Larue clapped her hands. "Oh, how wonderful. Thank you. Now, I don't have to worry about what to have for supper."

She met Rob halfway down the steps to take

the stringer of fish. "Come in, and I'll get you that drink."

Immediately upon entering the cabin Rob took an involuntary step back. The room smelled of… foul body odor. It wasn't coming from Larue, but from someone lying in the bed.

Larue noticed his hesitation. "I'm sorry for the smell. I have become so accustomed to it that I rarely notice it anymore, but my daughter will no longer even enter the house when she visits. It isn't like I don't bathe Amari regularly. I do. It's just that the awful… death smell will not leave her body."

Ignoring the shriveled woman on the bed, who was straining to see the visitor, Rob asked, "So you is stayin' heah now."

"Poor Amari apparently had a stroke and can no longer care for herself. I have been here two months now and I must soon return home. I just have to decide whether to take her back to Savannah with me, which I would rather do, or hire someone to care for her here. The problem is, she doesn't want to leave her home."

"I can understand dat." Rob took the glass she handed him. "My name be Rob, ma'am."

"Larue," she said. "It's very nice to make your acquaintance, Rob."

He nodded.

"You are a free man of color and work for the Jordans, is that correct, Rob."

"Yas'sum, I'se a free Negro."

Larue noticed how Rob was trying to hold his breath and talk at the same time, and motioned for him to follow her outside. "Let us sit on the porch where the air is fresher."

Rob sat in a rocker and took a sip of the tea she offered. It would look suspicious if he didn't drink it, and he had watched closely to make sure she hadn't added anything to the glass. "Ma'am, I knows you is a voodoo queen, ain't you?"

"Yes." Her eyes lit up as Rob witnessed the pride in them. "That is how I am most often described."

"I was wonderin' if you could he'p me wit' sumphin'?"

"Of course, Rob." Larue leaned back in the rocker, giving him her full attention. "I would be happy to."

"I figure you smarter about dis stuff dan most."

"Thank you, Rob." She laughed, a tinkling sound that echoed through the quiet forest. "What can I help you with."

"Well, ma'am, you see I was on dis plan'ation in Gawga fo' many year. An' de Mastuh dere, Mastuh Hawkins was de meanest man God ever put on dis heah earth. He be a evil, evil man."

"I'm sorry to hear that, Rob. I have no qualms with cursing people who go around causing harm to others. What can I do to help?"

"I needs one of dem voodoo spells."

"You must be more specific, Rob." Again her tinkling laughter filled the air. "There are many voodoo curses. I could make him lose his hair, cause him to go mute, deaf, cause sickness, or even death. What exactly do you want?"

"Death," Rob answered, staring into her cold dark eyes. "I want him dead fo' all de pain an' sufferin' he done cause'."

"I understand, Rob, and I can help you." Larue sipped her tea, peering out across the unkempt lawn with dead tree limbs scattered about. "By the way, how is the Jordan baby doing?"

Rob kept his eyes cast toward the ground, hoping not to give away the fact that he was lying. "I don't talk ta de family much. I stays in my cabin. But from whut I hears, she ain't doing so good. Po' lil baby."

"Yes, poor thing," Larue agreed, halfheartedly. "Wasn't that Joshua Jordan's son you had with you at the river the day we met?"

"Yas'sum. Lucille, my neighbor woman, tends ta de baby sometime an' I jus' took him ta de rivah dat day ta get him outta her hair fo' a spell."

"I see." Larue smiled, showing straight white teeth. "Do you know what ails the new baby?"

"No ma'am, de las' I heard she was in a coma or had some bad sickness. I don't be thinkin' she gittin' no better."

"How awful for the family."

"Yes'sum, from whut I hears dey sho' is to'e up 'bout it." They sat in silence for several minutes, listening to the crickets chirp and bullfrogs getting tuned up for their nightly concert down by the pond. "So, will you he'p me git even wit' Mast' Hawkins."

"I will be happy to help, Rob. I know it's a long shot, but do you happen to have a piece of clothing that Mr. Hawkins wore, or even touched?"

Rob thought about this a minute before answering. "Yas'sam, I took a old coat of his from de barn de night I run."

"Excellent. If you will go out in the yard and gather two twigs about the length of your hands and a strand of moss, we can begin."

"Is you gwine make one of dem voodoo dolls?" Rob expected a much stronger spell than a voodoo doll. "Ma'am, is dey pow'ful 'nuff ta kill somebody."

"Mine are." Larue laughed, a truly malicious sound. "I add a special ingredient to my dolls."

As Rob walked down the steps he passed a lizard sitting on the rail with his head cocked sideways. A bold lizard too. He didn't scurry away like most would. "I jus' git dem sticks."

When he returned, Larue took the sticks and laid them in her lap in the sign of a cross. She then took some twine from a basket on the floor at her feet and tied the sticks together. Next, she wrapped moss around the sticks to form a body. In deep concentration, and without a word, she deftly stitched buttons for the eyes, nose, and mouth.

Rob watched quietly as she took a knife and cut a hole in the moss where a heart would be located. When it was complete, she held the doll in front of her with her eyes closed, breathing deeply. Without opening her eyes, and in a voice that sounded strangely different, she mumbled, "Visualize the person you want dead, Rob. Infuse this doll with their energy."

She chanted a few words until a wisp of smoke puffed from the head of the doll, as if it were on fire. Rob watched, stunned to silence as Larue's eyes slowly opened. "The doll is now ready, Rob. Make clothes for the doll out of the clothes from Mr. Hawkens and dress him."

"Dat's all?" Rob couldn't believe it was that simple to cause someone's death. "Den dis doll will work?"

"Not quite." Larue slumped back in her rocking chair as though every ounce of her energy had been drained. "There is one more thing you must do."

"Whut's dat?"

"You must place a beating heart where I have cut out the hole in the moss, where the doll's heart would be."

"A beating heart?" Rob mumbled. "Were is I'm s'posed ta git a beatin' heart from?"

"The heart of a rat would work best. But remember, Rob, it has to be beating, so you must work quickly. It must be done on the night of a full moon. Place the beating heart in the chest of the doll, lay the doll on a hard surface in full moonlight, and stab a pin through the beating heart."

"Dat will kill him?"

She offered the doll to Rob. "He will never harm another living soul."

"Thank you, ma'am. I sho' do 'preciate it. You gwine he'p me take a mighty bad person outta dis world."

A bright smile lit Larue's face as her eyes twinkled in the growing twilight. "Always happy to help, Rob. Please don't hesitate to call on me if I can be of further assistance."

"I sho' will ma'am. Now, I bes' be on my way fo' it gits too dark."

"Come back soon, Rob," she called, as his horse galloped into the dark night. "I enjoyed our visit."

Rob doffed his hat. "Take care, ma'am."

Larue waved, smiling brightly as she turned to go inside.

Rob sat on a stump in the woods for over an hour, waiting patiently for Larue to blow out the candles. He intended to sneak on the porch and grab the handkerchief she had carelessly tossed in the basket to make clothes for the doll.

Then, he could begin counting the days until the next full moon when he could stab a pin through the evil witch's heart, thereby putting an end to her wickedness forever. Rob was *determined* to prevent her from ever casting another spell on a Jordan.

Chapter 24

Rob stood at the rail of the *Windjammer* inhaling the salty sea air. They had been at sea for two weeks and finally a full moon floated in the sky above him.

Tonight was the night.

Although it was midnight, the full moon illuminated the ship as bright as day.

Could he do it?

Could he kill someone?

Better yet, should he even have doubts about ridding the earth of someone as evil as Larue Fontaine?

The way he saw it, he really didn't have a choice. The devil woman was determined to harm the people he loved. Deep down in his soul Rob knew he wouldn't have a problem killing anyone who threatened Buttercup, or her children. One look at Makenna, especially when she struggled so desperately to draw her next breath, was all the impetus he needed. Larue Fontaine had intentionally brought sickness on Buttercup's baby, and she would pay.

Rob had fallen to his knees many times over the last few weeks and prayed, beseeching the Lord to allow Makenna's tiny lungs to fill with air. During those times he wished he could breathe for the innocent baby, all the while fearing that she had already slipped away from them to live with the angels.

The few times that Joshua had been busy with running the ship, and Lynna and Clara were so exhausted they couldn't remain on their feet a second longer, Rob had been asked to sit by the bed to assure that the baby didn't stop breathing while no one was awake to witness it. Even Beau had sat silently during those times, gazing out the window as though he were beseeching God on his sister's behalf.

Rob grew more afraid with each passing day, fearing the little girl wouldn't live to see Trinidad. He worried about Buttercup's sanity if her baby girl didn't survive the trip.

If only they could reach the island in time, and Doc Buzzard could successfully remove the curse from the baby and the entire Jordan family. Maybe then, Buttercup could live the rest of her life in peace. That was Rob's most fervent prayer. That she find peace. He had never known a more selfless woman.

Buttercup was positive that Doc was powerful enough to uncross the curse, so Rob kept that hope alive in his own heart as well.

Amari was surely suffering for all her wrongdoing. He had rarely witnessed a more pathetic sight than the shriveled up old woman with the awful smell, moving only her rheumy eyes. Now it was Larue's turn to pay for her sins.

Rob laid the doll on the ship's rail and raised the pin, sparkling in the moonlight.

"What do you have there, Rob?" Joshua

startled him, coming up to lean against the rail. His haggard appearance assured Rob that he had passed the last several nights without sleep, choosing to watch over his daughter. They were all bone tired, drained, and almost at the breaking point.

Should he tell Joshua the truth? Would he try to stop him? Rob couldn't lie to Joshua. "It be one of dem voodoo dolls I done got from Larue Fontaine."

"I see." Joshua studied the doll with interest. "What is the purpose of the doll? My guess would be that it's not to promote someone's health and well being."

Rob looked him straight in the eye, speaking without hesitation. "To kill Larue Fontaine."

Joshua didn't seem surprised in the least. While he would never be a strong believer in the occult, any chance at taking down Larue Fontaine or her ilk was worth a shot. "What is that in your hand?"

"A rat."

That did surprise him. "Pray tell, why are you holding a rat?"

"I gots ta put his beatin' heart in dis doll. Den I gots ta stab dis pin through de heart. When I do dis, on de full of de moon, Larue Fontaine will die."

Joshua didn't appear to be entirely convinced. "You're sure of this, Rob?"

Rob shrugged his massive shoulders. "Yassuh, as sho' as I kin be."

"Then, please." Pushing up his sleeves, Joshua held out his hand. "Allow me to help."

Rob grinned, his white teeth glowing in the

moonlight as he handed Joshua the pin. He then removed a knife from his pocket and   swiftly removed the heart from the rat. It was done with such precision that Joshua knew he had practiced on a few of the ship's rodents. Without any wasted motion, Rob immediately dropped the still beating heart into the chest cavity of the doll.

With a smile on his face, Joshua raised the pin high into the air and plunged it squarely into the center of his target, forever stopping the beating heart.

Larue Fontaine sat on her balcony in Savannah, the beam from the full moon causing her face to glow. Although a party was going on in the room behind her, she rushed outside at the stroke of midnight when she knew Rob would be performing the spell.

At first she had been upset that the man thought her incompetent enough not to realize his sham. A curse for Mr. Hawkins indeed. A curse against Larue Fontaine was what he sought.

Larue had seen the way Rob interacted with Joshua Jordan's son. He was no mere sitter for the child. What poppycock. He was a trusted member of the family. Anyone could see that. Still, the poor deluded man thought to outsmart the voodoo queen of Savannah? *Ha!* She sincerely hoped that Rob was enjoying his last night on earth.

Larue knew from the kitchen helper at Sea Grove, whom she paid a tidy sum each month for information, that Joshua, Lynna, Rob, Clara, and both children were headed to Trinidad. They had set sail on a fool's errand in search of a shaman to remove *her* spell on the infant.

How stupid they all were.

Traveling so far from home, when they had a person onboard Joshua's ship with the ability to remove any curse that Larue Fontaine or any other root worker cast. Clara's natural born ability came from her heart and soul and was a hundred times more powerful than a few chanted words or any spell, powder, or potion that came from a bottle.

"I hope she rots in…" Rob's words were cut short as he dropped to his knees, clutching his chest as an explosion of flames ripped through it.

"Rob," Joshua cried. "What is it?"

This was wrong.

Terribly wrong.

"What have I done, Rob?" Joshua grabbed his shoulders, wanting to somehow make this right again.

This wasn't supposed to happen.

The gentle giant crashed to the deck, lying deathly still. Too still. Blood bubbled from Rob's lips to roll down the side of his face and dribble onto the wooden deck. Joshua could only stare at the puddle, in shock, as Rob's body started to shiver. "I's cold." Rob's teeth chattered against each other. "So cold."

"Rob, is there a way to reverse this? For the love of God, man. How could I have been so stupid?"

"Look like dat bad woman done gots de las' laugh, don't it?"

Clara was in a deep sleep when she heard a

loud thump. It sounded like something heavy had crashed to the deck. She slowly opened her eyes, shaking her head from the terrible nightmare. She sat on the side of the bed, careful not to disturb Lynna or the baby as she tried to clear her head, yet, the vision wouldn't go away. As clearly as if she were standing before him, she saw Rob place a bloody, beating heart into a moss doll.

Rob and Joshua were on deck now.

Performing a voodoo spell.

She had to stop them. She raced toward the door and heard the sleeping baby's breathing suddenly become labored. She stopped to look back at her. Makenna couldn't breathe unless she was close to her.

She raced back to the bed and lifted the tiny bundle, then threw open the door to race down the dimly lit narrow passageway as she clutched the baby to her breast. Just as she reached the deck, Joshua raised the pin high in the air with a triumphant smile.

I can't reach him in time.

"Joshua... no!" Lynna screamed, out of breath. She had been awakened when the cabin door was flung open and rushed up the stairs on Clara's heels. "Stop!"

Joshua hesitated. "I was about to perform a voodoo spell to kill Larue Fontaine."

Clara shook her head rapidly and pointed to Rob.

Lynna gasped and clutched at her chest. "The spell would have killed Rob, wouldn't it, Clara?"

Clara nodded.

"I be damned," Rob muttered, tossing the doll into the sea.

Clara didn't hear him. As if in a trance, her mind sped across the sea to a strange room where Larue Fontaine was dancing with a handsome man, laughing gaily. The evil woman had one hand on the man's shoulder, while the other hand held a fluted glass of sparkling liquid.

The handsome man twirled Larue around the room without a care in the world, and leaned toward her to whisper, "Why is the voodoo queen of Savannah so happy all of a sudden?"

Larue's eyes twinkled mischievously. "Let's just say that I have a list of enemies, and tonight I was able to mark a name off the list."

"I would imagine the poor fellow never even saw it coming."

"He didn't see it coming, because he tried to trick me. I couldn't let him get away with it."

The man feigned shock at her words. "He actually thought to trick the great Larue Fontaine?"

"Exactly." Larue grinned. "Now, to begin marking the other names off my list."

Clara jerked when she heard those names clearly in Larue's mind.

Beau.

Makenna.

Joshua.

Lynna.

Clara jerked again, still clutching the baby to her breast as she fell to her knees on the deck.

Larue Fontaine had to be stopped.

Clara's entire body shook as she focused every ounce of her energy on the sinful woman. She directed every thought, every emotion, and every feeling toward the voodoo queen. She would *not* allow her to hurt the ones she loved.

Ever.

Again.

Clara heard the now familiar buzzing in her ears and felt as though fire flowed through her veins, instead of blood. All the energy in her body rushed to her fingertips, waiting for her to distribute it. She had no idea what was happening, but her greatest wish was to put a stop to Larue Fontaine's evil forever.

She laid the baby on the deck between her knees, then she twisted her body slightly to the east and held both hands toward her target.

Lynna, Joshua, or Rob didn't breathe a word.

Larue never suspected a thing as the liquid in the fluted glass she held began to bubble. Even as the liquid took on a blood red tint, she was too busy laughing gaily to take note of it. As her partner spun her around, a drop spilled over the edge of the glass, but she was too busy flirting to notice the hole it left in the fabric of her dress.

As a tiny crack snaked down one side of the glass, she simpered, "While you dance divinely, sir, let us pause for a moment while I have a sip of champagne. I am simply parched."

In a celebratory mood, Larue raised the glass and downed half of the contents before lowering it.

Then, she was... gasping for breath. Her eyes widened in disbelief as she realized her throat was on fire. About the same time, her dance partner was slowly backing away and looking at her lips with a look of revulsion on his stunned features. His face appeared to be frozen in complete horror. Why on earth was he behaving so strangely and drawing attention to them?

Since his eyes seemed to be focused on her mouth, Larue's hands went there. When her finger reached her lips she was stunned to feel huge, hideous blisters. They covered her lips, her gums, and her tongue. She could feel them rising in her throat, cutting off her air supply. Her tongue, mouth and throat were on fire. Yet, how could this be?

She was the great Larue Fontaine.

Who would have the courage to curse her.

She threw the glass to the floor and watched, paralyzed with fear as the floor smoked where the liquid was eating a hole in the wood. Larue tried to speak to the man who had been holding her so intimately only seconds earlier, but her swollen tongue no longer formed words. She could feel it swelling, and hanging grotesquely from her mouth. Her throat was closing.

She couldn't breathe.

The severe pain in her throat, and now her stomach, was unbearable beyond description. Feeling what she thought was hot bile rising in her throat, she vomited a pool of bright red blood that covered the front of her expensive pale yellow Chantilly lace dress.

She was dying. Larue accepted this. She had poisoned enough people to recognize the signs. Her one question was, who was powerful enough to curse her?

Only one person.

Clara.

As she fell to the floor writhing in agony, with excruciating pain radiating from her stomach and infiltrating every part of her body, Larue saw Clara's smiling face vividly in her mind.

The cunning little bitch.

As Larue took her last breath, she realized that even though she wouldn't be around to exact her revenge on Clara and the rest of the Jordan family.

Her daughter Jerica would.

Chapter 25

Lynna stood at the rail of the *Windjammer*, gazing across the frothing whitecaps as clouds swirled overhead. The seas had been rough for over a week now, with intermittent spells of heavy downpours and wind gusts. Lightning had flashed well into the night as she lay in her bed and never once closed her eyes. She had lain awake for the better part of the journey, praying that her daughter's tiny lungs would continue to fill with air and keep her alive for one more day.

Just one more day.

One day closer to Trinidad and Doc Buzzard.

The ship was damp and chilly. How she longed to feel the heat of the sun on her face. She leaned back as the wind fanned her hair out behind her and she breathed deeply of the salty sea air. Her cabin smelled like sickness.

Like death.

They had only been at sea for four weeks, with four more to go before they reached Trinidad.

Could Makenna hold on that long?

The baby wasn't thriving. She had no color. She had lost so much weight that she looked emaciated. Her once chubby little arms were bone thin, so fragile.

While they were feeding her around the clock, she was only swallowing a drop at the time and that wasn't nearly enough to sustain her. She needed to nurse at her mother's breast until her little stomach couldn't hold another drop, but she couldn't. Lynna gave thanks daily that she could at least swallow one drop at a time, enough to keep her alive.

She dumped another cup of life giving breast milk over the side of the ship and sighed despondently. The nourishment her tiny daughter so desperately needed was expressed from her breasts and dumped into the sea. What a horrible, horrible waste.

Tears filled Lynna's eyes and spilled over her lashes as she was forced to accept a brutal truth. Her daughter was starving to death. A four week old baby couldn't receive enough milk from an eyedropper to nourish her body.

Joshua came up behind her unnoticed, slipping his arms around her waist. His touch startled her. How long had it been since they had held each other? Since before Lynna gave birth. Her every thought and action since then had been directed toward keeping her daughter alive. She leaned her head on her husband's shoulder and closed her eyes for a few moments to pray.

He longed to ease her suffering, if only for a short while. Lynna wasn't eating or sleeping and she was losing weight. He thought about drugging her with a dose of laudanum in a glass of wine and forcing her to rest, but he knew if anything should happen to their daughter while she slept, Lynna would never forgive him. "What are you thinking,

Lynna?"

"How I'm going to live without her," she whispered, so softly that he barely heard her.

"Don't give up, darling. We're getting closer to Trinidad with every passing hour and that little girl in our cabin is a combination of us both. Makenna is a fighter. She is incredibly strong to have made it this far, and I have faith that she can hold on for a few more weeks. You have to believe that, Lynna. You can't lose hope now, not when our daughter needs you so desperately."

"Makenna took a turn for the worse last night, Joshua." A sob caught in Lynna's throat and it was several minutes before she could speak. "Clara is doing all she can, but Makenna is refusing to swallow her milk today. She's so pale, and gaunt. I caution you to hold her while you still can and show her how much you love her."

With a heavy heart Joshua took Lynna's hand, leading her down the ladder and through the narrow dimly lit hall to his cabin. He found Clara sitting in the window seat with the baby resting against her chest.

One of Makenna's little legs had fallen out of her blanket and it looked no bigger than Joshua's finger. Her skin was so white he could see every vein crisscrossing under the pallor of her skin. Her breathing was shallow, and since early morning she had been taking agonizingly long pauses in between breaths.

Joshua moved to the window for a better look. His daughter reminded him of a wax figure in a museum she was so still. He wanted to smash his fist through the glass, scream to the heavens at the injustice of it all.

Hadn't Lynna suffered enough?

Her life had been constant trials and tribulations since the day they met. If her child died in her arms, it would be a final blow that she might never recover from.

Joshua closed his eyes and silently chastised God for turning his back on them. He rued the day he had brought Lynna into his miserable life to suffer because of him and the curse on his family. He was so lost in his own misery that he didn't notice when the clouds finally parted and the sun's rays broke through the heavy clouds, shining through the window to fall on Clara and the sleeping baby.

Clara's eyes slowly opened when she felt the sun on her face, reveling in the warmth as it seeped into her chilled body.

She felt... funny.

She held her hand out in front of her, becoming slowly aware aware of a tingling sensation that started in the tips of her fingers and slowly worked its way throughout her entire body. It wasn't the typical fire in her veins that she had grown accustomed to feeling when she was angry. It was something else. Something entirely different.

Something pure and innocent.

Something good.

She shook her hand, yet the tingling remained. What were these strange new feelings coursing through her blood?

Today was her birthday, but she hadn't bothered to tell anyone. There would be no celebration with the looming fear that Makenna might take her last breath today.

Still, she felt so… different.

She lifted the tiny infant from the blanket, holding her emaciated little body up to feel the warmth of the sun. Tears streamed down Clara's cheeks. She had done all she could for this baby, and it hadn't worked. She could feel Makenna's tiny heartbeat slowing under her thumb.

Slower and slower.

It was almost over.

Her young life would be cut short before it began.

"Live!" Clara cried, standing to hold the child above her head. "I will not… let… you… die!"

When she spoke the words Clara heard roaring in her ears and felt a tingle that turned into a current of shock waves pulsing throughout her entire body. She felt a jolt rush through her arms that caused the baby to jerk violently.

Clara gently lowered the baby and acting on pure instinct, she brought the baby's lips to hers and forced air into her mouth. Using only her mind she commanded the tiny lungs to fill with air. Over and over she breathed for the child until Makenna's heartbeat fluttered under her fingers and began to beat faster. Clara's hands seemed to burn where her skin touched the baby. She turned to Lynna, and urged, "Put her… to your… breast."

Lynna and Joshua stood rooted to the spot for several seconds, amazed by what they were witnessing. Finally coming to her senses, Lynna jerked down the bodice of her gown and held out her hands. When Clara placed her daughter in her arms Lynna guided the tiny lips to her breast.

The baby didn't move.

She hefted her swollen breast and forced her nipple into the child's mouth. When nothing happened, she squeezed until a drop of milk fell on Makenna's lips.

And... their miracle happened.

For the first time, they saw Makenna's tiny pink tongue flick out to lick her lips. She opened her mouth slightly. Since she was too weak to suckle, Lynna expressed milk into her mouth and the baby swallowed and swallowed and swallowed until her little belly extended.

Joshua held Clara close to his chest, watching the amazing scene before him with tear filled eyes. Lynna moved to the window seat and placed the baby on her shoulder to tenderly pat her back. When Makenna burped it was a musical melody from heaven.

Joshua knelt at Lynna's feet with tears of joy, thanking God for His blessing. He placed a hand on his daughter's back that spanned the breadth of her tiny body. He bowed his head and continued to give thanks as he felt the steady thump of Mckenna's heart against his palm.

"Clara, you spoke," Lynna whispered. "How?"

Had she?

Clara shrugged, unable to explain what had happened in this room. All she knew for certain was that Joshua and Lynna's daughter had left this earth for a brief moment in time and, somehow, *she* had brought her back to life.

And she had talked.

For the first time in her life, she had spoken.
Could she do it again?

Lynna leaned against the window seat to get comfortable. She propped her feet up, smiling contentedly as she felt a sliver of happiness for the first time in weeks. "Thank you, Clara, for giving our daughter a fighting chance."

Clara smiled shyly, massaging her arms and legs where the tingle was slowly beginning to subside.

Lynna smiled wearily at Joshua over her daughter's head, her own head occasionally nodding as the need for sleep almost overwhelmed her.

Joshua saw an opportunity to convince her to rest. "Why don't you both try to get some sleep? Neither of you have slept in weeks. Makenna shouldn't be hungry again for a few hours at least."

"That's the best idea I've heard all day." Lynna yawned, her eyelids so heavy she could barely hold them open. "When Beau is ready for his nap will you bring him down, so Clara and I can cuddle with him as well?"

"Of course I will, darling."

Lynna stood from her window seat and took Clara's hand to lead the exhausted girl to bed. She placed the sleeping baby between them and joined her in dreamland.

Chapter 26

Suzanne opened the door to Magnolia House, tired and dusty after the long carriage ride from prison. No one was up to greet her at this late hour, and she was starving. She entered the kitchen and banged a few chairs around to gain someone's attention. Iris, Jasmine's daughter, stumbled sleepily into the room.

"Where is Jasmine?" Suzanne demanded. "I need her to warm me a bite to eat."

"She ovah to Cedar Hill hepin' wit' Miz Beth's new baby gal."

Suzanne determined then and there to put Jasmine in her place, and remind her that her responsibilities lay at Magnolia House, not flitting about the countryside. The woman had been coddled for too long and Suzanne intended to put a stop to it. When the old woman returned she would never be allowed to leave the plantation again. "Did my parents go as well?"

"Deys gone ta Savannah ta visit wit' Miz Mary's sistah, den deys gwine ta 'lanta so as Mist' Silas kin change his will."

"When did they leave?"

"Yestidy mawnin'."

Suzanne beamed brightly upon hearing this news. Her mother would visit with her sister for at least a fortnight before continuing on to Atlanta.

Father has gone to Atlanta to have his will changed and leave everything to me.

"Dey sho' will be 'prised ta see you when dey gits back, Miz Suzanne. Dey thought you gwine be in dat ter'ble place fo' five year."

"I'm sure they will," Suzanne snapped. "For now, please warm me up whatever you have available. I'm simply ravenous."

"Yas'sum."

"And have my bath drawn."

"Yas'sum." Iris eyed the girl strangely. She was sure the *thing* before her was Miz Suzanne, but she surely didn't look like the girl she remembered. Her hair had been bleached practically white in the sun, and it sprouted from her head in all directions. It brought to mind dried straw laying in the field. Her once wrinkle free forehead and the corners of her eyes were creased with lines from squinting against a blazing sun.

Why, Suzanne's skin was as dark as hers and looked as tough as shoe leather, while Iris's skin was as smooth as butter. Her mistresses shoulders slumped and her back seemed permanently stooped from months of hoeing and picking cotton. Iris was quick to realize that even the dress *she* was wearing was of a better quality than Suzanne's. The former southern belle was a fright.

Suzanne didn't care for the fact that an uppity servant was eyeing her with disgust. "I will be in the parlor. Call me when the food is ready."

"Yas'sum."

On her way to the parlor Suzanne passed by

her father's office. Meandering into the room that smelled of cigar smoke, she inhaled deeply of the pleasant aroma. The smell reminded her of her father, the only man on earth she had ever trusted completely.

As she pondered what he had been up to all these months without her, she went to his desk and opened a drawer to find several sheets of paper in her father's handwriting. As she was terminally nosy, she picked up the first sheet and slumped back in his chair to read.

The more she read, the more her blood boiled.

I, Silas Fletcher, being of sound mind and body, do hereby bequeath that all my belongings be divided equally between my sons Daniel Fletcher and Samuel Fletcher upon my death.

Suzanne threw the paper on the desk as though she had been burned.

He had lied to her face.

"Yo' food ready, Miz Suzanne."

She walked numbly to the kitchen and swallowed the tasteless food that settled in her stomach like rocks.

They would pay.

All of them would pay.

First, her father must be stopped from changing his will. She *would* inherit Magnolia House, but first things first.

She needed a hot bath, her own clothes, and a good night's rest. In the morning, she would be refreshed and ready to begin dishing out her own special form of revenge to all those who had wronged her.

The first person on her list was the backstabbing Pearlie, for helping Joshua make such a stupendous fool of her.

Suzanne was awakened by sunlight streaming through lacy curtains. She stretched luxuriously between clean sheets on a mattress filled with down and released a contented sigh, vowing to never lie in another hammock as long as she lived.

She raced to the top of the stairs before getting dressed, and bellowed, "Iris, for breakfast I would like pancakes swimming in maple syrup, ham and eggs, and a sausage gravy biscuit."

"Yas'sam."

"Oh, and a bowl of grits."

"Yas'sam."

"And don't be dawdling because I have a busy morning."

"Yas'sam."

What to wear? She opened her chifforobe and was astonished to find it only contained a small portion of the dresses that would normally have it stuffed to overflowing. She rushed to the top of the stairs, and screeched, "Iris, where are my dresses? If you good for nothing thieves have been pilfering my clothes I swear I will tan every last one of your hides."

"It ain't us been messin' wit' yo' clothes." Iris raced to the bottom of the stairs with her hands on her hips and her eyes blaring. "Yo mammy done give mos' of dem ta de po' white folks down at de church. She say you ain't be needin' dem fo' five year an' dey be outta fashion by den." Knowing just when to twist the knife after inserting it into Suzanne's gullet, Iris added, innocently, "You ought ta see dem white trash gals struttin' 'round in yo' fine dresses."

Suzanne's shout of outrage echoed down the stairs and into the kitchen, causing Iris and the kitchen workers to beam with joy.

She yanked one of her last remaining dresses from her wardrobe. It was a demure pale blue cotton with white embroidery around the neck and hem, and short puffed sleeves. Hardly one of her favorites, since it revealed zero cleavage, but it would have to do until she could have more becoming dresses made.

She returned to the top of the stairs, and shouted, "Iris, send Rose up to do my hair."

"Yas'sam."

She was sitting at her vanity and patting her foot impatiently when Rose entered. Rose could always work miracles with her hair. "I want an updo, Rose. My hair has been hanging in my eyes for over a year now. You know how I like it." As an afterthought, she added, "Just make me beautiful."

Rose stood, unmoving, having no desire to even touch the knotted, dried up straw mess on Suzanne's head.

"Well, hurry up." Suzanne spun in her seat to cast an evil eye toward the young maid. "Do you think I have all day to waste?"

Rose finally found the courage to stick her hands in the mass of brittle tangles. When she parted Suzanne's hair she found a scalp riddled with angry red, pus filled sores. She jerked her hands back, fearing the girl might have something contagious, and cried, "Whut's wrong wit' yo' head?"

Suzanne met her eyes in the mirror. "My head was infested with lice during the entire year I spent in prison. Some of the sores have festered, so I will need Miss Fanny to concoct a healing balm." Suzanne refused to allow her mind to return to that horrid place. "That is of little consequence, compared to some of the other atrocities I suffered while incarcerated."

She glowered in the mirror, appalled to see that her skin was actually darker than Rose's. Granted, Rose's father was white, but still, here she towered over her mistress with skin several shades lighter. Suzanne peered closely into the mirror and noticed dark blotches of scaly skin across the bridge of her nose and forehead. "I will need several applications of buttermilk to bring my skin back to its normal creaminess."

Rose continued to glare at her.

Miz Suzanne would need the good Lord to perform a miracle if she ever had a notion of getting her lily white skin back.

"Well, get busy," Suzanne snapped. "These tangles are not going to remove themselves."

"If'n you axk me, it be better jus' ta cut it all off an' grow sum' new hair."

"Well, since nobody asked you, I think you should just pick up that comb. Cut off my hair? Why that is the most absurd thing I have ever heard. My hair will be soft and silky again after a few milk and honey treatments."

"Yas'sam."

Rose dug the comb into the tangles and

struggled for several minutes just to get it back out. By the time she finished, several hours later, it was time for lunch.

Granted, Suzanne's hair was tangle free for the first time in over a year, but it felt like a horse's tail. Rose twisted the mess into a loose bun and pinned it atop Suzanne's head.

Suzanne placed a hand to her forehead and wished she could massage her throbbing head, but her hair looked decent for the first time in forever and she was not about to loosen a single strand. "I'm surprised I have a hair left on my head after all your pulling and yanking."

"You done tol' me ta git all de tangles out."

"I know what I told you," Suzanne snapped, before changing her tune abruptly. "Tell me, Rose. How is Pearlie faring lately?"

"She be doin' fine." Rose loved few things more than gossip. "She done jump de broom since you been gone. He old nuff ta be her daddy, but she say she love him."

"Oh, really? Pearlie finally found her a man and got married, did she?"

"Yas'sam."

"I just may have to pay her a visit this morning and congratulate her on her wedding."

Rose's eyes met Suzanne's in the mirror. Every last worker and servant on the plantation knew that Pearlie had assisted Joshua by pretending to bring him back to life as a zombie. By doing so, she had helped him trick Suzanne into telling Joshua where his wife was.

Rose clearly read the revenge in Suzanne's eyes. She would need to warn Pearlie.

After lunch, Suzanne ordered a horse to be saddled as she donned her riding habit and a wide straw hat. While she wanted to feel the breeze in her face, she *never again* wanted to feel the sun on her skin. Her eyes scanned the cotton fields in every direction.

How could her father even consider leaving this land to her brothers?

They didn't have need of it, but it was all she had. With her past history with men, and that bothersome little stint behind bars, she wasn't likely to receive an invitation to be the mistress of another plantation anytime soon.

She gave the horse his head and galloped for over an hour, until she came to a ramshackle cabin deep in a hollow. When she dismounted and walked up the rickety steps, the door opened before she could even raise her hand to knock.

The man looked her up and down. "Well, well, well, looky who's back."

She swept past him into the filthy cabin. "Hello, Gil."

"I ain't seen hide nor hair of you since you hired me and my brother to git rid of that Jordan feller for you."

Suzanne spun around. "Which, as I'm sure you heard was a colossal failure. I'm sure you also heard that I was the one who received the punishment for your ineptitude by spending a year in prison."

"I heard you was spending a few years on the farm." He grinned. "How'd you git out so soon?"

"It's all on who you know, Gil." Suzanne smiled a secretive smile. "By the way, where is your brother?"

"He died a few months back in a bar brawl." He displayed not an ounce of grief at his brother's passing. "The boy never could fight."

"I'm sorry to hear that." His brother was definitely the more *masculine* of the two.

Gil licked his lips. Suzanne wasn't much to look at now, but she still had two legs that still opened.

"What brings you to my neck of the woods, gal?" When he unfastening her dress and slipped it from her shoulders, he swallowed a horrified gasp at the sight of the multitude of bite marks and sores that riddled her back. He closed his eyes as he tried to remember the way she was before her incarceration, since his balls had retreated into his belly at the sight of her hideous skin.

"I need you to do another job for me," she simpered, coquettishly.

"Who you want killed this time?" Gil closed his eyes to block out the sight as his hands moved around to cup her repulsive breasts.

Chapter 27

Joshua, Lynna, Rob, Beau, and Clara stood side by side at the rail of the *Windjammer* as the lush green tree line of Trinidad came into view. Lynna looked toward the peach colored house that was barely visible on a hill in the distance.

Would Sean be there?

Had he returned to sea?

Clara pointed to the jungle green water swirling past the hull of the ship. "Pretty water." She didn't speak often, only during times of excitement or stress. She pointed to Beau as he wiggled in his father's arms. "Can Beau swim?"

Joshua smiled at Clara. "Rob will take Beau swimming. It will be a treat after suffering the confines of the ship for so many weeks, won't it, Beau?" He tousled his son's hair before handed the grinning toddler over to Rob.

Lynna beamed at her son. Within a few hours, the ship would be docked and they could be on their way to Doc's cottage. She whispered a fervent prayer that the shaman of Trinidad would have the power to uncross the voodoo queen's curse and heal her daughter.

She remembered Sean telling her the shaman looked to be every bit of one hundred years old.

Dear God, let him still be alive.
He was their only hope.

While Makenna was swallowing the milk they forced into her mouth, she was a far cry from the rosy cheeked, plump infant Lynna had given birth to. Since they were barely keeping her alive she wasn't thriving and filling out as Beau had at her age. Lynna glanced at her son bouncing in Rob's arms, eager to put his feet in the sand and stretch his chubby little legs.

She relaxed for the first time in months. The long wait was almost over.

Rob spotted a shady area near the beach. "I's gwine take dis lil feller over ta de beach when we gits dere an' let him play til y'all gits back, if'n you sho' you don't need me ta go wit' you."

"Stay here, Rob," Joshua instructed. "I don't know what Devereux's reaction would be to seeing you. He might try to claim you as his property."

Lynna opened her mouth to defend Sean, but Joshua held up his hand to stop her. "It's not a risk I am willing to take."

Lynna walked down the gangway toward the island holding a parasol to keep the sun from burning her daughter's pasty white skin. She was undecided as to how to get her daughter the help she so desperately needed. She had no idea where Doc lived.

Of course, Lisbeth would help her.
Would Sean?

"Shall I hire a carriage, Lynna?" Joshua startled her by asking. "Do you know the way?"

"I remember Sean telling me of a trail to

Doc's cottage, and having to practically crawl when the undergrowth grew too thick." She looked toward the pink mansion on the hill. "We don't have time to wander through the forest searching for his house, Joshua. Listen to Makenna breathing. It's much worse today." She glanced toward her daughter, then to the densely populated forest and made a quick decision. "Hire a carriage to take me to Devereux Acres."

"You?" Joshua queried, with a *no way in hell will that happen* expression. "You are not going to his house alone. Please, don't even ask me to allow it."

"Joshua, I beg you to trust me. Nothing is as important as Makenna. You, me, Sean, nobody, and I will not stand here wasting precious time while you play the part of a jealous husband. My daughter is dying." Even though his steely eyes bore into hers, she refused to back down. "Please, don't allow your insecurities to stand in the way of our daughter's life."

"Lynna…"

"Please, Joshua." Her voice softened when she saw the pain mirrored in his eyes. "You have to trust me."

"I trust *you*, Lynna." Joshua hailed a passing carriage and helped her to the seat. "Devereux Acres," he told the driver as he paid the fare.

Lynna just needed a few minutes alone with Sean, if he was even on the island. She bent to place a kiss on her daughter's forehead, and promised, "I will return as quickly as I can."

Her heart pounded against her ribcage as the carriage delivered her closer and closer to Devereux

Acres. One part of her prayed that Sean wouldn't be home and Lisbeth could show them the way to the shaman. The other part of her wanted to see for herself how Sean was faring.

Her heart squeezed like a vise was tightening around it when the carriage entered the circular drive in front of Devereux Acres. She noticed Lisbeth sitting on the verandah, sipping wine. As the carriage pulled to a halt, Lynna breathed deeply of the sweet smell of cocoa and felt the gentle tropical breeze warm her soul.

She felt at home.

Before she could ponder the thought further, she opened the carriage door and stepped out. Her shoes sank in the soft sand as sea gulls swooped and cawed overhead.

She heard Lisbeth's sharp cry of surprise as she stood at the top of the steps, waiting to greet her with outstretched arms. "My darling Lynna, you have returned. I have missed you so. You have no idea how bereft my grandson has been without you."

She drew Lynna close for a welcoming embrace, smelling of coconut oil as her lavender eyes sparkled. "It seems that you took all his joy when you left us so suddenly. Our island has become a dismal place without you. Come sit with me, tell me all that has happened in your life since you left us so abruptly without even bothering to tell an old woman goodbye."

"I'm sorry that I left so suddenly, Lisbeth. It's complicated, and I promise to explain it all later." Lynna tried to focus on Lisbeth's words as she glanced through the doorway into the house. "Is

Sean here?"

"He should be home any minute. He has been in the cacao fields all day." Lisbeth peered into her haunted eyes, knowing that something was terribly wrong. Lynna was but a sad shell of her former bubbly self. Her very soul seemed bruised. "Tell me what is troubling you, dearest."

Tears spilled from Lynna's weary eyes, leaving a glistening trail down her cheeks. "My daughter is very sick, Lisbeth."

"You have a daughter?" Lisbeth cried, at once ecstatic, both hands moving to her chest to press against her heart. "Tell me all about the little darling. How old is she?"

"Eight weeks."

As Lisbeth glanced toward the sea, Lynna knew she was busily calculating past months in her mind.

"I need to take her to Doc, before it's too late."

Lisbeth seemed to be in a world of her own. Lynna had never seen her look so completely serene or at peace with her world. "Tell me about the child, Lynna?"

Lynna smiled, her face softening just thinking of her daughter. "She's beautiful, Lisbeth. Curly black hair, creamy skin, and rosy red lips. Actually, she is perfect in every way."

"And her eyes?" Lisbeth took Lynna's hands and held them to her chest. "What color are her eyes?"

"We don't know, yet. She is under the curse of a very powerful voodoo queen and Mckenna has never opened her eyes."

Lisbeth's hand went to her throat. "You have… never seen her… eyes?"

"Can we please talk about this later, Lisbeth?" Lynna gazed into her lavender eyes, beseeching her. "I desperately need to find Sean."

"Yes, yes, of course." Lisbeth called for a buggy to be brought around. "You know where to find him."

Lynna raced down the steps, eager to locate Sean and be on their way. There wasn't a second to waste. She hopped on the seat of the buggy and flicked the reins to set the little pony in motion.

Lisbeth started to call for her own buggy, but changed her mind. She ordered that a horse be saddled immediately.

By the time Lynna turned the last curve in the road leading to the cocoa fields, she was a bundle of raw nerves. She noticed that Mister Juarez was talking to someone.

Someone without a shirt.

Someone wet with sweat.

The skin on his sculpted chest glistened with sweat.

The sight made her knees go weak and her heart pound against her ribs. Her body went liquid. Her limbs were limp as if they didn't belong to her at all. Her breathing became shallow as she licked her suddenly dry lips and prepared for the sudden assault to her senses.

She remembered when Sean had come to her bath chamber just before the Hammond's Ball so…vividly. She shivered, even though the heat on the island was sweltering.

As if he felt her presence, Sean leaned to the

side to peer around Mr. Juarez, certain that he had spent too much time in the sun today. He rubbed his eyes, yet the vision remained. "Excuse me, Mister Juarez." He shielded his eyes from the blazing sun, and whispered, "Lynna?"

"Sean," she mouthed the word, unable to speak.

"My God," he cried, dropping the bucket he was carrying to run toward her. With a beaming smile he wrapped his arms around her and held her close, lifting her off the ground and twirling her around and around as he laughed into her hair. "Lynna, my darling, you have come home."

He held her against him for several seconds, enjoying the feeling of having her body against his, breathing her in. When he at last placed her feet back on the ground he was afraid to release her, afraid she might disappear again.

It had been too long.

Much too long.

"I knew you would come back to me." He smoothed a few wayward strands of hair from her face and tucked them behind her ear, grinning his devilishly handsome grin. "What took you so long?"

"I… I," she stuttered, when no words were forthcoming.

"Did you get my letter?"

"Yes, Sean, I did."

His lips fell to hers softly, so softly that it was as if a feather was brushing across her lips, or a hummingbird's wings fluttered there, causing her insides to knot into a delicate bow. The caressing touch of his lips was more potent than if he had crushed her against him. It sent a shockwave coursing through her body from head to toe as his hands stroked her back, causing her to remember... too much.

To feel... too much.

With both hands behind her head to hold her steady he slanted his mouth across hers, savoring her taste, reveling in the feeling of having her once again in his arms where she belonged. He vowed then and there to never let her go again.

"Where is Beau, my love?" Sean knew she would never be happy on the island without her son.

Lynna hated to forever dim the light that sparkled so brilliantly in his eyes, but she had no choice. "Beau is on the ship."

"Then let us bring him to Devereux Acres where he belongs." He took her hand to lead her toward the buggy.

Lynna stopped him with a gentle tug on his arm as her eyes glistened with unshed tears. "We sailed to the island on the *Windjammer*, Sean."

Her words stopped him dead in his tracks. Sean refused to even look at her as he gazed toward the harbor where the *Windjammer* rode anchor. "Jordan is here?"

"I beg you to hear me out, Sean." He remained still, his back rigid. "Sean, please look at me."

He took a deep breath and tried to harden his heart toward this woman who had caused him so much heartache. "I can't live through the pain of you leaving me again, Lynna," he said, with all seriousness. "I would rather be dead."

Lynna's heart constricted in her chest when

she heard the catch in his voice. Her return to the island would bring him nothing but pain. Was she being selfish to put her daughter first, above all else? "I need your help, Sean."

He laughed harshly. "My help?" When he finally looked at her his eyes were filled with pain and confusion. "Haven't I helped you enough, Lynna? What more can I give you? My blood? My first born?"

Lynna refused to allow her heart to be swayed by his pain, her mission was too great. "Please, Sean, I beg you. Start by simply giving me your help. "

He knew his words were snide, yet he couldn't control them. "What could be so important that you would travel all the way to Trinidad with your… husband?"

"One of the two most important things in my world, Sean. My daughter."

She watched as the blood drained from his chiseled features. "You have a daughter?"

"Yes, and she is dying, Sean. She has been cursed by a powerful voodoo queen, and if Doc cannot remove the curse she will die." Lynna paused to look deep into his eyes, into his very soul. "Please, help us, Sean."

Her words twisted the knife she had already plunged into his heart. "So, you and Jordan have another child."

"I beg you to help me, Sean. We can have this, or any discussion you wish to have, afterward. Right now, nothing matters except my daughter's health. Nothing."

Sensing Lynna's genuine distress, Sean was

unable to hide the love he felt for her. His anger left him, to be replaced by tenderness for the fragile, heartbroken woman. "What can I do to help you, my love?"

Ignoring his *my love* for the sake of her sanity, Lynna forced herself to remember her purpose. "Take us to Doc, Sean. That's all I ask." Suddenly, the events of the last several months overwhelmed her and Lynna gave vent to the emotions she had kept bottled up inside for so long. She'd had no one to share her fears with back home, not even Aunt Judith. Scalding tears slipped down her cheeks as she gazed toward the harbor where the Windjammer rode anchor. "My daughter could be seconds away from death, Sean."

"How old is she?" Here was yet another complication standing in the way of her spending the rest of her life on the island, with him.

Lynna's stomach clenched into a tight fist as her legs suddenly felt too weak to support her weight. She took a moment to lean against his muscular chest and gather her bearings. "Eight weeks. She's waiting in town with… Joshua."

Sean looked away, unable to face her. "I still can't believe you brought him here."

"Sean, please, I beg of you. My daughter's life is at stake. Put aside your petty quarrel with Joshua and assist me in getting my daughter the help she needs." Lynna took his face in her hands and spoke straight from her heart. "Only when my daughter is well and healthy will I be happy."

Sean led her to the buggy. "You knew when you came to the island that I would help you in any way I could."

When he made to lift her into the buggy, she clutched his arm. "Promise me, Sean, that we will speak of nothing except my daughter until after we leave Doc. I assure you that my nerves are at their breaking point, and the smallest amount of added stress could tip me over the edge. Please, I beg you to give me your word on this."

He had never been able to deny her, and now was no exception. "I promise, Lynna." He paused with his hand on her arm. "On one condition."

"What is it?"

"That you will not leave the island until we have had some time, alone."

"I promise, Sean." She would agree to anything if there was a possibility that it could save her daughter's life.

"We both know that you always keep your promises." A twinkle caused his eyes to dance merrily before his face erupted into a full smile. "I remember with great clarity the last promise you kept, like it was only yesterday. In fact, I remember it several times a day, especially at night."

Lynna's blush deepened as Sean placed his hands around her tiny waist and lifted her into the buggy.

He was intrigued by the smell of her, the feel of her luscious curves, the almost overpowering desire to taste her inviting lips. His lips lowered to hers for the briefest touch, but he wanted more.

Much more.

"Sean, you have to know that I thought my husband was dead or I never would have…"

Sean put a finger to her lips to silence her

protests as his other hand lingered on her waist. He had waited too long for this moment, imagined it in his mind too many times to allow her to spoil it.

Lynna felt liquid fire race from his hands to rest in the pit of her stomach as his lips lowered to hers.

Her finger went to her lips to caress where his lips had been. Their eyes met as she gratefully took her seat before collapsing onto it.

"We will continue this later, little one," he promised.

Sean drove the buggy down the hill, dodging numerous potholes and deep ruts that were left over from the rainy season. He heard Lynna's irritated sigh when they were forced to stop and wait while an iguana casually meandered across the road. "Sean, we must hurry. Makenna needs us."

"I understand, darling. Still, if I run the creature over and bust a wheel we will have to return for another buggy. That would take twice as long." He felt a rush of sympathy for this woman whom he loved above all others.

Lynna looked like she hadn't had a decent nights' sleep in months. She was too thin. What Sean wouldn't give to pull the covers over her body, in his bed, and hold her until she slept. To watch her sleep peacefully as he had the night in the hotel in Port of Spain. "Just try to relax, Lynna. We will be there soon, I promise."

When the path was finally cleared of amphibious traffic Sean clicked the reins, with his mind far from the flower-bordered dirt road in front of him. So many thoughts, hopes, and dreams crashed against each other.

Since he had promised not to discuss anything except her daughter, he quietly relished the fact that Lynna was so near. So achingly near. How many nights had he dreamed of this very moment? Now, here she was.

All he had to do was convince her to stay.

With every bump in the road his thigh brushed intimately against hers, sending a blossom of heat searing through his midsection. He noticed her flinch. She felt it too.

Never in his wildest dreams, and there had been many, would he have expected this exquisite creature to show up at his door, pleading for his help. She knew he would move heaven and earth to help her, whatever the peril. But there was also the risk that this could be a trap, set by her husband.

The worry was never far from Sean's mind that Jordan could turn his whereabouts over to the authorities, leaving him to be captured and tried for piracy. He would then be, as the Queen had so eloquently proclaimed, hanged by the neck until dead.

He watched Lynna brush a tear from her cheek decided to trust her. If the truth be told, it would be physically impossible to do otherwise. "Tell me about your daughter, Lynna."

"A voodoo queen named Larue Fontaine placed a wasting spell on my daughter. She has been in a comatose state since birth. She never moves, and only swallows a drop of milk at the time. And she is so... frail and weak. If something isn't done soon..."

Sean squeezed her hand reassuringly. He knew all too well the devastating effects of a wasting curse. "We will get her the help she needs, Lynna. Trust me."

"I always have, Sean," Lynna murmured, softly, meeting his steady gaze.

The look she gave him allowed Sean the slightest glimmer of hope. He wanted to discuss them.

Him and her.

What their future might hold. Still, he had given his word. "Are you telling me that your daughter is eight weeks old and has never awakened?"

Not… once."

"What was her medical diagnosis?"

His question provoked another flood of tears. "She is either in a coma, or she contracted an illness that left her unable to move."

"You don't believe that do you?"

"No." Lynna lifted the hem of her skirt to dry her eyes. "Not when Larue Fontaine admitted to placing a curse on the entire Jordan family."

"The entire family?"

"Yes. When Doc removes the curse from Makenna I need to speak with him about removing the curse from the Jordan lineage as well. I pray that Beau or Makenna are never made to suffer as their parents and grandparents have."

When they arrived at the docks, Lynna's lips curved into a smile at the sight of her daughter. Joshua, Clara, and Makenna waited in the shade under a shed.

"Captain Jordan." Sean offered a brusque nod of his head. He couldn't begin to imagine how much hatred the man must feel for him.

"Captain Devereux," Joshua responded, stonily, attempting to hide his true feeling for his wife's sake. "We are grateful for your help."

Sean nodded. "Glad to offer any assistance that I can."

Clara handed the baby up to Lynna and climbed into the back of the buggy. Joshua took the seat beside Lynna.

Sean smiled at Clara. "Who do we have here?"

Lynna reached for Clara's hand. "This is Clara. Without her, Makenna wouldn't have made it this far."

"How so?" Sean was obviously puzzled. How could a young girl help such a sick baby when doctors were unable to?

"Clara was born with the gift of healing. Only when she is close to Makenna can my daughter even swallow. For some reason, and one that I will be eternally grateful for, Clara has the ability to ward off evil."

"I see." Sean clicked the reins as his gaze fell to Makenna. He was finding it difficult to disguise the alarm he felt at first sight of the sleeping infant. Lynna's daughter was extremely ill. She didn't move or make a sound. Her eyelashes didn't flutter, nor did her lips twitch. He had never witnessed a more malnourished child.

It crossed his mind that they might be too late for even Doc to help the little girl. "How can anyone be so heartless as to cause harm to an innocent child?" Sean wondered, aloud.

"The world is full of greed and evil," Joshua

responded, with a knowing look toward Sean. "How could anyone steal a wife and mother away from her son for his own personal greed, without a thought for those she loved."

"To save her life," Sean was quick to answer.

Joshua leaned forward to face the pirate. "Can you honestly tell me the only reason you took my wife was to save her life?"

"It was only after I discovered that Suzanne was going to murder your wife that I decided to take action." Sean returned Joshua's glare. "I would not have taken her had she been well and healthy. If you know Lynna at all, you know she would have fought me tooth and nail if I had attempted to ferret her away from her son."

Lynna took Sean's hand to squeeze. "I will always be grateful to you for saving my life."

"My pleasure." Sean turned to Joshua. "I'm not the man I was before, Jordan."

"I have been told that a leopard cannot change his spots, Devereux."

"Believe what you will." Sean had a sobering recollection of the days on his ship when Lynna was so sick. "But know this. Lynna would have died if I had done nothing."

"If you expect my gratitude you will have a long wait."

"Your wife has already thanked me." Sean's smile spoke volumes as he met first Lynna's eyes, then her husbands.

"Stop this at once," Lynna cried. "Both of you. Now is not the time for your childish bickering. I can't stand another second of it."

"I'm sorry, my love." Joshua gently nudged her head to his shoulder as his eyes conveyed a warning to the pirate. *She is mine.* "You're right of course, darling. I will settle the score with the pirate at a later date."

Sean would enjoy settling a number of things with Joshua Jordan. "Name the time and place."

"Please." Lynna glanced toward Sean and pleaded with her eyes. "No more."

Sean glanced down at the bundle in her arms, fearing that Lynna was in for an incredible amount of suffering. If the worst happened, he hoped and prayed that he would be allowed to help her through the nightmare.

"We'll ride as far as we can, then walk through thick underbrush the rest of the way. It's been a while since I've had cause to visit the shaman, but I think I remember the way." His eyes met and locked with Lynna's.

He turned on a dirt road at the end of the main square and followed the road for about twenty minutes, before steering the horses toward a little side road.

Lynna was stroking her baby's downy soft curls as she whispered sweet nothings to the comatose child. If she was as aware of the contact when their thighs brushed as he was, she was doing a stellar job of hiding it from her husband. Sean forced himself to look straight ahead as they followed the road for another fifteen minutes.

Steering the horses into a cluster of trees by the side of the road, Sean pointed to a path. "We'll have to go on foot from here. We should move as fast as we can since it will be dark soon."

Joshua took Clara's hand and pulled her forward to walk in front of him, always keeping her close to Makenna. "The path appears to be little more than an animal trail, Lynna. I will carry Makenna since I wouldn't want you or Clara to trip and fall." He nodded toward Sean. "Lead the way, pirate."

Sean grinned, loving the fact that he was getting under Jordan's skin.

Thick underbrush turned out to be a slight misrepresentation of the facts. The trail, what there was of one, was definitely overgrown with clinging vines and thorny briar bushes at every turn.

"Why would he want to live so hidden in the forest?" Lynna questioned, frustrated that it was taking so long. Her shriek of disgust echoed through the quiet woods when she ran headlong into a spider's giant web. She and Clara fell back and allowed Sean to lead the way. "Who can even find his cottage? Apparently, he doesn't particularly care for visitors." She slapped at a mosquito on her cheek. "How can that be good for business?"

"Those who have need of Doc's services will find him." Sean was remembering his earlier trek through this forest, when Lynna suffered from Suzanne's curse. "Just as I found him for you."

Joshua didn't fail to notice the look that was exchanged between them, and it set his blood to boil. The urge to choke the life from the pirate was strong, and getting stronger by the minute.

They stopped about half way for Lynna to rest against the trunk of a tree and squeeze milk into the baby's mouth. Surprisingly, she didn't appear at all embarrassed by the fact that Sean was practically drooling at the sight of her bare breast. This puzzled Joshua until he remembered the pirate had… bathed Lynna while she was a hostage on his ship.

Suddenly, it hit him.

Of course, they had been intimate.

It was at that very moment when Joshua realized that his wife had not been truthful with him. Lynna and the pirate had been lovers, he was sure of it now. One glance at the pirate and his smug smile as he feasted upon the sight of Lynna's full breasts, convinced Joshua that his thoughts were correct. He would kill the lowlife stinking scum.

Before this day was over, Sean Devereux would draw his final breath.

Sean watched Lynna with a look of awe and wonder spreading across his face, ignoring Joshua's rising anger. "Is that how you have been keeping her alive?"

"For eight weeks now." Lynna didn't look up, but kept squeezing out one drop at the time. When the milk ran out of the sides of baby's mouth she would squeeze Makenna's lips together to hold it in until she swallowed. "She needs so much more. I pray that Doc can help her."

"As do I," Sean agreed.

"We all do, darling." Joshua moved to kneel before her. "Here, give my daughter to me. There is a rising moon to guide us."

Lynna took Joshua's hand as he pulled her to her feet. "The spell has to be performed when the moon is full."

When they finally broke through the forest

into a clearing, after what seemed like hours of trudging through thick brambles, Lynna felt the urge to laugh out loud.

Finally, after eight long weeks, they had arrived at the home of the only person alive with the ability to save her daughter's life.

Chapter 28

Daniel and Samuel sat in the parlor at Sea Grove across from Jeremiah and Nathan. "We have come bearing terrible news." Samuel attempted to speak several times, but choked up, forced to wait until he could compose himself enough to continue.

"What is it, Samuel?" Jeremiah pushed his chair closer in order to place a comforting hand on the young man's shoulder. Whatever the news, it promised to be bad.

"Something so awful that it is beyond comprehension, Jeremiah."

Jeremiah and Nathan waited patiently to hear what had the brothers so distraught.

A sob caught in Samuel's throat as tears streamed down his cheeks. "Our parents have been murdered."

"What?" Jeremiah gasped, wishing he could pace the floor as Nathan was doing. "How? When?"

"A few days ago, from what I can gather. My parents were visiting my mother's sister in Savannah for a few weeks, before leaving to attend an appointment with my father's lawyer in Atlanta. It seems they were set upon by highwaymen before they could make it to the city." Samuel's voice cracked so that he was unable to speak further.

Daniel cleared his throat, continuing when

his brother couldn't. "They were robbed and shot execution style between the eyes." He dropped his head in his hands as heartbreaking sobs overwhelmed him.

"I don't know what to say." Jeremiah and Silas had not been on speaking terms since the trial, but he had certainly never wished harm to befall the man, or his wife. "You have our deepest sympathies. Please, don't hesitate to let us know if there is anything we can do for either of you."

"Thank you, Jeremiah." Daniel removed a much abused handkerchief from his pocket and dried his eyes. "You and our father were always friends until this drama with Suzanne. She ruined everything. My father would still be alive if not for her."

"How so?" Jeremiah asked.

"Father was going to Atlanta to have Suzanne stripped from his will. He sent me a copy of the new will he had written. I only hope it will hold up in a court of law and Suzanne never gets a single acre of Magnolia House."

Samuel swiped his hand across his eyes and blew his nose. "As bad as all this is, there's more."

Nathan stopped pacing, waiting for the other shoe to drop.

"We recently discovered that Pearlie, known far and wide as the voodoo queen of Magnolia House, was found… hanging from a tree."

Nathan and Jeremiah exchanged glances, it was not uncommon for folks to be hung in the South.

Samuel continued, "Pearlie had been coated with honey and left in the swamp so the bugs and night creatures could feed on her body. She died an excruciatingly painful death. Now there is an uproar as the workers refuse to leave their cabins for fear they could be next. Meanwhile, the cotton rots in the fields."

"Sounds like you two should head to Georgia and get your affairs straightened out before it's too late," Nathan advised, sinking down into a plush upholstered wingchair.

"I agree." Samuel walked to the window, a defeated man. "There is more bad news."

"For the love of God," Jeremiah cried. "What more could there be?"

Samuel looked from Jeremiah to Nathan. "Our sister was recently released from prison."

"What!" Nathan and Jeremiah shrieked in unison.

Nathan was aghast, leaping to his feet. "That's impossible. My lawyers assured me that she would be forced to serve the entire five year sentence."

Samuel sighed dismally. "According to my dear sister's letter, she was released early for good behavior, mainly due to the fact that the prison is overpopulated."

"How could they even consider releasing someone who is as inherently evil as…" Jeremiah paused, his face flaming. "Samuel, Daniel, please forgive me. I didn't mean to disparage your sister, especially at a time like this."

"Disparage her all you want," Samuel mumbled. "I have no doubt that she deserves every word."

Daniel nodded in agreement. "One of the

reasons we stopped by was to ask you to keep an eye on Cedar Hill while we're gone. Since Malinda is too far along to travel, Beth will remain here with her while Samuel and I return to Magnolia House to attend to our parents' affairs."

"How long has Suzanne been out of prison?" Nathan queried.

"We didn't know she had been released until a rider arrived with a note stating that she was in residence at Magnolia House. She even included a copy of her pardon, officially signed and sealed by a Warden Jerica Fontaine. It was almost like an afterthought in her letter that our sister even bothered to mention that our parents had been murdered."

While Samuel continued talking, Jeremiah stopped listening and turned alarmingly pale.

Warden Jerica Fontaine?

Jerica Jordan Fontaine.

Suzanne sat regally atop her steed as she trotted through the quarters. Not a creature stirred. She had never seen it so quiet. The hands refused to return to the fields.

This would never do.

Samuel and Daniel would think her incapable of running the plantation if they found the cotton decaying in the fields while the lazy workers trembled behind closed doors.

In truth, she had forgotten how superstitious they were, or she would have had what little was left of Pearlie's body taken down and buried before anyone could find her and spread word of her tortured demise.

Suzanne hid a yawn behind her gloved hand, remembering Pearlie's pitiful screams of torment. It was well past midnight when Suzanne had left the swamp with a bright smile on her face after hearing the satisfying snap of an alligator's huge jaw. Pearlie should have known there was room for only one voodoo queen at Magnolia House.

Suzanne went to the overseer's house and knocked.

Opening the door a crack, Jake Almond peered out at her. "What can I do for you, Miss Suzanne?"

"You can get your shiftless workers back in the field," she answered, haughtily. "That's what you can do."

"I'm afraid I can't do that." Jake shook his head. "Not until Silas gets back and has a talk with the workers. Most of them are afraid of their own shadows right now."

"Well, unfortunately, that's not going to happen."

"Why not? They should be back in a few days."

"No, they won't, since both my parents are dead."

Every ear in the quarters was pressed to a door or window, listening, because a wailing suddenly filled the air the likes of which Suzanne had never heard.

"Who will run the plantation with Silas gone?"

"I will, of course," Suzanne responded with a satisfied smile.

The wailing only increased.

The funeral for Silas and Mary Fletcher was a solemn affair. Daniel still couldn't accept the fact that his parents were gone. There had been harsh words between him and his father after his engagement to Malinda Jordan had been announced and they had been estranged since, but he loved his parents dearly.

Now he would never get the chance to make amends, tell them how much he loved them. He bowed his head as a single tear slid down his cheek when the reverend finished his prayer.

Daniel couldn't keep his eyes from straying to his sister, or the person claiming to be his sister.

Suzanne was hideous.

Her hair was like broom straw pinned atop her head and she had tanned leathery skin. And her hands? They more resembled lumps of connected calluses than hands, with dirt permanently embedded under her freshly manicured nails.

Daniel glanced up to catch her glaring at him. Her eyes were so cold and hard they didn't even appear human. Maybe Jasmine was right. Perhaps his sister's mind had snapped. Jasmine stood off to the side, eying Suzanne warily.

Since their arrival Daniel had noticed that his sister seemed to take a sinister enjoyment from tormenting Jasmine. She never let up on her demands or gave Jasmine a minute's rest, and it was taking its toll on the old servant woman.

He was still in the dark as to how Suzanne had convinced the parole board to give her an early release? Four years early? It was almost impossible to fathom. He knew Joshua would be livid, as he should be.

Daniel was furious and intended to write a stern letter to the warden at his first opportunity. Of course, he and Malinda would move back to run the plantation once she delivered their child. That was not a problem. Living in the same house with his sister *was* a problem. Malinda detested Suzanne.

Daniel allowed the preachers words to sink in as he gazed across a sea of mourners who had gathered to pay their last respects to his parents. The house servants stood in front and there wasn't a dry eye among them. Rose and Iris were almost prostrate with grief when the reverend spoke of Mary's gentle nature and how she was always willing to help those less fortunate than herself.

After the funeral, friends and neighbors gathered at the big house for lunch. Samuel and Daniel felt immense shame when their sister held out her horrid hands to greet their guests. While they heard the snickers, if Suzanne was aware of the insults she refused to acknowledge them in any way.

The girls that Suzanne had made fun of and lorded her father's wealth over made a point to come up and have a few words with her. They all wanted a close up look at what the high and mighty Suzanne Fletcher had been reduced to.

They each had beaming smiles and laughter in their eyes when they walked away to huddle in groups and whisper behind their gloved hands.

"When is Malinda's baby due?" Suzanne asked her brother, ignoring the two giggling fools who had just passed by her in the line.

If they only knew what I am capable of

doing to them.

"Any day now." Daniel removed his handkerchief from his pocket to swipe across his eyes. "That's why I can't stay. I need to get back to my wife."

"I understand, Daniel." *The sooner the better.* "Don't worry about the plantation. I have everything under control."

"How can you say you have everything under control when the workers refuse to return to the fields?" Daniel seethed, annoyed that she didn't seem to have the slightest grasp on reality. "The cotton has been ready to pick for days, and trust me, it will not pick itself."

"Don't concern yourself with those ignorant fools, Daniel Fletcher. I can handle them." She turned to meet Jasmine's cold black eyes. "They have been petted and spoiled far too long. They need a sterner hand than our father used. You just wait and see. I will have them whipped into shape in no time at all."

"No, Suzanne, you won't. Contrary to what you might think, you don't know the first thing about running a cotton plantation the size of Magnolia House. For that reason, Samuel will remain here until my child is born, then Malinda and I will return to see to the running of the plantation."

Absolutely not.

"Daniel, that isn't necessary at all," she wheedled. "Jake Almond is more than capable of overseeing things around here, just as he always has."

"If that were the case the workers would

have been in the field yesterday when we arrived, instead of locking themselves in their cabins." He held up his hand to stop her from begging. "No, Suzanne. Samuel and I have discussed it and the matter is settled, since father left the plantation and acreage to us."

Even though she *should* have just as much say in the running of the plantation as her brothers, they would never agree to it. The rights of a female didn't amount to a hill of beans.

Damn him!

Just what she needed. Daniel and that mealy mouthed Malinda, and another screaming brat, underfoot.

Chapter 29

Sean knocked on the door of the cabin in the rainforest, and waited. "Doc doesn't move fast, so this may take a while. I will give you the same words of advice that were given to me."

"What are they?" Lynna asked.

"Don't do or say anything to piss Doc off. I gather from Mister Juarez that it would be neither healthy nor wise. His exact words were, 'You don't want him on your bad side'."

"I will remember that." When Lynna had all but given up hope, the door finally opened just a crack and a blistering wave of intense heat rushed out the door to sweep over her. When her watering eyes cleared she noticed a sideways face peering out from about the height of the door handle. A face with a mouth filled to capacity with rotting and decaying teeth.

"It's a little late to come calling, ain't it?" The man had obviously already retired for the night and seemed more than a little perturbed at having his sleep interrupted. "Come back tomorrow."

Before he could shut the door in their faces Sean wedged his foot in the door.

"We cannot come back tomorrow," Lynna cried. "A curse has been placed on my daughter and she is dying as we stand here wasting valuable time.

Please, you must help us."

This got his attention. "What kind of curse?"

"A wasting spell." Lynna squatted down so she was eye level with the short statured man, but took an involuntary step backward when she felt the full effect of his breath in her face. "Can you make a salt packet to remove the curse from my daughter, like the one you made for me?"

"That would not work for one so young. We would have to take an entirely different approach." He yawned noisily, shaking his head and running a hand over his balding head. "Let me see the baby that is causing such commotion in the middle of the night when a man is trying to rest."

Lynna unwrapped her daughter's frail and withered body, holding it up to Doc's face so he could get a good look at her. He studied her for a minute by the light of the moon, touching her feet and limp hands, wiggling her fingers and toes. "Whoever cursed this child knew what he or she was doing. It ain't easy to get a spell to take on a newborn. It was cast while the infant was still in the womb."

Lynna had a pained flashback of Amari's mumbled words and crippled hand on her stomach. "It was a she," Lynna spat. "Her name is Amari and she is a dear friend and pupil of Larue Fontaine."

"Larue Fontaine." Doc actually cringed upon hearing the name. "You sure know how to make enemies, don't you girl?"

"I suppose I do."

"Larue Fontaine used this Amari to cast her spell. I've heard many a tale about the voodoo queen of Savannah."

"Can you remove one of her spells?" Lynna asked.

Doc glanced toward Sean. "Like I told you before, removing a wasting spell, especially one cast by the likes of Larue Fontaine, ain't going to be easy, or cheap."

"Name your price," Joshua assured the man. "My daughter's health is all that matters."

After hearing those words the wizened old man opened the door and invited them in. "You're in luck. The moon is full tonight. Come in, while I toss another log on the fire."

Another log?

Lynna already feared her dress might spontaneously combust into flames. She peered around the stifling hot cottage where a bubbling cauldron sat above a roaring fire. Every surface in the room was cluttered with strange bottles and jars filled with... unusual specimens.

"Close the door, will you," Doc wheezed. "It's freezing outside."

Lynna wiped sweat from her brow and made eye contact with first Sean, then Joshua.

Was he crazy?

At any rate, she needed more action and less talk. "Can you remove the curse from my daughter?"

"I won't make false promises, but I will do what I can." He went to the cabinet and began removing bottles and jars of different sizes, shapes, and colors. When he passed by Clara he rubbed his arms as a sudden warmth rushed over him, causing him to pause long enough to peer into her eyes. "Remove the baby's clothes and lay her in the center of the table."

Doc mumbled to himself as he tied nine knots in a black string, counting each knot out loud. Handing Lynna a paper, ink bottle and quill he instructed her, "Write the full name of the person who cursed this baby."

Taking the paper and dipping the quill in ink Lynna wrote, *Larue Fontaine.*

Doc spread a black cloth on the table, placing the paper on top of the cloth beside Makenna.

One at a time he added powdered herbs until the paper was covered. He then sliced a layer of bloodroot over the herbs. Next, he lit the black candle and dripped ten drops of wax, covering the herbs and paper.

He pointed to Lynna and motioned for her to come forward as he ground a clove of garlic and added drops of water to make a paste. "While I rub this mixture on the souls of your daughter's feet, I need you to visualize the person who has cursed your daughter and say her name three times while tying the bag shut with the knotted string."

"I have never seen her," Lynna cried. She wouldn't be able to bear it if the spell failed because of her. "I cannot visualize someone I have never seen."

"Then the child's father must do it." Doc instructed, firmly.

Lynna looked from Joshua to Sean, her fear and confusion clearly evident in her eyes.

Joshua stepped forward. "I haven't met the woman either."

"Then the mother and father of the child

must join hands and repeat the name together to break the spell."

Dropping her head in her hands, a sob of anguish tore from Lynna's lips as Joshua took her hand.

What was she to do?

"Are you ready, love?"

Something about the look of stark terror in Lynna's eyes made Sean slip quietly behind her and reach for her hand. She needed encouragement and he was happy to give it to her. "Thank you, God," she whispered, as she gently squeezed Sean's hand behind her.

Neither Doc nor Clara missed the exchange.

"Larue Fontaine," Joshua and Lynna chanted three times, as Sean repeated the words softly behind them. Lynna immediately released their hands and made to reach for her baby, but stilled when she heard Clara's pained gasp.

Joshua rushed to Clara's side, holding her steady as she suffered an apparent seizure. Her eyes rolled back in her head as drops of spittle gathered in the corners of her mouth and her body twitched convulsively. He helped her to a bench in the corner and wiped the sweat from her brow.

"There is no cause for alarm," Doc stated calmly, not seeming overly concerned. "The young lady is gifted. She is absorbing the evil as it flows from the child, that is all. It will pass."

Lynna reached for her daughter, "Can I hold her now."

"Do not touch her," Doc warned. "Not until the last remnants of the curse have passed from her body. The young lady was born with the power to ward off evil. The rest of you were not. You are like lightning rods and the evil will seek you out." No sooner had he said the words than a slight mewling sound was heard from the vicinity of the table.

"Makenna?" Lynna cried.

Her cry of joy echoed throughout the cabin as she rushed to gather her angry daughter in her arms. Her tiny fists were flailing the air, her eyes were squeezed shut, and her little mouth was wide open as she let anyone in hearing distance know how displeased she was at the injustice of being naked on a hard wooden table.

Doc grinned smugly, more than a little pleased that he was able to remove a spell cast by the great Larue Fontaine. "I do believe your daughter is hungry, ma'am."

Lynna slipped down her bodice and brought Makenna to her breast, laughing out loud as the greedy baby latched on and began a loud and vigorous nursing. Happiness overwhelmed her as she beamed a breathtaking smile that stole Sean's breath away as tears shimmered on her lashes and fell to her daughter's head.

Sean was amazed and pulled up a chair to witness the miracle that had taken place in this room tonight. Suddenly, a weary sadness overwhelmed him. Now that her daughter was cured, Lynna would sail into the horizon, again.

He almost wished that she had never returned if he would be forced to endure the pain of losing her all over again. What he wouldn't give if mother and child could be his. He would move heaven and earth to make them happy.

He still had one last chance to convince

Lynna to stay. She had promised to meet with him before leaving the island and she would keep her promise.

Joshua moved to bend down beside his wife, lifting Makenna's tiny foot in his hand and giving thanks for their miracle. He had never loved his family more than at that moment.

The only noise in the room was the crackling of the fire, an owl hooting in a tree above the cottage, and the sound of Makenna's noisy nursing. They all waited patiently until the child had her fill, then she slowly opened her eyes to view the world around her.

And Sean... gasped.

His startled gasp echoed through the stillness of the room as a look of pure unadulterated joy lit his features and caused his hazel eyes to twinkle merrily. He could no longer sit still and moved to lift the beautiful little girl from Lynna's arms, holding the tiny, fragile, yet perfect bundle against his rapidly beating heart.

Joshua stood, outraged that Sean would dare take his daughter from Lynna's arms.

What was the meaning of this?

He made to move toward the pirate, when Lynna put a hand on his arm to restrain him. The look of sadness in her eyes assured him that this situation would not end well.

Clara was puzzled by Sean's sudden display of enthusiasm. Although, she had to admit that the darling little girl had been blessed with the most exquisite lavender eyes she had ever seen.

The End

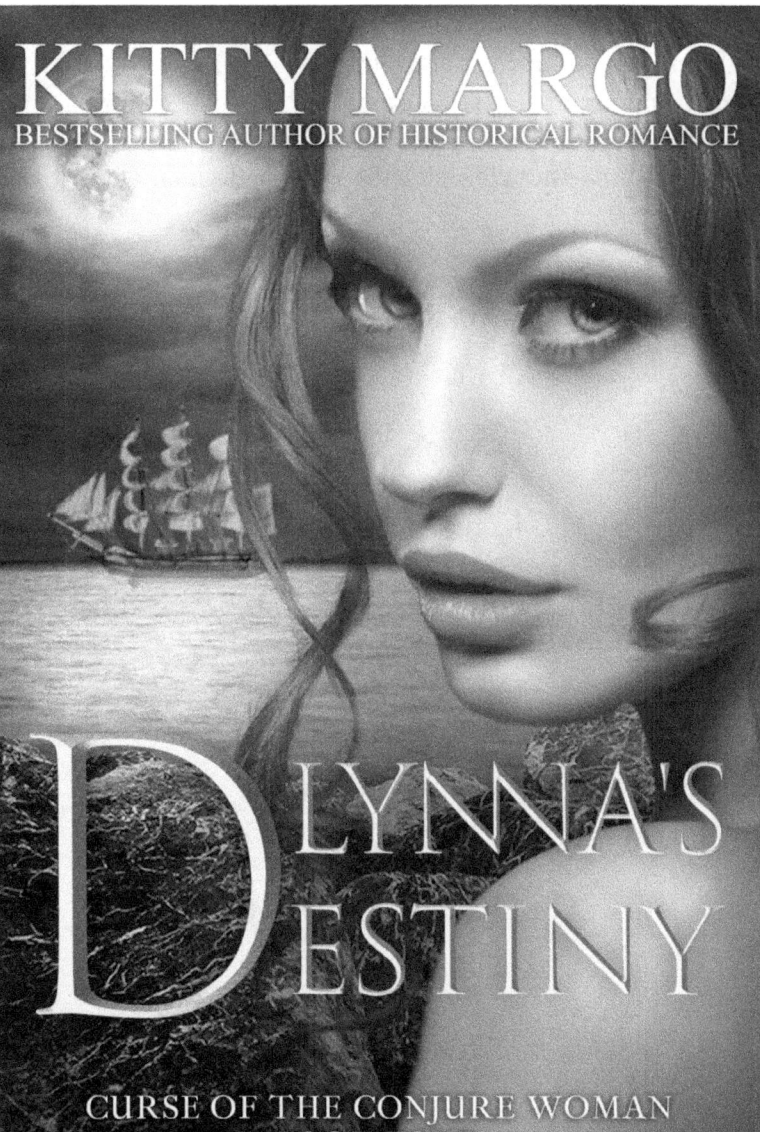

KITTY MARGO

BESTSELLING AUTHOR OF HISTORICAL ROMANCE

LYNNA'S DESTINY

CURSE OF THE CONJURE WOMAN
BOOK FOUR

Thank you so much for reading *Lynna's Promise*. I am truly honored that you chose one of the books from my collection. I hope you can read my entire series of bestselling novels featuring Joshua, Lynna, and Clara..

The Curse of the Conjure Woman

Lynna's Rogue

Lynna's Beau

Lynna's Promise

Lynna's Destiny

Jerica's Pirate

A Heartbeat in Time Series

Clara's Song

Clara's Heart

Clara's Desire

Clara's Temptation

Clara's Forever

A Note from the Author

If you enjoyed this book I would *greatly* appreciate a review to help spread the word.

Thank you again for choosing one of my books to read.

Kitty Margo